THE INVASION OF AMERICA

THE INVASION OF AMERICA

FREDERICK C. PAINTON

ILLUSTRATED BY
SAMUEL CAHAN

COVER BY
EMMETT WATSON

POPULAR PUBLICATIONS · 2022

TABLE OF CONTENTS

THE INVASION OF AMERICA

This is the story of the second World War—the conflagration kindled by the world's unrest and fanned into flame by one man's ruthless ambition to become the master of mankind. Beginning a powerful novel of Fascism tomorrow

1

THE STEEL FIST

AT PRECISELY TEN seconds less than quarter to nine o'clock the engineer of the Foreign Broadcasting Corporation stuck his head through Spike Brenn's door and said, "Okay, Spike, you're on the air."

Brenn hauled his great body out of the chair, took the stubby pipe out of his mouth and said to his companion, "Stick around, Dave, and we'll go to the dinner afterward."

He walked to the table where the small microphone was, took a quick glance at the scrawled notes he had made during the day and began to talk in the rapid, staccato fashion that had brought him twenty million listeners.

"Hello, America, this is Spike Brenn, your roving radio reporter, talking to you from Brussels, Belgium, where the naval limitations conference got under way today. As I told you yesterday, this conference among the naval powers was called by the President of the United States to stop the mad bankrupting race to build bigger and better battleships, and as the first move by the United States to promote better international understanding and keep the world at peace. I'd like to say at once that the doves of mutual love hovered over Parliament Building today and that the spirit of concession and sweet friendship lived in the hearts of

the delegates. But being an honest reporter, I must say that this is not true.

"There was jealous bickering—polite, of course—stubborn just the same. And tonight it looks as if the conference was on the rocks, sunk before it fairly got started. If the conference is to succeed, then old Uncle Sam will take the rap and pay the price. There is an old saying that the United States has never won a conference or lost a war, and it looks as if the old bearded gent is about to keep his record a hundred percent.

"Here is the crux of the situation: cruisers. Let me explain to you what that means. There are two types of cruisers, big Class A cruisers carrying eight-inch guns that can, for instance, cross the Pacific and come back to old San Pedro without refueling. The Class A cruiser is a dangerous weapon in case of war, and could menace, for example, Japan's sea traffic, or England's.

"Then there are Class B cruisers—five-thousand

HANNIBAL

tonners—and they carry only six-inch guns, and could cruise only three thousand miles. Those cruisers couldn't get very far away from their bases unless there were other naval bases in the direction they were steaming.

"Except for Pearl Harbor in the Hawaiians, old Uncle Sam hasn't any naval bases outside of his own country unless you could call Guantanamo a base. So small cruisers would keep our navy hugging our own shores.

"England and Japan have scattered bases where small cruisers could refuel, so they want small cruisers. Japan wants America to build small cruisers because in case of trouble with Uncle Sam our fleet couldn't strike at Japan. England wants us to have small cruisers because her navy would then be superior in cruising range.

"Uncle Sam wants big cruisers so, in case of war, our fleet could meet the enemy far enough from our shores to protect us from invasion.

"So, getting back to today's tiffs, England and Japan, backed by Italy and Germany, want to limit the size of cruisers to five thousand tons, thus handcuffing the American Navy. Admiral Tendor, our naval adviser, says no, and let's all hope he wins, even if the conference sinks, because with this jittery old world staggering along from one crisis and one undeclared war to the next one, Uncle Sam has got to be ready. I'm no jingoist, and I want peace maybe more than people who haven't seen as many battles as I have, but the fact remains that with the aggressive powers on the march, looking for more land and more power, the United States is isolated and hated today, and the backbone of our defense is a stout and sound navy. Let them shackle our navy and trouble may begin any time.

"This may sound alarming, but I am now on the track of an exclusive story which, if I can verify it, will make you understand just how much of a powder keg this world is at the moment. If I'm off the air for a few days, you will know I'm digging up this story for you.

"Now, let's see about the rest of the conference. The submarine question went over for committee consideration, and the limitation of battleship size to thirty-five thousand tons will be held over until the cruiser problem has been threshed out. The Belgian government is giving the delegates a big dinner tonight and I'm going over there. If I hear anything you'd like to know, I'll be on the air again at midnight, Belgian time, seven o'clock New York Eastern Standard time. Goodnight, everybody, I'll be on the air tomorrow at this same time."

Brenn switched off the microphone, hauled a white silk handkerchief out of his broadcloth trousers and wiped his brow.

"They're going to raise hell in New York at what they call my jingoism in that broadcast," he grinned.

David Farnham looked up the length of Spike Brenn, and seemingly ignored the point. "You're a big man, Spike," he said.

"Six feet, five," Spike said. "It's plenty of handicap when you can't get a plane berth or a train one, either, that's made for a guy over five feet eleven. My feet get chilblains most of the time."

He reached for his silk hat, muffler and topcoat. Farnham, studying the big, reddish face of Spike under the crop of prematurely white hair, thought he could understand why Brenn had the reputation of utter fearlessness. The very hugeness of Brenn had overawed smaller people; his boyishness and eager sense of adventure made him an utter stranger to fear. Farnham, who possessed considerable literary taste, did not think highly of what Brenn wrote, or of his radio broadcasts, but he had to admit that the man's personality made him always interesting.

"It was a little alarming, your broadcast," Farnham said, getting up and putting on his own top clothes. "Just why?"

Brenn's mouth clamped tight. "You'll know later when I dig it out. Then you business men will see that there's something else astir in the stymied globe besides selling more motor cars."

Farnham, who was president of American Motors which made two million automobiles a year, smiled good-humoredly at the jibe. He was glad he had a letter of introduction to this huge Spike Brenn who called him Dave after the first minute of association. The man had a brain and was a grand companion besides.

"Let's go," Brenn said, "and watch the witches stir their brew."

AT NINE O'CLOCK John Hannibal finished the last of his fine old brandy (trust the Belgian government to furnish the best when it gives a dinner), wiped his lips with the napkin and pushed gently out of his place. The Belgian prime minister at the speaker's table was warming to his subject and beside welcoming the delegates to the conference, was earnestly imploring world peace and future prosperity. Every one listened politely except Hannibal. He made his way to the rear with many *"excusez-moi's."* A lot of heads turned to glare at his interruption of the red-sashed speaker.

At the door Hannibal paused to light an excellent cigar. A familiar deep voice said, "Hannibal, you're the only man who'd have nerve enough to walk out on Prime Minister Duval's pet speech."

Hannibal held the wax taper until the cigar was thoroughly kindled, and only then did he turn to face the speaker. His strikingly powerful face relaxed.

"Hello, Spike," he said. "I hate to attend wakes—and they're burying the conference under a blanket of words."

"Better than burying an axe in Uncle Sam's skull," grinned Brenn. "Listen, Hannibal, I want you to meet a kindred soul—David Farnham. He's president of American Motors and he's got within a hundred million dollars or so as much money as you."

Brenn turned to Farnham. "Meet John Hannibal, the only man who ever sold America short and got away with it."

Farnham felt a sharp wave of dislike and antagonism

sweep over him as he took the firm hand thrust out to him. Somehow he resented the tremendous power that he recognized in this quiet man, and yet he had no reason for his dislike. He was glad when Spike kept on talking.

"Hannibal fought the last World War as a captain," Brenn was saying. "He'll probably be a general in the next. Any man who can make two hundred million bucks speculating in the late depression ought to be a military genius."

The three talked about the conference for a while and Farnham explained that he was in Europe inspecting American Motors' different plants.

"And you?" he asked Hannibal.

Hannibal chuckled. "Spike will tell you I attend all these conferences. I get a macabre joy, it seems, out of watching these stupid diplomats bungle toward the next war."

Again Farnham had the sharp sensation almost of hatred. He could dislike a man who profited during the country's depression, because Farnham himself despised speculators. But this was a deeper antagonism—and an unreasonable one.

Brenn was loading his pipe. He said slowly, "Hannibal, you get around. Have you heard of an organization that calls itself the Steel Fists?"

"Steel Fists," repeated Hannibal. "Sounds Fascist. Brown shirts, black shirts—"

"I don't know what it is," cut in Brenn grimly. "But I'm going to find out. The tip I got said these Steel Fists have got the idea of starting a revolution in the United States."

Hannibal laughed. "That's amusing."

"A sort of international Fascism," Brenn said. "It's

supposed to have a big organization in every country in Europe."

"You hear anything in Europe," said Hannibal. "But I never heard of the Steel Fists."

"You will when I'm through digging," said Brenn. "Well, come on, and I'll buy a drink for you golden boys."

Farnham was about to excuse himself, but Hannibal spoke first.

"I've got to run along," he said. "I've taken the Château Brabant for a month, Spike, so come out for dinner. I'd like to hear more of the Steel Fists."

He shook hands with Brenn, and Farnham forced himself to give Hannibal's hand a firm grip. Farnham's eyes followed the tall striking figure until it vanished from view. In his mind was a picture of Hannibal's blazing blue eyes.

"An odd chap," Farnham said. "One feels a peculiar sense of power about him."

"Oh, he's brilliant," nodded Brenn. "When I met him in Shanghai when the Japs and Chinese were fighting, he explained every tactical move to me. Absolutely right, too. His hobby is military strategy and he knows his stuff." Brenn led the way to the bar.

"You know," he went on, "I've often thought Hannibal was a queer duck, but I never realized how queer until tonight when I saw you two together."

"In what way?"

"You're, both big men—big by millions, I mean. But you're young—you're thirty-four, aren't you?—and he's old. And he's ruthless; that man would do anything to get what he wanted. You, Dave, seem to have made a lot of money and still kept a decent conscience. Don't know how you did it."

Brenn grinned and ordered two brandy and sodas. "You didn't like him and he didn't like you." He paused, and a queer expression crossed his big face.

"Somehow, I felt as if I were with two men of destiny tonight." He looked at Farnham, and then he grinned again. "Pretty fancy phrase for me."

MEANWHILE, JOHN HANNIBAL went out to the Place Rogier. The doorman shrilled a blast and Hannibal's enormous Rolls Royce purred up to the curb.

"Step on it," Hannibal said to the chauffeur.

"Okay, boss. How was the dinner? I seen more brass hats in one spot than I ever seen before."

Hannibal laughed sharply. "The same brass hats that led us into the last slaughter—and will do it again if they can."

Les caught the bitterness. "Your head ache bad tonight, Boss?"

Hannibal suppressed a sigh. His head always ached; it had never stopped since that moment in 1918 in the Argonne Forest when, leading an attack on a machine gun, the world had blown up in his face. It would never stop until he died; the doctors said that.

"No worse than usual, Les," he said.

The car sped swiftly into the northeast section of Brussels, the aristocratic section, far removed from the slums. From the Rue de l'Aune the car turned into the Château Brabant. Under the full moon the place had real grandeur. Owned by one of the dukes of Brabant, the palace—for it was all of that—was set in a park of four acres which had been brought to perfection after three hundred years of care.

In the center of this sat the Gothic château whose spires and crenellated towers evoked the glory of an earlier time—of knights in hauberks and the gleam of lances. Hannibal had rented the place partly because of its beauty, but chiefly because there were four ways to enter and leave the château unnoticed.

Beake came down the steps of the *porte-cochère* when the car drew up. His legs and body glistened silkily in the full panoply of an European butler's livery.

"Good evening, sir," he said. "Young Mr. Stephen insisted on waiting up to have you er—tuck him in, sir."

Hannibal's face softened. "The rascal," he chuckled, but nonetheless his step quickened as he mounted the fine marble staircase to the upper floor. He found his son on the floor of the great bedroom, studying a chess problem. The chess pieces, however, were not the usual kind. The pawns were small replicas of modern tanks; the castles were huge siege guns, the knights were airplanes of the pursuit type; the bishops were armored cars; and the queen was an upright battleship; and the king a radio tower.

The blue blaze in John Hannibal's eyes dimmed; the drawn face relaxed. There was tenderness in his gaze at the bright-haired boy.

"White to move and mate in three moves, son," he said.

The boy, who was eleven, looked up quickly and jumped to his feet. His bare heels rapped against each other; he stiffened to attention and snapped his right hand to salute. "Private Stephen Hannibal reporting for bed, sir," he piped.

"Get your blanket, Private," said Hannibal.

The boy whirled, took a single blanket from the bed and marched stiff-kneed to the door which led to an outdoor balcony. As he opened it a blast of chill May air stiffened his thin suit of silk pajamas against his lean torso. But he did not flinch. He went out onto the porch, draped himself in the blanket and lay down upon the floor.

John Hannibal followed. In the light from the room he could see the flush of healthy color under the boy's clear fine skin. Color and health that he, John Hannibal, had spent eleven years in building. Bess—his heart flinched even now as he thought of her—would have adored the boy, and spoiled him.

"How did the studies go?" he asked.

"I read Napoleon's campaign at Austerlitz in the French, sir, and made two mistakes."

"Soon," said Hannibal, "you'll make none. Anything else?"

"I swam in the pool for twenty minutes with the water at freezing."

"Did you mind?"

"Not any more, sir. I went in without hesitation."

Hannibal bent down and offered his cheek to the boy's lips.

"Goodnight, Father."

JOHN HANNIBAL DID not lock the bedroom door when he went in and left the boy to the hard boards. Steve might shiver all night with the cold, but he would not come in to the huge canopied bed where he could have been snug and warm. Hannibal had trained the boy too well for such deceit.

"He's not soft," murmured John Hannibal. "I'll make a man out of him, Bess—a great man."

Beake met him downstairs. "Colonel Dorsey's in the salon, sir."

Hannibal nodded. "Very well. You can retire." He paused. Then: "Are Jerry and Nick at their posts?"

Beake frowned. "Yes, sir. And if I might make so bold, sir, it seems a pity that two such—such er—unsavory persons should be part of our entourage."

John Hannibal smiled. "Jerry and Nick were in my regiment during the war, Beake, both snipers. They are two of the finest marksmen in the world."

Beake saw the expression on his master's face. "Quite so, sir. Goodnight, sir."

Hannibal went into the great salon where once Madame Sevigny had entertained Napoleon. It was a vast, lovely room from the white and gold piano to the great chandelier dripping crystal. High-ceilinged, its walls covered with tapestries of a loveliness scarcely found nowadays, it had the dignity of great age. In the center of the room stood a large elliptical table that seemed strangely out of place here. There was nothing on it but a large glittering steel gauntlet doubled up to make a fist. The gauntlet had come from a complete set of plate armor in the next room.

The light from the chandelier winked in a hundred places on the polished steel fist.

John Hannibal gave it scarcely a glance. He moved to the sideboard to make certain there was a sufficient supply of liquor, cigarettes and cigars. This done, he stepped back to the center of the room and looked first at the east wall, then at the west.

"Everything under control, Jerry, Nick?" he called.

From the east wall came a chuckle. "Boss, I could shoot them pearls outa your shirt."

"And me the buttons off that swallowtail coat," this from the west wall.

John Hannibal smiled thinly. "Good. But, remember, do nothing unless I give you the signal."

"Okay," came the chorus.

Colonel George Dorsey entered just then, with a huge Mercator's projection of the world. He placed it on the table and weighted it down with the steel fist. Hannibal watched him abstractedly. Dorsey had a shark-like face, big nose, thin protruding mouth and a small chin. But the great semi-bald dome of his head belonged to a man of acute intelligence.

Hannibal said, "You'd better put a man to trailing Spike Brenn. He's investigating the Steel Fists."

Dorsey's thin mouth turned down at the corners. "Why trail him, John? He could be er—liquidated."

Hannibal's eyes blazed anew. "You're a bloodthirsty devil, Dorsey."

"How so? I've only—"

"You murdered Pierre Lachard and Otto Zeiger. But for that no one would have heard of the Steel Fists until I was ready."

Dorsey looked up from putting a box of cigars on the table. His face flushed with anger.

"You don't understand," he cried furiously. "In a game like this it is our lives or theirs."

"But you'll stop this killing," said Hannibal curtly. "I made you my chief of staff because you're a tactician and an organizer. But you kill any one else without my order and I'll break you, Dorsey, as I broke Halldale before you."

Dorsey did not quail.

"If you lose this game we play it is because you didn't purge enough. Take lessons from others—dictators."

"Where death is necessary, I inflict it," said Hannibal. "In Brenn's case, merely watch him. And—" he broke off, for Beake came in and bowed.

"Your guests have arrived, sir."

HANNIBAL NODDED AND stood with folded arms while Dorsey shook hands with the men who entered. Each man as he entered clicked his heels, struck his chest over his heart with his clenched right fist. Each one wore on the silk lapel of his full dress coat a small silver steel fist.

Hannibal did not bring a conference air to the meeting as he had them sit down. He casually inquired about the crops in each nation these men represented. And they knew what was meant; without good crops the world cannot make war. Each reported prospects of a bumper crop.

Hannibal nodded, blew smoke from his pursed lips.

"We've been six years preparing," he said at length. "Now is the time."

"You mean this fall?" asked Della Volpi of Italy.

"I mean September—after the harvest—for you and Von Eitel."

The big German general stirred at mention of his name.

"You have planned well in six years, Mein Herr," he said. "But we must have some guarantee of success before we take the final step."

"*Si, si,* Signor Hannibal," murmured Della Volpi.

Hannibal studied their faces; power there, ruthless, brutal power. Cool rational men who must face the balance of the scales in their favor before making a decision.

"You mean war with Japan?" Hannibal asked.

"Jawohl," said the German logistics expert. "Bring that about and we shall act at once."

"Si," said Della Volpi. "War with Japan is the crux of the problem. America is peacefully inclined. She will endure much for peace."

Hannibal glanced around the circle of faces.

"You agree? Knowing my plans and organization, do you agree that success will come if war is made with Japan?"

A chorus of assent went up. They had studied the scheme, knowing their own lives hung upon it. And they were certain.

"If war with Japan is declared on or after August first," Hannibal said, "you will act no later than September?"

"Possibly before," rejoined Von Eitel promptly. "Time will be the essence of the affair then."

"Quite," nodded Hannibal. "Very well. You are the Five of the Grand Council. You have your orders, your plans, the money."

He paused. Then: "The United States will be at war with Japan on August first. That is the signal for the rest of you."

He moved the map slightly and stabbed its surface with his pencil.

"Now here is the three-part plan. And here are the final details."

He began to talk swiftly, his blazing blue eyes completely dominating these men who were rulers themselves.

2

FASCISM FOR CHILDREN

ON THE NIGHT of July 28th in Paris a man was murdered, and Spike Brenn returned from a swing across Europe and Asia. Both were incidents of prime importance in the events that were to come.

John Hannibal ordered the man killed. In the house he had taken in the Bois de Boulogne district, facing the Avenue de la Grande Armeé, Hannibal sat talking with his son Stephen. The house below hummed with activity; dozens of secretaries labored; dozens of specialists carried out his peculiar orders, all supervised by the saturnine Dorsey. But here all was quiet save for the boy's childish treble.

"You mean, sir," he said, "that there are two types of people in the world; those who rule and those who are ruled. Those who are ruled are the peasants."

"Yes," assented Hannibal. "The theory of democracy as you have studied it in that book is a fraud, a delusion, the product of weak minds who would bind the strong."

"Please explain, sir."

Hannibal studied the boy's bright hair and unconsciously his hand came out to stroke its golden softness.

"There are two theories of government in the world,

boy," he said in what was a gentle voice for him; "one theory is called democracy. That is to say, all men, no matter how ignorant, how lowly born, shall have a vote as to their own destinies. This theory is based on the superstition that in the mass of people there exists an instinctive rightness—that they cannot be wrong. This is a fallacy, of course, for the bigger the mass, the greater its ignorance, the surer it is to be wrong.

"The theory of democracy is promoted by those who, by bribery, strength and cunning, hide behind it and exploit the masses to their own ends. That is why America has been denuded of its resources. That is why I can become rich and other men must remain poor. Democracy has been tolerated heretofore because no matter how much was stolen, wasted or destroyed there was sufficient left over to feed even the lowliest. That time has passed for good.

"The second theory—my theory—is that there are two classes of people in the world; those meant to rule, and those meant to be ruled. By rigid discipline—regimentation is the present popular word—the ruling class controls the nation, conserves resources, cuts down the prohibitive cost of self-government, stops theft by those elected to office and moulds the nation in preparation for its manifest destiny."

"I believe in the second theory," said Stephen stoutly. "When I'm grown up I want to rule, not be ruled by ignorant peasants."

"When you grow up," said Hannibal musingly, "you will rule. I am training you for nothing else. You will be—"

He stopped speaking as the door opened. He turned, frowning. Dorsey's shark-like face thrust through the opening and a raised pair of eyebrows brought Hannibal to his feet.

"Reveille at six, son," he said, "so go to sleep."

He kissed the boy, heard, "Goodnight, sir," and went out of the room. Dorsey drew him to one side and whispered, "Miguel Lopez is downstairs."

Miguel Lopez was the head of the Steel Fist echelon in Mexico. His presence was not unexpected, and Hannibal frowned.

"What of it? He was sent for to report on the border situation."

Dorsey smiled. "That is true. But this is *not* Miguel Lopez."

"Not Miguel Lopez," Hannibal looked angry. "Don't talk in riddles."

"It is not Miguel Lopez," repeated Dorsey. "This one speaks Spanish; he looks like Lopez except that this one has a scar on his thumb ball which Lopez never had."

Hannibal was instantly alert. "You're certain?"

"I'm more than certain; I'd stake my life." Dorsey smiled again. "This one asks too many questions. Oh, cleverly, but he asked them."

"Let me have a look at him—unseen, of course."

Dorsey led his chief to a gallery overlooking the library. The swarthy man, unaware that he was seen, was examining papers in the wastebasket. At some sound he looked up. Hannibal got a look at his face. Hannibal's headache was acute tonight, and so were his perceptions. He had an uncanny memory for movement and faces. The way this man straightened sharply told him it was not Lopez.

"You're right," he said harshly. "Have you recognized him?"

"No, but he is an American. That is stain on his skin or I'm a Chinaman."

Hannibal turned back to the neighboring room. "Send Nick and Jerry after him. We cannot afford to take chances now." His voice remained hard.

Dorsey nodded. "Right away. And the cable, has it gone yet?"

"Not until tomorrow," said Hannibal. He turned back to his own study. Dorsey went downstairs and sent word to Jerry and Nick. Then he returned and bowed the pseudo-Lopez out by saying Hannibal was indisposed now but Lopez was to come back at ten in the morning.

"The boss is very interested in your report," Dorsey smiled.

Lopez went out. Jerry and Nick followed him across the Bois de Boulogne. Ten minutes later Jerry and Nick came back. Dorsey let them in the side door.

"Well?" he said.

"A Maxim-silenced gun can only fire one shot and it has to be good," grinned Jerry.

"This one," said Nick, "was perfect."

Dorsey smiled. "Good enough," he said and departed.

SPIKE BRENN CAME into Le Bourget on the Imperial Airways Express from Brindisi, and, of all persons, David Farnham met him.

"I was in Harry's New York Bar when your cable came, so I drove out myself," Farnham said. "I'm sailing for home Tuesday and I wanted to see you again."

"Appreciate it," said Spike, dropping wearily into the

back seat of the car. "Good Lord, I'm tired. I'm so tired—" he accepted the proffered flask of brandy and took a stiff three fingers.

"Still on the trail of the Steel Fists?"

Spike Brenn screwed the top back on the flask. He tamped his pipe full, lit it, and a cloud of smoke swirled from the bowl.

"Let me give a monologue," he said. "I've got to straighten out my own thoughts. Right now I have a hard time believing them."

Farnham sat very quietly, but now alert. Brenn rubbed his hands over his face.

"I've been in Germany, Bulgaria, Hungary, Yugo-Slavia, Italy, India and China and Japan," he said. "I found Steel Fists everywhere except in China and India. It's an international Fascist organization, all right, but I can't find out much about its purposes. Except one thing."

"What?" asked Farnham.

"The Steel Fists are extremists," said Brenn. "In Germany they want to overthrow Hitler and put their own man in. I've an idea—though I can't prove it—that Oberst-General Burghard Von Eitel is the leader. The Steel Fists want to make war now. I heard a hint that the objective is to conquer and colonize South America."

Farnham nodded; he had been in South America during the winter. "Fascism is making inroads there. What else?"

"In Italy it's Giovanni Della Volpi. The idea is, as I get it, that Mussolini is in his dotage and Count Ciano is a dumb cluck—and Volpi would make a better dictator. There was talk here, too, *sub rosa,* that Italians could colonize Argentina and Paraguay very easily."

Farnham's car reached the Grand Boulevards. Brenn interrupted himself long enough to say, "Drive to my office. May have to broadcast tonight."

Farnham gave the necessary order. "What about Japan?"

Spike scowled. "In Japan the Steel Fists are all extreme Army and Navy men. It's a political party that wants all of China, Borneo and Java—wants to fight Russia. At once." He paused, added, "The Steel Fists is a war party."

"I see," said Farnham. "Then the Steel Fists are aware of international anarchy and want to take while the taking's good."

"All they need is a leader to point the way," assented Spike moodily.

"They must have such a leader," said Farnham. "What else could bind such groups together internationally?"

"Right, but who?" The car stopped, and the two men went up to Brenn's office together. There, after a moment's silence, Farnham said: "You said in Brussels that the movement had for its purpose the conquest of the United States. Did you hear anything more of that?"

"A false rumor, I guess," said Spike wearily. "They must have meant South America because even in Japan I kept hearing about South America as the promised land for have-not peoples."

Farnham got up and walked to Spike's desk, got a package of matches and returned.

"Did you ever hear of the Monroe Doctrine?" he asked.

"Sure. The United States guarantees the independence and integrity of South American countries. It's an order from us to Europe to keep hands off—" Spike broke off as a sudden perception of what was in Farnham's mind came to him. "Holy Joe!" he exclaimed. "If these Steel Fists got control in their countries and wanted to go into South America, they'd have to fight us first."

"They would," said Farnham.

Suddenly Spike Brenn looked back and chuckled in relief. "Then there'll be no war. We've got the Atlantic Ocean. No European power or combination of powers excepting England could fight our fleet. It's just another Fascist pipe-dream for home consumption. But it's a swell Story."

"Yes," said Farnham, thoughtfully, "it's a swell story. "But—" He broke off and turned toward Brenn's office door. "Is that a dog or something scratching there?"

In two strides Spike Brenn reached the door and jerked it open. A man, stiff-legged, with hands partly raised, plunged at him and would have fallen if Spike hadn't caught him. Spike dragged the man into the room.

Farnham had hastened over to aid. Now, as he saw the blood seeping through the stiff shirt, he cried in a startled tone, "He's been shot!"

3

FIVE YEARS TOO LATE?

SPIKE CARRIED THE man to a couch and sent Farnham for a bottle of whisky in a drawer. He looked down at the swarthy pale face.

"He's dying," he said. "But you'd better get on a phone, Dave, and try to raise a doctor."

"Never mind doctor," muttered the wounded man. "Give me another shot of whisky—and listen."

"Take it easy," said Spike gently.

"No time," growled the man. "Whisky! I'm dying—I've got to talk. Prime me."

Spike poured a half-tumbler full of whiskey into the man's mouth and it brought a flush to his face. His voice, when he spoke, was stronger.

"I met you, Brenn, in China—on the *Panay*. When they shot me I remembered your office was closest. Now listen."

He tried to lift himself up, failed and sank back.

"I'm Lieutenant Norman Carstairs of the U.S. Navy," he said distinctly. "Take this message to the Embassy. Either Miles or O'Hara will do. Tell them—give me another drink."

"Take it easy, fellah," began Brenn. "You—"

"A drink," gasped Carstairs.

Brenn gave him the liquor. Carstairs gagged but got it down. It stiffened him, gave him back his speech.

"Listen, when this liquor goes I go. Tell Miles or O'Hara that John Hannibal is the leader of the Steel Fists. His organization in the United States is the League of Unemployed. He's a traitor. He—" Carstairs' voice broke. Then: "Tell Kay—tell Kay—" His jaw dropped and he died between two breaths. The room became strangely silent. Neither Spike nor Farnham moved.

Finally Farnham said, "Did you know him on the *Panay?*"

Spike replied dully: "I met a Carstairs—Naval Intelligence." He looked at Farnham. "Hannibal's in Paris. He murdered this man."

Farnham silently assented. Quickly Spike went to the telephone and finally got the Embassy and was given Lieutenant Burton Miles' home address. "Miles is the Naval attaché." He gave the number and waited.

Farnham said, "Hannibal murdered him but you can't prove it."

"No," said Spike. A voice came on the wire and Spike said, "Burt? This is Spike Brenn. Pick up O'Hara and come to my office right away. Don't ask questions. Get moving."

He hung up. "Hannibal!" he muttered. "Steel Fists! What does it all mean?" In sudden decision he went to his traveling bag, took out an automatic pistol and snicked back the collar. "Stay here," he said to Farnham, "and talk to Miles. Tell him I'll hurry back."

"Where are you going?"

"To see Hannibal."

JOHN HANNIBAL WAS on the transatlantic telephone

talking to Paul Martin, president of the League of Unemployed. Hannibal was issuing orders crisply.

"Keep them marching," he said. "You've got enough ex-service men to teach them squads right and left. I want discipline. And I will have it."

He listened for a moment to Martin's report; six hundred and fifty thousand members in twelve thousand units— echelons was the technical name they were known by. Hannibal nodded but his face did not relax.

"Recruit up to eight hundred thousand," he said. "And get them all young—and dissatisfied." He issued a few more instructions and promised to put four million dollars on deposit for expenses.

As he hung up Dorsey tiptoed into the room. Dorsey's shark-like face was dark.

"Spike Brenn's downstairs. He wants to see you."

Hannibal rubbed his throbbing head.

"Well, send him in."

"He looks tough. He may have discovered something."

Hannibal shrugged. "In a few days it won't make any difference whether he has or not. Send him in."

Spike's very hugeness made his entry into a room an impressive event. Hannibal, rising to greet him, regarded the two hundred and twenty pounds of bone and muscle almost with envy. Not a small man himself—six feet—he was dwarfed by this giant.

"Back from the wars, Spike?" he smiled and held out his hand. Spike let him hold it out.

"When I saw you in Brussels," he said, "you told me you knew nothing about the Steel Fists."

"Yes."

"You lied. You're the head of it."

John Hannibal relaxed and lowered himself carefully into a chair.

"I'd say offhand," he murmured, "that your approach is bull-headed and stupid."

Spike ignored the remark. "You had a man murdered tonight. An agent of Naval Intelligence. Made up like a Mexican."

"I deny that."

"The man lived long enough to tell me so."

"But not long enough to tell any one else. Furthermore," Hannibal went on coolly, "I can prove I was elsewhere at the moment—if I have to."

Spike said: "Yeah? Okay! You can. But you've practically told me you did it, and that's what counts."

He stared down at Hannibal. "What's the big idea?"

"What do you mean?"

"You were a captain in the World War. You were probably a good soldier. But organizing the Steel Fists—working with other countries against your own—that's treason in my language."

Hannibal's blue eyes blazed brighter. "What was it Patrick Henry said, 'If this be treason, make the most of it.'"

Spike moved closer to Hannibal and leaned on the desk. His eyes, glancing down, noted a pad of cable blanks.

"I'm an honest reporter," he said at length, turning to face Hannibal. "I had to verify what the Naval Agent said. I've done so. If you don't want to explain, I'm now at liberty to draw my own conclusions."

HIS BIG HANDS played with the cable blank pad. Carelessly he ripped off a couple and began folding them. His mouth was drawn taut.

"And those conclusions are?" Hannibal said quietly.

"You've got a scheme to overthrow the government—perhaps put yourself in as dictator. Form an international coalition of Steel Fist dictators. Perhaps you're thinking about world power. I'd say you were insane enough."

Hannibal smiled grimly. "Do you believe I could overthrow the government?"

"No, but you could make trouble."

"Well," said Hannibal, "since you're not leaving here immediately, I don't mind talking with you about the possibility. I've always admired your brawn, Spike, and you have above-average intelligence."

Spike heard the threat and ignored it. He waited silently.

"Do you think democracy is functioning well in the United States?" Hannibal asked.

"Good enough for you to start from scratch and make a couple of hundred million dollars."

"That's not democracy. It's theft."

"Theft?"

"Yes. I stole the money. I had some capital. I got more abroad. I sold the market short. People, desperate, threw their securities on the market to sell at any price. I paid them a tenth of the value."

Hannibal leaned forward. "In a country where individual anarchy does not exist as it does in the United States, such theft of people's wealth could not happen."

Spike stared in amazement. Hannibal was really serious with this nonsense. And Hannibal went on, his blue eyes blazing.

"What does democracy give the worker?" Hannibal cried. "The privilege of laboring all his life for food and the privilege of starving to death in his old age.

"Don't tell me that democracy gives every man a chance to be wealthy. It doesn't. Ninety per cent of the people—the peasants, peons, slaves if you will—never had a chance from the beginning. No chance to learn, no chance to be smart, no chance to be healthy."

Hannibal leaned back, his lips curling. "All your so-called democracy does is remove the responsibility from the wealthy of taking care of worn-out workers. They are allowed to die of malnutrition and industrial diseases."

Spike said slowly, lowering his face to Hannibal's, "And what would you put in its place?"

"An industrial government, run on business lines. One boss, whose sole task would be to distribute the nation's wealth so that all had security and no one was so incredibly wealthy as, say, myself or your friend Farnham."

"And that's what you intend to do—substitute this ideal of yours by force in the United States?"

"I was merely talking," Hannibal said.

"And you've talked plenty." Brenn strode to the door, but there he paused and swung around. There were deep lines around his mouth. "I don't like your little idea, Hannibal—and I don't like you. But I'm going to give you some publicity; tomorrow I'm going to tell twenty million Americans about you and your tin soldiers."

"You're not going out," said Hannibal.

"No?" Brenn drew his gun and leveled it. "Why?"

"Don't shoot, Nick, Jerry," said Hannibal quietly.

"Okay, boss."

Brenn whirled. Listening to Hannibal he had never heard the little slot in the wall open. But he saw it now and the gun muzzle glittering in the aperture.

"Sit down, Spike," said Hannibal.

Slowly Spike shook his head. To him, suddenly, the solution was simple. He smiled.

"Tell your man to shoot," he said quietly. "He can't kill me before I kill you."

"True," admitted Hannibal. "But what good does that do?"

Again Spike smiled. "Three people—important people—know I came here. They'll know who killed me. Second, twenty million people in America knew me, Hannibal. And if anything happened to me—"

He paused significantly, then added, "It would be as good a way as any to blow up your incredible plan."

There was murder in John Hannibal's blazing blue eyes. The fingers of his left hand slapped the side-arm of the chair as an angry cat's tail slaps the floor.

Jerry called, "Shall I let him have it, boss?"

Spike's own trigger finger whitened. It is doubtful if in all his forty-three years John Hannibal had ever seen such calm, utter courage. He yielded to it grudgingly.

"You're right, of course," he said quietly. "You're more powerless alive. You may go."

Spike reached behind him and opened the door. "Keep your dogs leashed, Hannibal," he said. He backed through the doorway and vanished.

Jerry said, "Shall we take him outside, boss?"

Hannibal considered. When his head ached like this he thought with blinding clarity.

"No, Jerry," he said. "What he does can't make much difference now. He's five years too late."

SPIKE BRENN GOT back to his office shortly before midnight. He strode in, the blank cable form clutched in his hand. The dead body of Norman Carstairs still rested on the couch.

Besides Farnham he recognized Burton Miles, the Naval attaché, and Captain Glen O'Hara, the military attaché of the American Embassy. Beyond them he saw a tall, stunning girl in white satin evening dress. His glance took in her bright golden hair, her red lips and lustrous eyes, moist now with unshed tears. Silently he shook hands with Miles and O'Hara.

Spike's eyes shifted to the girl.

Miles said, "Kay Carstairs—Norm's sister! She came to Paris to see him. She was having dinner with us when you called Burt."

"Tough," said Spike. He went over to the girl and took her limp hand and squeezed it gently. "I'm sorry," he said softly. "He was a swell guy."

Miles spoke quickly to relieve the strain on the girl. "I remember the time in the last quarter at Franklin Field against Notre Dame. Norm was blocking and he tore a hole through the Irish line you could have driven a truck through. Kept his feet, too, to take out the secondary and yelling at me, 'Get the lead out and run.'"

"He must have been quite a man," said Farnham, his eyes on the girl. He walked to her. "He died in line of duty and he gave his last breath to deliver the information that cost him his life."

Her eyes swept past Farnham to Spike. "I'm Navy

enough to save my tears," she said. Her voice was soft, pleasing. "Who—who did it?"

"John Hannibal," Spike told her.

For the first time her frozen-faced grief disappeared in the face of astonishment.

"John Hannibal? Oh, no, not John Hannibal!"

"I'm telling you."

"But—but I know John Hannibal. I know him well. We've been friends. Friends for four years."

"It was John Hannibal," said Spike harshly. "I just talked to him. He as much as confessed."

She was staggered and silent. And she remained alone and silent while Spike whispered with Miles and O'Hara about what should be done with the body. Miles said they would take it to the Embassy and announce death from natural causes.

"We'll have to," he went on. "Carstairs was on undercover work."

"Looking for what?" Spike asked.

Miles shook his head. "You know I can't tell you. But I'll say this: he wasn't investigating Hannibal, which is why I can't understand why Hannibal shot him—if he did."

"I know he did," said Spike grimly.

He stood aside while the body was carried down to the Embassy car. Farnham offered to escort Kay Carstairs but she shook her head.

"I'll go with Burt and Glen." She came to Spike.

"Why would John Hannibal shoot my brother?"

"Come here tomorrow," said Spike, "and I'll tell you."

He stood quietly for some minutes after she and the others had gone. Then he turned to find Farnham studying him quietly. Without speaking Spike unfolded the cable form he had brought from John Hannibal's. "Take your knife and scrape that pencil for some graphite," he ordered. "Hannibal had sent a cable and he pressed hard with the pencil. I want to see what he sent."

He spread the graphite dust, talking as he worked, describing what he knew of Hannibal's Fascist plot.

"I expected that," said Farnham when Spike had finished. "It's incredible, but his intriguing could cause trouble—with a presidential election coming up in November and much discontent."

Spike did not reply. Under his skillful touch the indentations on the cable blank had suddenly become visible.

"Look at this," he said.

KURIHO, MACAIR,
MANILA, PHILIPPINE ISLANDS
THIRTIETH OFF CORREGIDOR NOON BEFORE
GOVERNOR ARRIVES
JOHN HANNIBAL

He looked up from the blank. "What do you make of that?"

Farnham pondered for a while and at length shook his head. "It was something to do with an event transpiring in Manila. You'll have to start investigating from that end. And you've only got two days."

Spike reached for the telephone and dictated a cable to the Foreign Broadcasting Corporation's reporter in Manila. When he turned back to Farnham, his broad face was twisted in a frown.

"Damn it," he growled. "I've got this thing almost in my hands—and yet I can't reach it." He stared at his huge clinched fists.

At last he got up, fixed two drinks of cognac and water and handed one to Farnham. He sat down again, aware of a sense of comfort in Farnham's presence. The man exuded a confidence, a calm power that soothed Spike's tired nerves.

After a while Spike said, "The League of Unemployed. Hannibal's organization!"

"And very Fascist," Farnham pointed out.

"But not big enough," growled Spike. "He'd have to have plenty of men—a million—and even then it couldn't be done." He stood up. "It's impossible. The country's too big."

Farnham sipped his drink. "Keep one thing in mind, Spike. Hannibal may be a megalomaniac but he's clever. He's colossally rich. He's dangerous."

Thus they sat there talking while in Manila on the other side of the globe John Hannibal's fateful message was delivered to a bright-eyed young Chinese named Kuriho.

4

SPEAK TO TWENTY MILLION...

LATE IN THE afternoon of July 30th Spike Brenn sat writing furiously in his office. He was preparing his broadcast for the American public. And it concerned only the mysterious Steel Fists.

At the moment the world was in a critical stage. Hitler was threatening Czechoslovakia, and demanding colonies on pain of drastic action. Mussolini was mobilizing troops on the Libyan border, threatening to invade Egypt. England was having another cabinet crisis and the anti-American prime minister, Joseph St. John, was castigating the United States bitterly for failure to back up England's protest to a new Japanese invasion of China. The Spanish Rebels had launched the final offensive against Valencia. Russia was purging itself of anti-Stalinites.

But all this Spike ignored. He was preparing, he told himself, a broadcast that would bring every one of his twenty-million listeners popping out of their chairs.

He'd smash Hannibal's Steel Fists with one powerful blow of publicity that would brand Hannibal a traitor and a maniac. He was three-quarters done when his secretary came in and said, "Miss Kay Carstairs to see you and she says it's important."

Spike frowned, then said, "Show her in."

He was remembering her bright head, and it was as lovely as his memory of it when she stood offering him her hand. He could find nothing to say, so for a moment there was an awkward silence.

Finally she sat down, crossed her slim legs and said, "I came about Norm."

"Yes," Spike said.

"He's been buried, and nobody over there can do anything to make Hannibal pay. You can't even mention he's been murdered."

"No," Spike told her. "The Embassy asked me to suppress it—on grounds of national safety."

"They won't do anything to Hannibal, then?"

"You can't have a man arrested for murder unless you can prove it. Furthermore, the government wants secrecy in investigating the Steel Fists—for a while anyway."

She nodded. "And what are you going to do?"

Spike told her about his broadcast. "They can't stop me doing that," he added defensively.

Again she nodded and remained silent for a space. Then quite suddenly she said, "I'm going to John Hannibal today."

"Why?" Spike protested.

"John Hannibal is in love with me—at least, he wants to marry me." She stared straight ahead. "I'll prove he's a murderer—and then you can broadcast it. I'll tell you all I find out."

Abruptly Spike touched her hand. "With you on the inside we could—but it's dangerous."

She stood up, ignoring his warning. "Tell me where I can reach you besides here at the office."

Spike gave her his telephone number. At the door she halted a moment, studying Spike's face. Then swiftly she smiled. "You'll hear from me," she said.

Downstairs she entered a taxi and gave John Hannibal's address.

SPIKE WENT ON the air at nine o'clock. This time, standing before the microphone, he read each word of his broadcast and he spoke slowly so there could be no misunderstanding.

"Hello, America, this is Spike Brenn, your roving reporter, talking to you from Paris. And I want you, please, to listen carefully because the future of the United States, your country and mine, may depend on what you do in the next few days.

"First of all, from time to time I've talked to you about the Steel Fists. This international order of Fascism—another way of saying international gangsters and racketeers—has for its purpose the overthrow of the American government and the establishment of a dictatorship as brutal as those now existing in Europe. Presently I'll tell you the name of the head of it.

"These European extreme Fascists who hate America are backing the Steel Fists to win. How they hope to win I don't know yet, and that's why I'm appealing to you. There must be in the United States an organization of Steel Fists, but not known by that name. They must be a big outfit, for no small one could hope to overthrow our present government. So I appeal to you.

"Have you heard of the Steel Fists? Have you heard the

members of any organization known by any name speak of destroying our government? Favor a dictatorship? Speak about some impending change?

"I appeal to all of you to speak out if you know anything. And I especially appeal to my pals, the 'Hams' of the American Amateur Radio Association. As your honorary president, I'm asking for real help. This is deadly serious. With a presidential election coming up, with the world in a state of anarchy where gangster nations can muscle in, America is in danger. You've got to help.

"The head of the Steel Fists is an American. He is a megalomaniac who would destroy two hundred years of American tradition to put in his own insane conception of government. His name is—"

"Spike!" called the radio engineer.

Spike looked up at the gesticulating man.

"His name," Spike repeated.

"Lay off, Spike," the radio engineer said. "You're off the air. They cut you off in New York. You can't get away with, libel on the air."

"You mean I'm talking to myself?" Spike cried.

"Sure, for the last minute or so."

Spike cursed and threw down his manuscript.

"Libel!" he cried bitterly. "That's a laugh."

"You can't scare America," said the engineer. "Not while there are thirty-five hundred miles of water separating them from this European bonfire."

Spike looked at the man who spoke a short ugly word....

Kay Carstairs was sitting with John Hannibal in his library when the broadcast was burked. She was listening to Spike's strong friendly voice and feeling in it tonight a deep sincerity that held her tense in her chair.

"This is deadly serious," the radio said. "With a presidential election—" the radio was silent for ten seconds. Then a suave voice said, "People of America, atmospheric conditions prevent the continuation of Spike Brenn's broadcast from Paris. He—"

John Hannibal clicked off the powerful radio.

"I was getting it from New York," he said.

"They cut him off the air," Kay said.

"A flannel-mouthed, rabble-rousing piece of hysteria," said John Hannibal. "I don't blame them."

"And you don't believe what he says?"

"Of course not."

John Hannibal rose. "How about the Perroquet for a dance and a spot of champagne?"

Kay nodded. But she was thinking, "John Hannibal had the power to stop that broadcast."

As Hannibal was helping her into the fur bolero jacket, Dorsey came in with a cable. His face shone with excitement but he said nothing.

Hannibal glanced at the cable.

WHEN YOU RECEIVE THIS IT WILL BE ALL
OVER WE LEAVE IN ONE HOUR
KURIHO

The cable was dated from Manila at eleven o'clock. Hannibal computed the difference in time swiftly and handed the paper back to Dorsey. Then he smiled and offered his arm to Kay.

"You look lovely tonight," he said.

IN A LARGE cleared section of land in the hills of Luzoiq a low-winged airplane, her twin motors covered with tarpaulins against the heavy moisture, rested under a canopy of brush camouflage. Nearby was a small khaki tent, completely covered with mosquito netting. Within a man reposted on a cot, reading a copy of the Japanese daily, *Nichi Nichi*. He was Mongolian, but there must have been white blood in him, too, because he was taller than the average Chinese and had a fairer skin. Only his hair, stiff and black and thick, and the peculiar cheekbones and beady eyes told of his mixed ancestry. He was consuming cigarettes chain fashion as he read.

The news was all Japanese flavored; that is to say, in the present crisis of Japanese-American relations over the conquest of China, only the Japanese view was presented. The shooting in cold blood of the American consul at Hankow was presented as a dreadful accident that no one could have foreseen. In almost the same breath the story said:

> But if this is an accident, the fact that nearly a hundred American aviators are flying and fighting with the Chinese against us is not. These American pilots are flying American planes, armed with American machine guns, and while our peerless flyers have been superior to them, the fact remains that several Japanese pilots and planes have been shot down as a result of these American depredations. If America wants to maintain the traditional peace and amity which has always existed between our countries, then it would be best for her to demand, and promptly, that Chiang Kai-shek and his rebels

force the withdrawal of these Americans.

The young man smiled sardonically. He turned the page to a long interview with Vice-Admiral Togo Matsu.

The world is arming against Japan, trying to wrest forcibly from us that which is our manifest destiny—Asia for the Asiatics. At the moment Japan has the preponderance of power. With the treaty of joint action existing between Germany, Italy and Japan, we stand in a position to enforce our will in the East. Now is the time to do it.

Borneo and Java possess raw products which we will need in the long struggle to come. The Philippines offer a sound base to outflank the British sea power based at Singapore. It is for us to seize the moment, occupy these islands and ensure to us the material most vitally needed by our expansion.

At the moment the British cannot detach their fleet from the Mediterranean to oppose us. The American fleet has no close bases on which to base the operations of their fleet so far from home water. Neither can stop us; but the next turn of the wheel may find America and England aligned so that we shall have to fight for our very existence. A blockade by the combined fleets to cut off our fuel supply would be a stroke at our jugular vein. Borneo, Java, the Philippines will amply supply such fuel and place us in a position to meet their offensive with a counter-offensive. Our present Japanese ministry must realize this and act, or there are others, including myself, who will appeal to the Emperor to dismiss the traitors and begin a more favorable policy for Japan's future.

The eyes of the young Chinese gleamed. "You are not

done with us yet," he muttered. "China will fight on and you will see—" He broke off as the sound of a motor car struggling along the rutted road came to ear. The Chinese stood up and reached for a gun but more as a precaution than with any expectation of hostility. This haven was too well hidden to be discovered in the brief time the plane had stayed there. A dilapidated Ford with fenders rusted off, pushed through the thick green vegetation and came into the clearing. The youth put down his gun and, pushing aside the mosquito netting, ran out to where the hot motor hissed and boiled.

"Kuriho," he exclaimed with pleasure.

THE YOUNG CHINESE jumped to the ground. His Oriental features were twisted with emotion. "I have sent the cable," he said and repeated in a harsh whisper, "I have answered him—and we obey this order."

He held out the blue bit of paper. The young Eurasian, Sung Kai, looked at it and his own face split in a huge smile. He handed back the cable which Kuriho immediately tore into bits, put in his mouth and chewed into a soggy wad and then spat it out.

They touched their foreheads. "For China," they repeated in unison.

Then the younger said, "Did you go to the harbor?"

"Yes," nodded Kuriho. "I saw her lying just off Corregidor. There is to be a big fete and tea aboard this afternoon at one. Every one of importance will be there."

"Then let us depart," said Sung Kai. "We will go in an hour," said Kuriho.

"*Tso Tak*," said Sung Kai.

They walked quickly to the huge plane that they had

flown secretly from Hong Kong. The three-thousand-pound pay load now consisted of three enormous cylindrical bombs of a thousand pounds each, held to the ship by brackets controlled by electrical toggles from within. Sung Kai looked at these while Kuriho examined the motors. There was not much gasoline supply aboard, in order to assure a quick take-off.

"We shall not need much gasoline anyway," Kuriho said.

"No," nodded Sung Kai. "Just enough to get there."

The plane was a Douglas heavy bomber capable of two hundred and fifty miles an hour. On the leading edge of the wings were mounted, in tandem, four machine guns of .50 calibre each and synchronized so their combined fire converged at a hundred yards ahead. In addition there were two machine guns in a glass-covered cupola in the nose. These the pilot operated with another lever.

Belts were checked to make certain cartridges were greased and not likely to jam. These checking operations passed the hour swiftly. Sung Kai climbed in and took his place. Kuriho checked the starters, got the radial fifteen hundred horse power motors choked, and pressed the starter. First the starboard motor rattled, choked, roared, then the port. At quarter throttle Kuriho let them warm up. At the end of twenty minutes he pivoted on his seat.

"Ready, Sung Kai?" he asked.

"Ready, brother," said the other, and gestured to the electric toggle.

"We'll dive vertically from fifteen thousand feet," Kuriho said. "And at all risks I shall go down so close that you cannot miss."

"I will not miss," said Sung Kai.

Kuriho cracked the throttles and as the propellers revved up the big ship trundled down the field to turn into the wind.

5

HANNIBAL'S WAR

OFF THE FROWNING walls of Corregidor in Manila harbor the Japanese battleship *Mutsui,* 56,000-ton dreadnaught, was gaily bedecked with bunting and lanterns and there was a great coming and going of launches from her starboard quarter ladder. A great battleship, the pride of the Japanese navy, was paying a friendly visit to the American colonial high commissioner of the Philippines. The nominal reason was to represent Japan when the Philippines celebrated the act of independence for which they had fought for years.

As an added friendly gesture from Nippon the *Mutsui* carried aboard His Imperial Royal Highness Prince Hirita and his new young wife from the powerful Antzi clan. They were celebrating their honeymoon, and at the same time the young crown prince would speak at the festivities and pledge to the Filipinos that Japan would never encroach on the new independence but would always be the big brother to the north. Truly a great gesture from Japan.

The short broad Japanese officer of the day, dressed in spotless white and gold, strolled toward the gangway, his sword clanking. He gave the order that the boatswain's mate should pipe the high commissioner aboard when the launch came off from shore with the American.

As he turned away, he heard a thin drone from the sky above. His head craned, but the plane was too high to be immediately discerned. He thought to himself that it was probably one of the Philippine military aircraft come out to circle and stunt as a sign of welcome; it was frequently done so.

The drone thinned to nothing, then came back slowly like a big fly buzzing off a hot window pane. The officer of the day turned his attention to shore. The government barge was already getting under way. He called a midshipman and sent word to the captain that the American high commissioner would come aboard in a few minutes.

As the midshipman walked swiftly aft the drone from above became suddenly louder. The officer of the day lifted his binoculars, tracked the sound with his ears and eyes and located the plane. It was slanting downward, but not too swiftly, and he could make out on the under side of the wings the red, white and blue cocards with the superimposed star—the American air-force insignia but also adopted by the Filipinos.

The motor-roar grew ever louder.

A sharply hissed word caused him quickly to lower his binoculars and leap to rigid attention. His Imperial Highness, the Crown Prince, was coming down the deck with his young bride. With them came the captain. The officer of the day understood; as a final gesture to make amends for the tense feeling now existing between Japan and the United States, His Imperial Highness would himself welcome the American high commissioner aboard.

At the officer of the day's sing-song shout rising high
and thin at the end, the lines of sailors became rigid stat-
ues. He had to shout so; the noise of the plane above was
getting louder.

The barge from shore was a quarter of the way out to the
huge floating Japanese fortress.

Louder came the roar; the almost human howl of high
speed motors turned up to the last notch. Even sailors violated rigid attention to steal a peek at this diving
plane. It was perhaps three thousand feet up now, standing straight on its nose, directly over the battleship's stern
where the flags idly flapped in the tiny puffs of wind.

The officer of the day stole another look. Two thousand
feet or so, he estimated; about time to level off.

THE CAPTAIN WAS staring up as the plane above streaked
down a thousand feet, a reasonably safe altitude in which
to pull out. The captain's face suddenly became livid. He
uttered a harsh, screaming cry. He turned and seized the
prince and started to wrestle him toward the side of the
battleship. The prince, not realizing the captain's purpose,
resisted, and for a few brief, fatal seconds they tugged and
wrenched.

And now the plane above pulled out with a groaning
human howl that drowned all other sound. But as it pulled
out, the officer of the day was looking up and he saw, falling
like plummets, three glittering objects that were shooting
as straight as bullets toward the squat funnels of the huge
battleship.

The officer of the day barely saw them. The plane had
been diving at nearly four hundred miles an hour. This
terrific speed plus the gravity of their own weight, made

the three bombs merely slashing gray streaks against the blue sky.

Before the officer of the day could open his throat to shout, the bombs struck. All three hit almost simultaneously.

A great cloud of smoke and flame erupted. The terrific concussion as the bombs exploded, broke windows in the hotels four miles away. The huge thirty-six-thousand-ton battleship seemed to squat in the water beneath the impact; then she rolled until her starboard chain rail hung beneath the water.

Her entrails flew up in a gigantic cascade of debris, one bit of which struck the governor's barge a thousand yards off, and sank it.

The plane above soared, banked, turned and came back diving, and her machine gun bullets stormed in a steel rain along the shattered top deck of the stricken battleship.

There were brave men among the Japanese sailors. The bombs had slaughtered them until the scuppers boiled with a flood of crimson. There was no order, no discipline

But out of the bloody fragments sailors crawled to the 3.2 inch anti-aircraft gun that had escaped demolition. There were four live shells still in the munitions locker from target practice.

The Japanese gun-pointer spotted the huge Douglas coming in to machine-gun the ghastly decks. The gun-pointer fired the four shells between the time the plane reached the battleship's stern and the time it was over the amidships section. The fourth shell was a direct hit.

The plane jumped, nosed downward and struck squarely in the center of the *Mutsui's* blackened hulk. The plane exploded like a gun crash, caught fire and was utterly consumed.

By that time the governor was yelling for aid because he was swimming, and he was afraid of sharks. Before another boat rescued him, the *Mutsui* was down by the head and sinking fast.

FOR ENDLESS HOURS during the week following the sinking of the *Mutsui*, dispatches from the four corners of the world poured onto Spike Brenn's desk.

Here was the *Berliner Tageblatt:*

JAPANESE CROWN PRINCE AND WIFE KILLED
AS AMERICAN BOMBER SINKS MUTSUI

The story below referred to the deed as outright, brutal murder. Adolph Hitler sent condolences, saying, "Japan has no recourse but to wipe out this stigma by blood, and any policy she pursues will have our ardent sympathy."

Premier Benito Mussolini not only sent his sympathy but concluded his editorial in *Popolo* by saying:

THE UPSTART OF THE WEST SHOULD BE
PUNISHED AND A BITTER LESSON ADMINIS-
TERED. NOW IS THE TIME FOR THE JAPANESE
TO PROVE THEIR WORLD POWER.

The Tokio newspapers wept, for the young Crown Prince was not only sacred but beloved.

England was strangely silent save for the *Record,* anti-American, which said:

IF THE UNITED STATES HAS CHOSEN THIS
MOMENT TO CREATE AN INCIDENT FOR WAR,
SHE HAS SUCCEEDED.

The American newspapers insisted there was some
mistake. Secretary of State Crull immediately cabled the
government's sorrow, denied the plane was American or
authorized to such a dastardly attack, and promised swift
investigation.

For three days the Tokio government remained silent.
But Spike spotted one ominous development: The Japanese Emperor ordered convened the Imperial Conference,
a sign of crisis, for only twice in the past thirty years had
such a conference been called and both meetings had been
followed by war.

Another fact that worried Spike was the Department
of State's silence and refusal to divulge the contents of the
Japanese note handed in Friday by the Japanese Ambassador, Yardai.

Spike himself was held off the air because he had wanted
to accuse John Hannibal of deliberately manufacturing the
tragedy to cause war between Japan and the United States.

On Saturday Spike called Atterbury of the F.B.C. on
the transatlantic telephone and pled for ten minutes time
on the air.

"You've got to," he shouted. "Hannibal sent a cable
ordering that bombing, and I've got a copy of it."

"I tell you, Spike, you're crazy," Atterbury yelled over
thirty-five hundred miles of ocean. "You can't prove the
cable has any connection. Divers have been down to

the *Mutsui* and the plane and the men in it were utterly consumed."

"But—"began Spike.

"It's out. Hannibal could sue us out of our grave."

"But, he's making a war."

"There won't be any war. Calm down, Spike, in heaven's name, and broadcast the news, not suspicions of Hannibal and the Steel Fists."

Spike groaned. "No war! Why doesn't the State Department release the Japanese note?"

"The terms are too stiff. Replacement of the battleship *Mutsui* and public apology to the Japanese flag by the president. Negotiations will calm the Japs down."

"That's what you fools think," cried Spike. "It's war. And you'll wake up to it when the Japs strike."

A week passed during which rumors and gossip only accentuated the ominous absence of real facts. Spike did his news broadcast under a promise not to mention the Steel Fists or Hannibal. He compromised by imploring his radio audience to sit tight and be calm. It was well he did; a tabloid reporter got access to the Japanese note (no one ever found out how) and the publication of its terms wiped out sympathy for Japan and substituted anger. The consensus was that Japan was deliberately trying to humiliate the nation.

The only two incidents to disturb Spike's routine were Dave Farnham's departure and a note from Kay Carstairs.

Farnham dropped by to say farewell. He was catching the Pan-American plane to New York.

"I'm going home because it's war coming," Farnham said.

"Can't you convince those stupes that Hannibal is behind it?"

"Do they care?" asked Farnham ironically. "The president wants a second term. With a war on he'll be voted back into office."

"And the Jap militants want war, or they wouldn't put out such impossible terms and refuse to arbitrate."

Spike leaped to his feet. "Dave, what is Hannibal's purpose? How can he hope to become dictator with America involved in a war with Japan? A war always binds a nation together."

"Suppose Japan wins?" Farnham said quietly. "No government has ever stood in face of defeat. Look at Napoleon the Third after Sedan. Look at ex-Kaiser Wilhelm and the Emperor of Austria after the last World War. They—"

"But Japan can't win," said Spike.

"Maybe we can't, either. It'll be a naval war—and it may last for years."

Spike looked down at a fresh dispatch with a Manila date line.

> Paul Levering, Philippine High Commissioner, announced today that in the opinion of his fact-finding board, the Japanese battleship *Mutsui* was destroyed by two Chinese fanatics desiring to involve the United States in the undeclared war in the Far East.

Spike's lips curled. He pushed the dispatch to one side and jabbed his pipestem at Farnham.

"Listen, Dave," he said. "You've got dealers for your cars

scattered all over the country. Couldn't you organize them to uncover these Steel Fists?"

"I could," nodded Farnham, "and it's one of the purposes taking me home."

"Then you believe Hannibal's deliberately promoting a world war?"

Farnham nodded. "Get me proof, Spike, and I'll see the president personally."

THREE HOURS AFTER Farnham's plane had left for Croydon a ragged Frenchman with a seafaring look, came into Spike's office. He held out a dirty gray letter, saying he had found it with a hundred franc note attached and instructions to deliver it to Spike. The latter gave him another hundred francs and eagerly tore open the missive. He saw Kay's name signed before he plunged into the reading of it.

> Dear Spike,
>
> By the time you get this (and it was the only way I could reach you) I'll be aboard John Hannibal's yacht bound for an unknown destination. I am not a prisoner.
>
> Here is what I have discovered. Hannibal does not know my brother is dead, so he must not have ordered him murdered. Not knowingly at any rate. Hannibal is in constant radio communication (in code, of course) with a German named Burghard von Eitel and an Italian named Count Giovanni Della Volpi. He has also communicated with a Japanese admiral named Araka Toga. Hannibal is up to something.
>
> Besides Dorsey, he has aboard twenty-two men who are constantly seeing him. About what I do not know, but they have maps and charts and endless statistics. He has sent

drafts for several million dollars.

Though I don't know our present destination, I do know we will be back in the States by the middle of October or thereabouts. He asked me about that—he wants to marry me by then. Lady Lucille Elton is my chaperone at present. She is an old mistress of his—and jealous.

Hannibal is sure war is coming and is glad. He talked quite wildly the other night (could he be a narcotic addict?) about the future of the country and said he hoped America would lose the war.

As nearly as I can quote it, he said this: "The present American government is so wasteful that it cannot endure. Between what the rich accumulate and what the government doles out to the poor and unemployed, the middle class, upon whom the country's wealth and prosperity depend, are being crushed. What the country needs is the abolition of state, county and other forms of archaic government. What is needed is a real boss and discipline. What the people need is work and security."

And he went on to cite how slaves of ancient times were better off because they were looked after in their old age.

He is imperious in his discipline with this secretariat, and they bow and call him Seneschal. He is mad, yes, but shrewdly so.

I will try to communicate later, but will leave him in New York because I cannot go on with this hypocrisy. Sometimes I hate him, sometimes I fear him—then again he arouses my pity.

Spike was to remember later that this was the first time

that he had heard the word "Seneschal" connected with Hannibal.

"Von Eitel!" he exclaimed aloud. "He's the arch enemy of Hitler—the leader of the military group in the Reichswehr who want to oust Goering and Hitler.

"And Della Volpi! He's the greatest opponent Mussolini has."

He leaned back and sat staring into nothing for a half-hour. He had, he knew, the clue to the truth here if he could but discern it. So he was still baffled when his secretary came in, trembling with excitement.

"Look," she cried. "It's come. Look what they've done."

Spike took the flimsy—it was from the Associated Press and as he read his heart sank.

> Manila, P.I., August 17: Japanese battleships believed to be of the first line, destroyed by shellfire the naval defenses of Manila early today. Afterward the battleship broadsides were trained on Manila itself and bombarded for more than two hours. Fires are raging through the city in a hundred places. The number killed and wounded cannot be estimated but it is believed they will run into thousands.
>
> Add Manila. Japanese marines and infantry units have landed and seized Manila. All communications… Add AP Paris Office—the report from our Manila correspondent was interrupted at this time. It is believed that Japanese troops have seized the cable and wireless offices.

Spike let his hand fall heavily on the desk. The flimsy slid slowly to the floor.

"It's come," he muttered. "It's here—Hannibal's war."

6

"I ASK THE CONGRESS..."

SPIKE BRENN WENT through the Embassy to Miles' office and found the latter packing. Miles grinned at Spike. "What's the use of having pull if you don't use it? I'm going back to the fleet."

It was three days since the Japanese seizure of Manila and though no war had been declared, the world knew it was war to come. Congress had met in extraordinary session and the president's message was sure to declare a state of hostilities. Spike knew all this, but he knew Miles had better information.

"What's the low-down?" he asked.

"The fleet is going to sail," rejoined Miles. "They're making ready now. I'm trying to catch them—on the fleet aviation staff."

"Any more talk of an expeditionary force?" Spike asked.

"Some. How right it is I don't know. O'Hara is pulling strings to be recalled to active duty so there may be something to it."

Spike nodded. Out of all the excitement in the States he had gleaned two facts: the American Third and Fourth Armies were being mobilized west of the Rockies, and the American Air Force was being concentrated on the west coast.

This latter came about because, already, hysteria had gripped California, Oregon and Washington. People were swearing they had seen Japanese warships, submarines and airplanes. There was clamor from these coast States to keep the fleet deployed along the coast so that the people would not be bombed in their beds.

One particular feat of the imagination had even made Spike smile mirthlessly. A heavy Pacific fog had rolled in near Bandon-by-the-Sea in Oregon while to the eastward a forest fire was burning. The citizens of Bandon swore that Japanese airplanes in the night had laid a gas barrage, and pointed to six in the hospital at Coquille to prove it.

Actually, as Spike knew, the Japanese had done nothing beyond taking Manila and issuing a statement through the Tokio Foreign Office which declared bluntly, "The government of the United States refusing to yield satisfaction for the murder of the Japanese Crown Prince and the sinking of His Imperial Majesty's battleship *Mutsui,* the Japanese Imperial government reserves all liberty to deal with the incident to achieve a fundamental solution."

But, as Spike knew, there was real worry among the military. The American Asiatic Squadron, small at best, and deprived of its base at Manila, was trying to reach Hawaii and Pearl Harbor. The Japanese Second Fleet had sailed under sealed orders and was presumably looking for the squadron. When they met, battle would follow.

The *President Hoover* of the Dollar Line, and the *Greta Maersk* of the Maersk Line, had been seized at Kobe, and the crews and American passengers made prisoners.

"What I came about," said Spike, "is to know what the Naval Bureau thought of your report on Hannibal."

"They want more information."

Spike smiled. "We've got a Mediterranean scouting squadron. Could they find Hannibal if I told you that he's at sea on that big yacht of his—the *Bess?*"

Miles whistled softly. "So? That does away with one rub—asking the French to arrest him." He dropped the papers he was packing. "I'll tell the chief."

Spike did not wait around. He had, as he went back to his own office, the same feeling of confusion that a man in a house on fire has when he has suddenly to do a hundred things instantly. He stopped on the way at the Imperial Airways and reserved a berth on the transatlantic plane. He noticed grimly, as he paid for his reservation, that a copy of the Paris edition of the London *Daily Mail* had this headline emblazoned on it:

ENGLAND DECLARES NEUTRALITY IN
AMERICAN-JAPANESE WAR

The clerk said, "You're an American?"

"Yes," said Spike.

"Watch yourselves," said the clerk. "These Japs, taking

them by and large, are great little fighters. You chaps have been lording it over the world too long."

"I see," said Spike.

"See what?"

"What England thinks."

AT HIS OFFICE he put in a call for Atterbury in New York, and while waiting for it to be completed, scanned the dispatches piled on his desk. Two facts suddenly revealed held him absorbed for a half-hour. First, while declarations of neutrality were pouring in from Turkey, France, Spain, England, Belgium, Holland, Norway and Sweden, there were no such declarations from Hitler or Mussolini. Indeed, there was no news at all from Rome or Berlin.

"Are they waiting for a chance to pounce?" Spike thought.

His suspicion was borne out by the second fact: an Associated Press dispatch from Rio de Janeiro. The dispatch was brief but pregnant:

> Fascist political groups headed by Paolo Armini, openly wearing Italian Black Shirts and armed, resisted all attempts today to break up a Fascist meeting called to attack President Ortegas' policies. Ortagas has declared martial law and called out the troops to suppress the riots. The large Italian and German minorities here are demanding a bigger voice in the government, and it is said that the Fascist groups are receiving support from Mussolini and Hitler.

Spike shook his head grimly. "Get the United States occupied with a good war in the Pacific and the Italians and Germans could steal South America from under our noses."

He was still striving to pierce the cloudiness of the situation when Atterbury came on the phone.

"I'm catching the night plane home," Spike said bluntly.

"No," said Atterbury. "You're catching the plane east to Shanghai. We've got to have somebody out there who can—"

"What goes on out there is not going to be of much importance in the next two months," cut in Spike grimly. "When the Steel Fists open up in America—well, the country will be fighting with its back to the wall."

"Nuts!" said Atterbury. "You and your Steel Fists!"

"I'm either coming home or I'm quitting," said Spike.

He banged his fist down.

He had his way, of course, for he was the most popular news commentator on the air. And even Atterbury got some idea of the home front as news when that night the coastwise Panama-Pacific liner, *California*, was stopped by a Japanese submarine in a calm sea off the Peninsula of Lower California, the passengers forced into boats and the ship shelled to destruction.

It was the first taste of long-range submarine warfare and Spike, sitting with dispatches in the Imperial Airways plane *Maiia*, perceived in them already the wild hysteria that would inevitably follow.

Atterbury greeted him with more news when he came to the FBC offices from the Southampton airport.

"Look," he said in an awed voice. He held out the wet sheets of the New York *Sphere* proofs:

AMERICAN ASIATIC SQUADRON
DESTROYED IN GREAT SEA BATTLE

Spike skimmed the tragic news that told how the small
squadron, composed chiefly of torpedo boat destroyers and
Class B cruisers, had been racing for Singapore, doubtless
with the intent of refueling and coming home the long way
around the World. They were spotted by Japanese reconnaissance planes and intercepted by the faster Japanese big
cruisers and held in play until the Jap heavy battleships
came up and pounded them to bits at long range.

The British correspondent, Lady Drummond Hay, sending from Singapore, believed that three Japanese cruisers
were sunk by accurate American gunnery, but the Japs
denied this. However, one fact remained, that the Asiatic
squadron, small though it was, had been destroyed, and first
blood had gone to the Japanese. It was not an important
victory, nor even a decisive one; indeed, none of the Japanese moves had inflicted any real damage beyond the loss
of life of the personnel involved. But the destruction of
the small fleet, the sinking of commerce vessels by long-
range submarines, the seizure of Manila (which no American naval or army officer ever thought could be held) had
resulted in a series of sharp blows to American pride and
morale.

These were, Spike knew, the fast sharp jabs of the beginning of a deadly fight. One look at Atterbury's face told
him that the effect on American morale was the most
important achievement.

SPIKE GLANCED AT a smaller dispatch from Lady Drummond Hay which said that the American light cruiser

Marlborough, detached from the Asiatic fleet, had escaped disaster and was attacking the Japanese oil tankers from Borneo.

"That's the item I'll use," he said to Atterbury. "Remember the *Emden* in the World War? The ship became a sort of hero—or heroine if a ship is a she—and we've got to keep up to morale."

"Six thousand lives lost, though," said Atterbury, wetting his lips. "And only the beginning." He braced himself. "But wait till our fleet gets that Jap fleet—we'll smash them."

Spike glared at him and crushed the dispatches in his big hands. "I hope you never have to hang by the throat until the American fleet catches the Japs," he said.

"Why, what do you mean?" bristled Atterbury. "Look, I've been reading Jane's *Fighting Ships of the World.* It says right here—read that—we've got seventeen battleships to their twelve; and nineteen battle cruisers to their nine. We've got more ships of every kind than they have, and you've got to admit our fleet is trained and ready."

"I do," said Spike wearily, "but listen, guy. If you were up against a bigger man than yourself, would you stay and fight when you could get away from him?"

"What?" Atterbury looked startled.

"Listen," said Spike. "The American navy is all you say it is. But if the Jap navy stays ten thousand miles away, we haven't got the fuel to get at them—how can you bring on an action?"

He went out, leaving Atterbury to ponder the point. A United Press flash had just come in that David Farnham, head of American Motors, had been appointed chairman

of the War Industries Coordinating Board. Spike wanted
to see Farnham.

So it happened that he arrived in Washington during the
special night session of Congress when President Henderson delivered what later became known as his "war speech."
It was broadcast so that Spike had only to listen and go
on the air at midnight with his comment. Spike thought
he had never seen a man so tired, drawn and haggard as
President Henderson as he stood up there under the blaze
of camera light and read the words that committed the
country to war *de jure*. It was a long speech, summing up
the crisis since strained relations began more than ten
years previous. It was not a rabble-rousing speech; indeed,
Spike thought its summation dull. But toward the end
Henderson became filled with emotion and struck a note
that thrilled them all with the seriousness of the moment.

"Japan has refused all efforts at mediation, has rejected
arbitration in any form. The Imperial Japanese government has submitted terms which no self-respecting nation
can consider. Without pause for consideration, the Imperial Japanese government has attacked and seized Manila
whose independence we specifically guarantee; the Imperial Japanese fleet has destroyed our Asiatic squadron with
a loss of six thousand lives. The Imperial government's
submarines, ranging along our coast, have sunk unarmed
American vessels.

"In the face of these depredations by an irresponsible
nation, the United States has no recourse but to resist.
We have no alternative but gird on the sword and resist
with force the force used against us. Our cause is just, for
we do not attack but defend. And so, putting our trust in

Almighty God and the righteousness of our cause, I ask the Congress of the United States to declare a state of war existing between the United States and Japan."

With two hundred and eighty-six dissenting votes Congress passed the resolution. The date, queerly enough, was September 1st. What concerned Spike was the number of opposition votes. Where had they come from? Did they mean a split in the nation in this crisis?

7

THE LEAGUE OF UNEMPLOYED

DAVID FARNHAM HAD a big suite in the Mayflower Hotel and Spike was in Farnham's private office the day after war had been declared. There were many things Spike wanted to inquire about (he was broadcasting every three hours from WAPX) but for the moment he stifled the questions. By the look on Farnham's face he knew there was something more critical.

"Just glance through this," Farnham said, and held out a grayish bit of newsprint paper, printed as a throw-around.

AMERICAN WORKERS, DON'T BE FOOLED

Workers of America: With millions of you on relief or made work, trying to exist on the miserable government dole, you elected President Henderson on the platform that he would tax the rich, control industry and supply security and jobs for all. *He has failed to do that.* You are worse off than before. And now, to avoid keeping his pledged word, he has deliberately trumped up a war with Japan to avoid the responsibilities of his action. He hopes that *patriotism* will prevent you from complaining, that you will submit to having your youth conscripted to fight in a war against people who have not harmed you. The trumping up of a war is an old excuse among plutocrats to distract the attention of the poor from the real issue.

Don't be fooled. Conscription laws to force you to work at mean wages, or to fight on land and sea, are to be considered. Resist them. Refuse to fight; refuse to work at the meager starvation pay that will be offered. Refuse to support this war, and stand for your rights, the control of the government for the people, by the people, of the people.

The throw-around was signed by Paul Martin, president of the League of Unemployed. But what took Spike's eye was a small replica of a Steel Fist directly below the signature.

"They've dared at last to step out in the open," he muttered. Then, looking at Farnham, he added, "How big is the League?"

"About seven hundred thousand. But being recruited— and they don't take everybody."

"What do you mean?"

"I sent one of my sales checkers around to join. Apparently he wasn't sufficiently hard-up, tough and desperate because he got what you call the bum's rush out. His report says these Steel Fists are scum, tough men with real hatred. They drill with wooden guns."

Spike compressed his lips. "They can be prevented from meeting."

"Not unless the president declares a state of emergency and suspends constitutional privileges."

"Well, why not? We're at war."

"The middle west and inland states don't take the war

seriously. They believe it's just some naval skirmishes. They can't imagine invasion."

"Neither can I—even with the Steel Fists," admitted Spike.

Farnham stoked his pipe and lit it. "Figure it this way, Spike. We know Hannibal wants to be dictator. We know he's laid his plans. If we give him credit with being clever, he will have seen just as many obstacles as we have to his plan. Won't he?"

"Yes, of course."

"Well, then, if you can't imagine invasion with a war with Japan on and revolt being plotted within, Hannibal must have other moves waiting that will bring about that end."

"Undoubtedly," Spike admitted, "but what?"

"I don't know—yet."

SPIKE SPRANG UP and began pacing the room, pipe clinched between his teeth. "You mean we've got to sit around and wait for Hannibal to spring his plan?" For a brief moment Farnham looked back across his own life and saw the planning and work that had brought him where he was.

"Hannibal's spent years on this, Spike—many of them. You can't uncover in a few weeks or a month what a man has spent half his lifetime building."

Spike supposed not; but to himself he declared that he would blast the Steel Fists on the radio. There was still the power of the press and speech. But for the moment he turned to his job as a reporter.

"What's the Chief of Naval Operations planning?" he asked.

"Off the record?" asked Farnham.

"Well, if you insist, I won't use it."

"I do insist because it's very secret. Well, here's the strategy: Raid and sweep the seas clear of Japanese shipping; try as best we can to block off her tank line to Java and Borneo. And by suppressing her shipping, force her navy to a fight."

"Not bad," said Spike, "but what will Japan be doing?"

"Watching her chance. As we detach more and more ships to protect our shipping and raid hers, she will, if she's wise, watch her opportunity to engage in a fleet battle with the odds more even than they are now."

"A long drawn-out affair."

Farnham shrugged. "Our plans call for an advanced base, possibly Guam. Lord knows how long it would take to establish such a base—if it can be defended. It's only two hundred and six square miles, and surrounded by Japanese-mandated islands—marvelous submarine base for them."

Spike rose; he had a sense of suspense, of unease, of a sinister gloom pressing hard on his nerves. He did not know, of course, that this was caused by the fog of war, the mantle of silence filled with rumor that drops when war comes. He attributed it to his fear of Hannibal's next move and swung his thoughts back to the man.

"I tipped the Navy he was at sea in his yacht. Why don't they pick him up? With him out of the way, at least there'd only be Japan to fight."

"His passport has been rescinded. A couple of destroyers out of the Mediterranean squadron are looking for him. But I wonder," Farnham added, "if it hasn't gone so far that, like an avalanche started down a mountainside, nothing can stop it."

"Maybe, but I've still got a voice. And I'll pound at the Steel Fists as long as it lasts."

He began that night, but he got orders the next day to stop. Atterbury talked to him personally.

"It's direct from the White House, Spike, and we'll lose our broadcasting license unless you obey. The president says he wants only propaganda news to go out, and they've called in George Clive as chief of the government press bureau—he's to be censor."

Spike could do nothing but agree; and under control of the press bureau he found himself suddenly limited to reporting cheerful stuff. Such as his visit to an army cantonment and candid broadcasts from soldiers interviewed. Atterbury tried to get him aboard one of the convoy destroyers, and failed because the Navy wasn't interested in publicity.

HE WAS ON the west coast when the *President Coolidge* was torpedoed between San Pedro and San Francisco and was at the shore with a portable microphone when the survivors came ashore in small boats. He broadcast their descriptions of the arrogance and brutality of the Japanese sailors in forcing them almost garmentless into the lifeboats. He described from them the arrival of the torpedo-boat destroyers that smashed the ocean surface for hours with depth bombs.

There were the victories, too; the destruction of the *Nagasaki Maru;* and the swift slashing triumphs of the cruiser *Marlborough* which was performing the amazing feat of breaking the Japanese tanker line and refueling from her victims. She had sunk eight tankers. It was said that twelve Japanese big cruisers were combing the ocean for her. Besides, the Japs were forced to put all tankers under cruiser convoy.

All this was cheerful but on September 20th came shocking news. Spike had difficulty in controlling his voice as he said, "Americans all, this is a time when you've got to stick out your chins and take it with a grin. News arrived ten minutes ago that terrific charges of explosive, buried near Culebra, Panama Canal, no one knows how long ago, were exploded today by two planes which managed to escape our anti-aircraft fire. The explosive started a slide which has completely blocked passage through the Canal and will continue to block it for months. As our main fleet is in the Pacific, this is only senseless destruction. The two planes were shot down, but burned with their crews so that no clues as to where they came from were obtained."

Twice more, in different ways, Spike Stressed the senseless destruction of the Panama Canal, and declared that the blow was not one to harm or in any way cripple America's war effort. But himself, he was not sure, and as soon as he was off the air he hurried to Farnham's suite in the Mayflower.

More and more, while he was in Washington, he was seeing David Farnham. He had recognized the power in the man, and the honest friendship beneath; and it was possibly due to Spike's constant reference to him on his broadcasts that Farnham had finally been made industrial czar of war industries, responsible directly to the president alone.

Spike came in to find Farnham just finished dictating to his secretary. Farnham looked unutterably weary. But Spike did not spare him.

"Japan didn't blow up the Panama Canal locks," he cried. "She didn't have to—for two reasons. First, she's not interested in our Atlantic coast. Second, under the Hay-Pauncefote Treaty, Japan had the right to use of the Canal even if we were at war with her."

"True," said Farnham. "You think Hannibal did it?"

"He must have, and since he doesn't do anything without a reason, it can have only one motive. He wants to cut our Pacific fleet off from the East Coast."

"Meaning that—" began Farnham.

"Meaning," said Spike hoarsely, "that we are going to be attacked on the East Coast." Swiftly he re-told what Kay Carstairs had passed on to him about Hannibal's connection with Von Eitel and Della Volpi.

"But my Lord, man," cried Farnham, "you're trying to tell me that Volpi and Eitel are going to take possession of Italy and Germany and come into this war."

"It's got to be," said Spike. "Why else was a Panama Canal made impassable?" He harked back into his mind for a fragment of an interview he had obtained years before. "Old Admiral Humphries once said that the only way the United States could be invaded was for the country's forces to be grouped on the West Coast and then a sudden declaration of war come from a coalition of European powers. Dave, don't you see? That's just what Hannibal is working for."

"Yes," said Farnham, "you're right. I've been fighting him in Italy and Germany through my agents. I'll know in a week whether I've succeeded."

JOHN HANNIBAL'S YACHT, the *Bess,* was longer than some ocean-going ships, and was itself a small replica of the most palatial of transatlantic liners. Five hundred and fifty feet in length, equipped with Diesel motors, and carrying a crew of seventy-five, it could voyage three-quarters of the way around the world without pause for fuel or food.

Sound-proofed and air-conditioned, it also possessed a radio sending set that could be heard at five thousand miles.

It was a complete world of its own—a man-made island.

On this pleasant afternoon John Hannibal himself was on the promenade deck, watching his son Stephen. The youth was in dungarees and old shirt, though the breeze was cool and fresh. He was polishing the yacht's bright work. Hannibal, watching him, noticed with inward pleasure that the boy did not slight the task, though, it must have been extremely distasteful. And as he knew from long ago, a normal boy, disliking a task, will slight it if he can. Though he was less than ten feet from the boy he did not speak, nor did Stephen look up.

Here was one thing he had achieved—perfection in itself; and Hannibal glowed proudly at his handiwork.

Presently Hannibal said, "Stephen, how do you like Miss Carstairs?"

The boy looked up and smiled eagerly. "I like her lots, sir."

Hannibal nodded almost to himself. She was that. "Suppose I were to—marry her? Would you like that?"

"Yes, sir," rejoined the boy. He flushed pink. "She kisses me and—and I like it."

Again Hannibal nodded. He thought to himself that he could give the boy a stout body and a fine mind. But it needed a woman's affection to round out the lad fully. Before he could say any more Dorsey strode briskly to him.

"You're wanted in the radio room, John."

Hannibal left the boy and ascended to the boat deck.

Dorsey trailed behind. His shark-like face scowled.

"I caught that Carstairs girl looking through some papers on your desk last night. I think she's spying on you."

Hannibal gestured his impatience with the suggestion. His eyes grew hard.

"Nonsense! She's probably curious. After all, we've been wandering around for a month or more and it does look queer."

"I don't like it," said Dorsey.

Hannibal pulled up sharply. "That doesn't matter," he declared coldly. "I shall probably marry Miss Carstairs, so bear the fact in mind."

"You can't stop me speaking my mind," rejoined Dorsey thinly. "Women and this business don't mix. With two American destroyers looking for us, suppose she managed to get off an alarm."

"She won't."

Hannibal entered the radio room. It was instantly apparent that something momentous had occurred. A half-dozen men, part of the Working Council, stood around the radio operator's desk. Their faces were flushed; their eyes bright.

They snapped to attention and stared eagerly at Hannibal.

"At ease," said Hannibal and looked at the radio operator.

"Dispatch from Count Volpi, sir." Hannibal took the yellow paper.

His eyes moved with swift eagerness over the slip of paper, and the words he read ran through his brain as smoothly as if they were printed on a rollertape.

STEEL FISTS HAVE TAKEN CONTROL OF ITALY. SLIGHT REACTION FROM BLACK SHIRTS BUT WILL END THIS IN TWENTY-FOUR HOURS. AM ANNOUNCING THAT NEW GOVERNMENT OF UNITED STATES, WHEN IN POWER, WILL GIVE ITALY FREE HAND IN COLONIZING AND ANNEXING BRAZIL. RE STATE THIS PREMISE IN STEEL FIST MANIFESTO. LONG LIFE STEEL FISTS.

VOLPI.

HANNIBAL HELD THE paper loosely in his fingers. Now that the result of long planning had been achieved, the fruition left him strangely unelated. He was thinking, indeed, that all things were easy to accomplish if you appealed to men's greed. Italy wanted good colonizing land, wanted to be a first-class world power. Offer her that and she could be lured into anything.

He was thinking, too, that before the Italian people could resent the Steel Fist government, they would be in a war and propaganda would keep them loyal. He handed the message to Dorsey.

"Send the manifesto at once," he ordered.

The radio operator handed him a Marconi news dispatch picked up a few minutes before Volpi's message came.

Benito Mussolini, premier of Italy, and his son-in-law, Count Ciano, were assassinated today as Mussolini was making a speech from the balcony of the Palazzo Venezia. They were killed by two rifle bullets fired from a hiding place across the thronged square. The assassin was an American believed to be Antonio Morelli, from Brooklyn. Captured by Black Shirt Guards, he was seized from his captors by an infuriated mob and literally torn to pieces.

The death of the Premier and his heir-apparent to the Fascist dictatorship was the signal for the revolt of a powerful opposition led by Count Giovanni Della Volpi, long the enemy of Mussolini. Well-organized, the Steel Fists, as they call themselves, had complete control of the army and the police. Ensconced in the Parliament House, Della Vopli tonight announced his acceptance of the premiership and promised swift vengeance on those who had insulted Italy by assassinating her premier.

The whole country is believed to be behind Volpi whose *coup d'etat* appears to be the result of years of organization.

There was more coming in but Hannibal waved it aside; he knew the necessary truth and the rest could wait.

To young Graven, the German, he said, "Get a message off to Von Eitel. Tell him not to waste a moment."

To another secretary, "Begin the commandeering of monster liners and other smaller transport. A minimum of a million tons."

To a third, "Send messages to Volpi and Von Eitel that the assembling of the fleet should begin at once."

He turned to the door of the radio coop. "Bring me immediately any word from Von Eitel."

Going down to the promenade deck, he encountered Kay. He saw from her face that she was in a grave mood.

She said decisively, "John, when are you going into port?"

"Are you unhappy?" he smiled.

"No, but I'm concerned and puzzled. You told me we would cruise for a fortnight. It is now over a month we've been to sea. Why? And I do not get any reply to my radio messages."

She had radioed friends merely to find out if the messages were sent. She knew they had not been.

She went on, "What is the mystery that keeps all these men working day and night? Why was Mr. Dorsey so rude to me last night?"

"War, my dear," Hannibal told her. "The United States is at war with Japan." She knew this, but pretended amazement.

Hannibal said, "We will land tomorrow night. We are only two hundred miles off the New Jersey coast. Are you, then, so anxious to see the last of me?"

"Don't be silly! I'm simply mystified, and somewhat concerned about what my friends will say, despite the presence of Lady Elton."

She paused. Then: "John, what are you up to? What is going on?"

HE STARED AT her absently, scarcely hearing the questions. In his great loneliness he needed her; and the urge was strong in him to tell her the huge scheme that had absorbed his life. But how would she respond? He could not be sure. He decided to test her out without revealing too much.

"Kay," he said suddenly, "do you believe the world is getting any better?"

Her heart exulted. At last, after weary days. "Well," she smiled, "steam heat, air-conditioning—"

"Oh, I don't mean plumbing, automobiles, two chickens in every pot. I mean, is the world—for the common man—is the world for humanity reaching any higher toward a goal than the Greeks were reaching twenty-five hundred years ago?"

"I don't know, perhaps I don't quite understand."

"Those who are religious—I am not—say a Divine hand guides our destiny. And because this is not true, humanity lives in anarchy save for such laws as keep the mob in order. The powerful can rob, steal, violate all canons of decency and honor.

"The ignorant remain ignorant, and fall even lower in the norm of human intelligence because the ruling class have few offspring and the feeble-minded breed like rats. The resources of our nation are wasted and destroyed so that unless a halt is called, within two hundred years we will be another China. China, the classic example of lack of supreme, intelligent control."

"And you would change all that?"

"If I can," he said. "I would breed a new class of rulers. I would sterilize criminals and morons. I would protect our resources and guarantee to the worker, work and old-age security—all they are entitled to."

"It sounds Fascist—and horrible," said Kay. "You would destroy all freedom."

"Freedom! Freedom for what?" Hannibal's blue eyes blazed. "Freedom to destroy the earth's riches that enables us to live? Freedom to breed indiscriminately and make humanity a race of drooling morons?

"There is no real liberty. Liberty now is the right of the strong to prey on the weak as a big fish eats a smaller one. No, my dear, there are more precious things than liberty. There is the goal of enlightened intelligence and finer mankind. There is—"

"You've cut yourself," she interrupted.

He had. In cutting the end of a cigar he had slit his finger. It bled freely. At sight of it a roaring came into his aching head. He staggered and would have fallen but for her aiding arm.

"Wrap it up," he said thickly. "The sight of blood—" his voice choked.

She bound the finger, wondering as she did so at this queer weakness in him. She did not know that the sight of blood aroused sharp, horrible memories of those days in the Argonne Forest in 1918. Presently he was recovered and she wanted to prod his ego again.

But the arrival of Dorsey prevented. "Radio from Berlin," Dorsey said. Hannibal excused himself and departed. Kay stood by the taffrail summing up what she had learned and its significance.

Hannibal had the megalomaniac's dream of power; he had caused the war with Japan. And his communications now with Volpi and Eitel meant he was using Italy and Germany. But how?

Out of her memory came a fragment of conversation. It was clearer now, old Admiral Jones talking with her, answering her childish questions as to whether the United States could ever be conquered.

"Kay, my child," he had said, "there is only one possible way our country could be conquered—and that might fail."

"How?" she had asked.

"Let Japan attack us on the west first and concentrate our power in the Pacific and on the West Coast. Then, while we are engaged, let a coalition of European powers attack from the east. Then—and only then if you had an internal revolt—could our country be invaded. But we should win even then in the long run."

Remembering this now, Kay suddenly gasped. It was as if old Admiral Jones was a prophet. Here was war with Japan; here was scheming and intrigue with Italy and Germany; and here were Hannibal's American Steel Fists, organized under the League of Unemployed.

At long last she saw the scheme in its full brilliance. The sheer boldness stunned her for a moment. But she shook off emotion.

She had penetrated the scheme. She had the full sweep of it. Now, if she could get evidence to prove it, and get ashore, there were still days, perhaps weeks, during which preparations could be made to defeat it.

As she went below her mind was planning how to ransack John Hannibal's desk.

8

THE WHITE HOUSE

SPIKE BRENN HAD his offices in the National Press Club Building and he was on the air three times a day, noon—six and nine P.M. From here he surveyed the heat and confusion of Washington and tried to keep a clear perspective on world events. It was difficult because he, as well as the National and Columbia Broadcasting commentators, were under the thumb of the Federal Radio Commission's censor.

When he wanted to comment on the rumor that the Italian and German fleets had been seen together cruising in the North Sea, he had been forced to strike out the comment and substitute, for example, a new victory by the dashing and elusive *Marlborough*.

"The fleets together are merely a threat at England," said the FRC censor. "Let's stick to our own war. You can announce that the Fourth and Fifth Army corps are one hundred per cent mobilized in the West and that the Universal Draft bill will pass the House this weekend."

"And I suppose," said Spike wearily, "that we're going to retake Manila."

"Well," said the FRC censor, "we will and we have to keep prodding it home. Make the people realize this is a long, tough war. 'Remember Manila.' That's the slogan to pound home."

"Oh, Lord, how long!" cried Spike.

But he did as he was told. He wanted more to be with Miles in aviation on the West Coast or with O'Hara with the Fifth Army corps. But this was his job, so he watched the ponderous, awkward, clumsy efforts the country made to get ready to fight.

These efforts were handicapped by definite opposition in Congress and by the League of Unemployed. Then there were the pacifists who poured propaganda on Washington.

"Let the Philippines go," they cried. "They're not worth the blood of one single American."

The college youth movement, pledged against war, swore to resist being drafted. "Either jail or freedom from the draft," they cried.

Had the war spirit been thoroughly aroused in the country, these protestations might have been squelched by mass action. But so suddenly had war come, so remote was its scene of action, that save along the West Coast, no deep emotion was engendered. There were many people who privately agreed the Philippines were not worth fighting for.

And so the days drifted past until the afternoon of the news that Mussolini and Ciano had been murdered. Spike read the fateful words and as their significance came to him, he leaped from his chair. Five minutes later he was in Farnham's suite at the Mayflower Hotel.

When Farnham had read the dispatch, he stood silent a moment and then turned toward the door.

"Come on," he said to Spike. "The president has called a conference and he should have this."

The big room in the White House was silent when the two men entered. Spike smiled grimly as he saw the faces of those gathered; queer, he thought, how the country called on industrialists in time of crisis and shelved the politicians.

He had met President Henderson several times in the preceding weeks but even so he was shocked at the change in the man. From a robust, hearty man of vigorous personality, he seemed to have withered like a dehydrated apple. There was a look of sleeplessness about his eyes, and his clothes hung slackly from a gaunt frame. Only his handshake had vigor.

At Farnham's behest Spike spoke his mind.

"I'VE PROVED TO you the connection between John Hannibal and Volpi and Von Eitel," Spike concluded, "and their connection with the Steel Fists. You've seen the British dispatches describing the Italo-German fleet maneuvering. I submit that Von Eitel, as leader of the Reichswehr rebellion against Hitler, will throw the Austrian out. As soon as that is done, Italy and Germany will declare war on the United States."

"War?" repeated Granlen of American Steel.

"War!" repeated Spike bluntly. "The two countries have built for war. The war preparations have burdened the people to the point of revolt."

"Perhaps," conceded Granlen, "but why would Italy and Germany fight us? What's the motive?"

"Suppose," said Spike, "we lost this war. Our government would blow up with it. No government has ever lost a war and survived. Look at Austria-Hungary and Germany in the last World War. Suppose we had a new government with John Hannibal as dictator."

Granlen and President Henderson were aware of Spike's obsession with Hannibal.

"Well," said Granlen, "suppose that happens. What then?"

"In return for aid, Hannibal abolishes the Monroe Doctrine. He offers Germany and Italy a free hand in South America. Freedom to colonize or even annex such rich countries as Brazil, Argentina, Chile—all having a white man's climate. Isn't that a stake worth fighting for?"

All conceded that it was, and then Spike pointed out the persistent reports of internal revolt from South America.

"Those prove the fact," he said finally. "And if Von Eitel overthrows Hitler in the next seventy-two hours, you can damned well bet that either declared or undeclared, we'll be at war with Germany and Italy by October 1st."

There was a silence. President Henderson said, "Thanks for your observations, Mr. Brenn. Anything is valuable during this period—"

"I was not finished, Mr. President," said Spike. "I suggested that the League of Unemployed are Hannibal's Steel Fists. I insist that they are boring from within to make America's war effort hopeless. I have said and I repeat that they must be dealt with harshly. A suspension of the constitutional privileges of free speech and free assembly. Arrest the ring leaders and abrogate the right of habeas corpus. Smash them before they smash us."

"Abrogation of civil rights might lead to revolt. Many

other factions are discontented with this war." It was Granlen speaking.

"A state of national emergency and martial law can be declared," said Spike.

"And I would be accused of aspiring to dictatorship," said the president.

The convention continued, but as Spike quickly saw, it was getting nowhere. He left the meeting with Farnham, discouraged and fearful.

His forebodings were borne out thirty-six hours later. Farnham was with him when the ominous dispatch arrived.

Berlin, September 2: Revolting elements of the Reichswehr, the German regular army, led by Oberst General Burghardt Von Eitel, tonight seized control of the German government and announced the abolition of Nazism. Adolph Hitler, Nazi Fuehrer, has been arrested. His fate remains unknown. Marshall Hermann Goering, number two man of the Nazis, was killed when he sought to resist those sent to arrest him.

MORE

Berlin, September 2: Hitler is dead. He was shot by order of General Von Eitel as a traitor to Germany.

The revolt was not a sporadic or palace revolution but was a mass rising of the Germany Army which has sworn allegiance to Von Eitel and the Steel Fist government. The army, alienated and disgruntled since the removal of Marshall Werner Von Blomberg, has long resented Hitler's domination and the introduction of Nazism in the military ranks. The army has also resented Hitler's apparent weakening in his South American policy. New announcements are expected on policy as soon as Von Eitel has formed his government.

Nazi SS troops and Gestapo (secret police) ranks have been decimated where resistance was encountered. Thousands are believed to be dead in the *coup d'etat.*

Spike leaned back, suddenly feeling inwardly exhausted. It was as if he had been standing taut on tiptoe, waiting. And now the blow had fallen.

He looked at Farnham. "Henderson must strike at Hannibal and the League of Unemployed."

"He has," answered Farnham. "Hannibal is outlawed and a price of fifty thousand dollars dead or alive put on his head."

THE YACHT CREAKED and groaned as it lifted and fell in the strong ground swell that was the aftermath of the storm. Each sound, soft as it was, made Kay's nerves jump. She tiptoed through the salon toward John Hannibal's private study. It was a long risk she was taking and she knew it. Her only excuse, if she were caught here, was the ship's library, and that was a poor one. But she was chancing it, nonetheless. Something had happened that day that she must know about.

Dorsey, who hated and distrusted her, had forgotten his usual caution of not speaking in her presence. Hannibal had been sitting aft talking with her when Dorsey had burst in. He was panting with excitement.

"They've started," he cried. Then seeing Kay, his mouth had snapped shut. His head gestured to Hannibal to leave. Hannibal did so. A half-hour later the *Bess* had suddenly throbbed to pounding engines. Despite heavy seas, she was being pushed at highest speed. Kay only knew they had headed southwest. But why?

The yacht, at the moment, was under bare steerageway, but for twenty-four hours she had been pushed regardless of strain.

The yacht slept save for the watch on deck, and these, accustomed to Kay, merely saluted as she passed. At the end of the salon she stared at a few titles in the library and then tried the study door. It was, as usual, unlocked (strange, no door on this yacht had ever been locked to her knowledge). She opened it and stepped within. Her heart pounded. There was, as she knew, a file of radio messages in the upper right hand drawer. In one of his moments of self-communication, Hannibal had said that he was saving every scrap of correspondence against the day when he intended to write a great document. He had never said what book it would be but she knew it was to be his memoirs, a justification of the course he was now pursuing.

She reached for the file.

It was there with three or four later messages thrust between the covers, waiting to be clipped. These she scanned first.

Prepared as she was against startling facts, the first message made her set her teeth against a gasp. It had been a coded message but below in Hannibal's precise penmanship was the decoded version.

Fleet sailed transports loading cruisers off American coast for raids timetable based on October one where is American Pacific fleet Von Eitel

The radio beneath was from Italy, signed by Volpi.

Yield to your reason coalition fleet will be commanded by
Admiral Morthau as long as mechanized divisions remain under
command of General Strella

She skimmed through the others but they were all messages relating to details in this vast scheme which at last was plain before her. This she knew; the combined Italian-German fleet had sailed under command of Admiral Morthau, its intent to dominate the Atlantic and clear the way for transports with an invading army, part of which would be commanded by General Strella.

She knew that this fleet had sailed secretly; it would attack without declaration of war, make a surprise that might be fatal to the American resistance. This, she suddenly realized, was what she had waited for, why she had stayed on the yacht. At home they would not suspect what was coming. It was plain that she must tell them. She must leave at once.

She thrust the file back in the drawer and turned to go. As she did so, the ship suddenly vibrated to the clamor of the huge Diesel engines and she could almost feel the spurt forward. She darted from the study.

JOHN HANNIBAL WAS just coming into the salon. With him was the chief radio officer, and Dorsey. They saw her before she could reach the rack of books. They stopped talking, and she stood very still. There was silence except for the quivering of the yacht to the thrust of the propellers.

Kay took from her dressing gown a packet of cigarettes, lit one and waited for them to approach.

Dorsey rushed at her. "What does this mean?" he demanded furiously.

"What does what mean?" She stared at him calmly. "I came to get a book. Isn't it permissible to read?"

She turned to John Hannibal who was watching her with opaque eyes. "I don't like the manners of your hired hand, John."

Hitherto he had always been kind and gentle with her. But this attitude had now undergone a change; and she saw the harsh, dominant, ruthless quality in him uppermost.

"It's nearly one o'clock," he said, "and no time to come for a book."

"I couldn't sleep," she said truthfully.

He suspected her; she felt that; but he did not make an issue of her presence then. He said in a softer tone, "We'll discuss it later. Please go now."

She accepted the dismissal but, going to her cabin, knew that it was merely delay. Whatever he had thought of her before, his suspicions were aroused. She wondered if she would tell him the truth. Weeks in his company had not changed her mind about him as the murderer of Norm, but had softened the full fury of her hatred. Sometimes she even liked him, often pitied him....

She sat up, trying to read. But the words were blurs, and she was only aware of the rushing speed of the boat, and the wild vibration of the timbers. The *Bess* was running as fast as she could go which meant something like twenty-five knots. Running where?

She finally sat in darkness, so that lights would not betray her wakefulness. She heard the chronometer strike two bells in the dog watch—five A.M. Already a dirty grayness had stolen the beauty of the night, and day would come swiftly.

And as she became aware of this she saw land—the first she had seen in six weeks or more. A low-lying sandy shore that gave way to a greenness, but no sign of habitation, and no sign of life. The trembling of the engines quit now and as the yacht turned to follow the coastline south, she saw that someone on shore had a car, for its headlights were flicking off and on as if they were spelling out a message. The yacht lost way.

She heard the trundle of the davits as they were swung outboard and an officer's orders to sailors about clearing the lines on the boat. A small motor was started, and she knew it was the tender of the yacht, a fast speedboat swung from the starboard amidships.

Someone was going ashore.

She determined to stay here no longer. Swiftly she dressed and went up the companionway to the deck. She was in time to see John Hannibal with suitcases and other baggage preparing to go down the ladder to the tender. With him was Dorsey who gave her a sharp bitter look and spoke under his breath to Hannibal. Hannibal, however, had changed.

He smiled and called to Kay. She came over, saying, "What is going on?"

HANNIBAL DID NOT answer the question. He said imperiously, "I've changed my mind, Dorsey. I'll take her with us."

"No, no!" cried Dorsey.

Hannibal stiffened. "Stop that!" he snapped. "See that the steward gets her baggage aboard. We've twenty minutes until full daylight. Time enough. Harkins, see to Miss Carstairs' baggage."

He turned to Kay. "I'm going ashore, and I'm going to take you with me."

"But what shore? Where are we? And why this landing before it's hardly daylight?"

"I'll explain going in the car," he said. "That's the New Jersey coast. We'll land south of Atlantic City."

"Well," grumbled Dorsey, "I suppose it will be safer if she's with us. But, Hannibal, I'm beginning to think you're a fool."

"You'll say that once too often," said Hannibal coldly. Then, to Kay, "Get your coat and a traveling suit. It's quite a long ride after we land."

Dorsey followed her. "It'll be a cold ride. I'll get you some coffee."

She ignored him, knowing he was merely wanting to watch her pack. He called the steward and while waiting for the coffee, he leaned against a bulkhead and watched her scramble her clothes in the cases.

"Why do you play up to Hannibal?" he asked suddenly. "You don't like him—I think, sometimes, that you hate him."

"That's nonsense," she said. "I respect John Hannibal a great deal. But I do not understand all this mystery, or why things are done secretly."

The coffee came and Dorsey handed it to her. "It's at least hot," he told her.

She drank the coffee. She had a feeling of emptiness inside which the heat relieved and her quivering nerves calmed. She followed Dorsey to the deck, and so down the ladder into the tender. The sailor in charge instantly started the boat as fast as it would go toward the shore.

The sea was calm, save for the ground swells which broke whitely along the level stretch of sand. She could see a road, now, inland perhaps three hundred yards, and the car was on the road. But a man was down on the beach, waving and pointing as if there was a deeper place where the tender could come in. However, the bow grounded on the sand perhaps ten yards from the beach. The sailor leaped out and heaved the baggage to the sand. He carried Kay ashore on his back and Hannibal and Dorsey, to her amusement, waded.

The man waiting on shore did a strange thing as Hannibal came onto the sand asking for a towel. He clicked his heels, came to attention and slapped his right fist against his chest over his heart.

"Hail, sir!" he said.

She saw he had a Steel Fist emblem in his buttonhole.

"At ease, Granger," said Hannibal. "Help me get this sand off."

Kay heard no more then. A strange sudden dizziness swept her. Her eyelids became so heavy she could not prop them open. She had an intense longing to lie down. She yawned. But as suddenly as the wave swept her, she began to fight it. She knew.

"Dorsey," she cried, "that coffee—you—" the blackness came in a huge, comfortable wave that swept her. Her knees went rubber and she sank to the sand. She rolled over, and sighed, and was instantly asleep.

Hannibal saw this. "Why, you idiot?" he shouted angrily.

"She knows too much now," snarled Dorsey. "With you in the States and a price on your head—and everything hinging on you—I don't intend she should spill the beans."

"Sometimes," said Hannibal through tight lips, "I don't know why I put up with you."

"Without me," grinned Dorsey, "your plan will fail. That's why. And I intend to see you don't fall into the hands of government agents." He gestured to Granger. "Pick her up and put her in the car."

9

WAR WITHOUT RULES

ON SEPTEMBER 26TH Spike Brenn got his first intimation of the "Pirate Cruiser." A man by the name of Coolidge, the New England Broadcasting Company's commentator, called up in a wildly excited voice.

"A Merchants & Miners' steamer, the *Montauk,* was stopped off Nantucket Light today, the passengers forced off, and the steamer shelled until it sank."

Spike Brenn's brain, already weary and thick, naturally assumed the obvious.

"Japanese submarine?" he said. And yet as he spoke he wondered how a Japanese submarine could be in the Atlantic attacking shipping.

The Jap long-range submarines could and did travel twelve to eighteen thousand miles without refueling, but even this remarkable range would not permit them to traverse the Horn or travel two-thirds of the way around the world through the Suez and the Mediterranean without being reported.

His speculations were broken by Coolidge. "It wasn't a Jap submarine. It was a cruiser flying no flag. But the survivors said the crew that boarded spoke Italian."

"Italian!" yelled Spike.

"That's it. And one of the passengers, Braccioli, who has been in Italy, said the uniforms were Italian Navy uniforms."

"Yeah," said Spike. He dropped the phone and stared dully at the wall.

The new warfare, he knew, had changed from the old days when war was formally declared between two nations and both nations took time to maneuver and mobilize. Such international protocol was no more. Since the Spanish Civil War, when Italian submarines had sunk Russian supply ships, and even attacked British ships and destroyed them, war was waged in the manner of the school bully who strikes another boy from behind.

This was some of the same medicine. The cruiser bore no flag, and the Italian government would deny all knowledge and that would be all until the next time.

However, the next time came swiftly enough. A Clyde-Mallory liner, the *Mohawk*, out of New York for Galveston, was torpedoed off Hatteras by a submarine that stood by and watched the lifeboats swamp in the heavy seas. Of the four hundred souls aboard, only sixty succeeded in reaching land. Sloops of war put out of Norfolk in answer to the liner's frantic S.O.S. but the submarine had vanished. It had raised no flag.

In rapid succession then the liner *Manhattan* bound for Rio was shelled and sunk, and the Navy Department radioed every American vessel on the Atlantic to head forced draft for port.

The sinkings were bad enough, but to Spike the public reaction was even more terrible. So long as the enemy had been Japan and the fighting and sinking confined to the Pacific coast, the eastern seaboard had supported the war but had not got excited. The public panic that had swept the Pacific coast from Vancouver to San Diego was frowned upon. The powerful eastern newspapers, guided by Washington, had sternly castigated the panic-stricken western populace which had called hysterically for the fleet to protect the coast against marauders. But now it was different.

From Boston to Savannah there came a violent demand for protection against marauding "pirate" cruisers and submarines. Convoys for ships, "Shall the American flag be swept from the seas by irresponsible piratic vessels taking advantage of our war with Japan? Is the Navy which we have supported with staggering sums of money for years unable to protect the people now?"

JUST WHEN THE turmoil was at its height, when rumors of vast enemy fleets seen in Atlantic fogs were driving the Navy distracted, there came the final blow which produced real panic. Two submarines—at least they were said to be submarines—came into Long Island Sound on a night of full moon. Off Bridgeport they trained their guns on the Sikorsky airplane factory—or hoped, apparently, they had—and shelled for three hours. Patrol boats and submarines were called from New London, but by the time they had arrived the submarines had disappeared beneath the surface, and no more was seen or heard of them then.

The shelling set a dozen fires that raged most of the night in Bridgeport; two hundred and ten people were killed and over three hundred wounded. The Sikorsky plant was not particularly damaged, but the loss of life sent a tremor of fear from one end of the Atlantic coast to the other.

There began then the agitation for taking part of the Pacific fleet to reinforce the Caribbean Special Service Squadron to protect the East Coast. The New York *Times*, most staid and conservative hitherto, wrote editorially:

> A Navy which cannot maintain the merchant marine on the sea in time of war, a Navy which cannot protect the rich and populous seaboards from death and destruction, has failed in its purpose. We do not pretend to be strategists or naval tacticians, but it does seem clear to us and to others, that instead of keeping the bulk of the American fleet idle in the Pacific as a "fleet in being" to stop the Japanese attack, it would be better to take part of that fleet and send it forced draft to the Atlantic and wipe out these pirate craft. Indeed, we believe this must be done. Not only to allay the understandable panic of people afraid for their lives, but to keep the American merchant marine flag flying. The United States is not self-contained. We must import vital material to prosecute the war. And if our vessels must cower in harbor, then a blockade has been established, and it is only a question of time before our war effort must slow down.
>
> From now on the motto must be *Bring the Navy to the Atlantic.*

Shortly after this appeared, Spike got a summons from the Chief of Naval Operations, Admiral Conlever. Spike knew something was up and he was certain of it when he entered the War, State and Navy Building. There was an air of anxiety and nervous tension there.

Conlever bore it out. And he came bluntly to the point.

"You swing more lead than any other publicist in the country," he said. "You've got to start fighting this agitation to bring part of the Pacific fleet to the Atlantic."

"Why?" demanded Spike, instantly antagonistic. "You know as well as I do that these cruisers and subs are Italian—maybe some German ones, too. They intend to support Japan and make war in the east. We need part of the fleet here."

Conlever stared at him coldly. There was weariness in his eyes, a haunting fatigue that betrayed many sleepless nights and worry.

"I've no time to give a course on naval strategy," he said, "but I can convince you, I think, that such a policy of separating the fleet is suicidal. You know old General Forrest's military motto, 'Be there fustest with the mostest men'?"

"Yes."

"Well, as matters stand now, we have more ships and guns in the Pacific than the Japanese. Save for a few submarines of theirs, we have driven their fleet into the South China Sea. Convoy service by torpedo boats and sloops of war is protecting our merchant marine—coastwise to South America, anyway, where we get the most of our raw products for war.

"Now, as long as we have the preponderance of ships and guns, the Japs will not force an action. We will be in a position to establish an advanced base and either cut their sea lanes completely (which they cannot afford to have happen) or force them to a battle."

"Meanwhile, the Italian-German fleet sweep the Atlantic and clear the way for perhaps an expeditonary force," said Spike.

"Wait a moment," snapped Conlever. "The Italians and the Germans are not fools. They would never send an army over thirty-four hundred miles of water so long as the possibility exists that we might turn our Pacific fleet and cut their line of communications. The Germans and Italians are using pirate tactics to cause us to split our fleet. Because then we would be no stronger or perhaps weaker than the Japanese, and the Japs could force the action while the advantage was with them. Perhaps destroy our Pacific Fleet. What we could detach to reinforce the Special Service Squadron would not equal the combined Italo-German fleet. So we should lose both ways—and then would come disaster."

"And your plan?" said Spike.

"To advance bases, bring the Japanese fleet to battle. Destroy or render it ineffective. Then turn to the Atlantic with the whole American fleet and if the Italo-German fleet runs for it—as it must—then undertake such punitive measures that seem advisable to bring peace on our own terms."

As Spike remained silent, the admiral went on, "Remember what Nelson said: keep the fleet together and destroy first one enemy and then the other. But do not divide."

Spike nodded; it was all familiar. "But the process of advancing a base, either floating or to some island, will take months. What is going to happen meantime to the East Coast?"

"What raiding is done cannot affect our war power. The attacks are only meant to raise panic among our people, try to bring about the very thing—division of the fleet—which we wish to avoid."

SPIKE WAS CONVINCED. "I'll do what I can," he promised, and was as good as his word. He pounded at the point, declaring people would have to sacrifice and suffer for the sake of winning the war. But the only result was to bring in furious telegrams, telephone messages, and there was a movement started to have him boycotted from the big eastern radio stations that re-broadcast his comments.

Worse still, congressmen and senators were deluged with telegrams and threats, and visited by delegations who threatened more than defeat at the polls unless the politicians voted for protection of the east coast.

The following Tuesday the *U.S.S. Falcon,* sloop-of-war, happening to be less than forty miles away, caught the S.O.S. of the Savannah liner *Chattanooga* and raced to her rescue. She came upon the submarine before it had a chance to submerge. With four shells from her three-inch guns, she hulled the conning tower and as the submarine was trying to fight back, charged her and with depth bombs accomplished the total destruction.

The submarine did not show a flag and no one was rescued. The submarine sank in two hundred and ten feet of water and the salvage tug *Macon* was rushed out and a diver dropped to the wreck.

The evidence brought up conclusively proved that the submarine was the Italian PV type, *d'Annunzio.* The State Department immediately lodged a vigorous complaint with the Italian government. Della Volpi did not reply then.

But two days later two cruisers stood in ten miles off

Atlantic City and shelled the city for two hours, from five o'clock until dusk. Then they turned seaward and the Atlantic squadron detachment of three battle cruisers failed to find them.

The shelling of the city accomplished what Spike had been fighting against; the Congress revolted. Such pressure was placed on President Henderson that an executive order was issued detaching three battleships, two battle cruisers, five light cruisers and suitable auxiliary vessels from the Pacific fleet. The ships were ordered at forced draft to report to the command of Rear Admiral Hugh-Dunning of the Atlantic Squadron.

Spike had just finished broadcasting this fateful news (wondering why the enemy should be informed by radio of such a vital move) when the door to his office opened and a girl came in.

"Kay!" he exclaimed.

It was raining out, and she was beaten by the rain and the wind, and streaming water.

Instinctively he took her into his arms. He saw that she was cut and bruised, exhausted physically and mentally. She slacked against him and began to shake. He roughed up her head with his hands vigorously.

"Get hold of yourself," he said gently. "Don't pass out on me now." She looked up at him. "Hannibal is arranging for the country to be invaded," she said. "There'll be between two hundred and fifty thousand and a half million soldiers. I found it out from a radio dispatch. Dorsey tried to kill me."

"And you escaped?"

"Yes, Hannibal's in New York."

"In New York?"

She nodded. "He has a penthouse on Park Avenue. I crept along the coping—the penthouse is thirty stories high." She shuddered. "Hannibal is in constant communication with the enemy. Short wave radio. He's engineering everything from New York."

Spike reached for the telephone. He called the Navy and Army Intelligence and told them what Kay had said. He called the Department of Justice and repeated the news.

"What name is he using?" he asked Kay, still holding the phone.

"Jeffrey Hanan," she replied.

Spike told them this and admonished them to hurry. But it was a useless suggestion. At midnight the Intelligence men chopped down the door and burst in. The penthouse of Hannibal was empty.

"He knew you'd tell where he was and left at once," Spike said gloomily. "Now, where could he have gotten to?"

But she did not know, and although the Intelligence services spread his description, John Hannibal was not found.

And in the scurry of the next few days Spike was forced to dismiss the man from his mind.

For on the thirtieth of September Italy, through Della Volpi, declared war. And on October first, Germany, under Dictator Von Eitel, followed suit.

10

ORDERS FOR DAWN

LIEUTENANT BURTON MILES stood on the flying deck of the U.S.S. aircraft-carrier *Wright* of the Atlantic Scouting Fleet and stared across the gray heaving ground-swell into which the great ship plunged her bow at twelve knots.

He held in his hand a letter from Spike Brenn, received just before the *Wright* hastily left Charleston to join the fleet; but he was not reading it. He was thinking that before many days had passed he would probably be dead. No, not exactly dead, because every man thinks he will live, but he was dwelling on the hopeless sacrifice which was presently to be made. He was thinking of the size and power of the combined Italo-German fleet, and the definite inferiority of the Atlantic fleet.

Within range of his eyes were twenty-odd gray ships lifting and falling to the swell, their grayness merging with the gray of the mist. Far ahead was the scout cruiser division, six ten-thousand-ton Washington Treaty vessels mounting eight-inch guns. Behind them was the submarine flotilla which might launch their attacks, or might retreat behind the screen of the main fleet.

Then came the scout cruiser division proper whose smoke he could just see. Just ahead of him, squat, powerful, was the battleship division, the infantry of the sea, the armored monsters with sixteen-inch guns whose hitting power decided naval supremacy. They were drawn up in two columns; the *New York*, the *Massachusetts*, the *Oregon* on the port line, the *Utah*, the *New Mexico* and the *Minnesota* at starboard.

Then there was the aircraft division of which his vessel, the *Wright*, was one, and the old *Lexington* and the *Concord* the others. Behind him, scarcely visible on the horizon, was the naval train, the base force with its repair ships and oilers, minesweepers and hospital ship.

To starboard and port he could see the smoke of the torpedo-boat-destroyer screen, a tight cordon against a surprise submarine attack.

Yes, here was the Atlantic battle force, bound to be outnumbered in all types of vessels, and particularly so in the battle force, six battleships against nine. They were ready and trained, these battleships of the line and battle cruisers. The wood had been ripped from the steel decks to prevent flying splinters; the chain rails and stanchions were down; it needed only the call, "battle stations" to swivel the huge guns on a target.

But the problem was—and a strange one—should the fleet fight or take refuge in Chesapeake Bay behind the mine fields and huge coast defense guns? Miles knew what he'd do. "I'd run for it and to hell with popular clamor," he muttered.

To shake his mind from the unpleasant thoughts, he turned again to Spike's letter. But it did not comfort him much.

I was rotten-egged last night, and in staid Boston of all places. At the order of the powers-that-be in the press censorship I went up there to broadcast from the Copley-Plaza. I broadcast in the huge ballroom so that the big-wigs could seat maybe five hundred people to watch me.

The idea was that I should talk technically about why things were being done the way they were. I had to explain that due to public clamor, the Pacific fleet had been dangerously reduced and had to retreat onto Pearl Harbor in Hawaii and surrender the initiative to the Japs. I had to explain that the Atlantic fleet might not be able to fight because, though it had reduced the Pacific fleet's superiority, it wasn't as big nor as strong as the enemy coalition fleet.

And—this between you and me—I had to begin laying the groundwork for what must come—suspension of civil rights, declaration of a state of emergency, and the adjournment of Congress with all its powers parsed into the hands of the president.

MILES PAUSED A moment to stare out at the tossing ships; then he went back to his reading.

Boy, I used to think I was popular when the fan mail came in bushel baskets in the old days. But evidently I wasn't popular last night. There was a bunch of Irishmen there to razz me. They started calling, "What about our babies and wives?" And "What about the Connell family?" (You remember that was the family in South Boston that was wiped out by a bomb last week. Six kids, the father and mother. One of the Italian Savoia-Marchetti planes the Italians must have sent from their hidden fleet.)

Well, I couldn't be brutal, but I had to say that war was no longer a war between armies but between peoples; and there had to be civilian casualties. I said that while the death of the Connell family was to be pitied, it was not going to affect the outcome of the war in any way.

The Irishman came back, "We want the fleet to fight, and we want airplanes to guard us. That's what you government guys are supposed to do."

I was sort of sore myself, and I told him if we dissipated our air force to protect every hamlet in the United States, there'd be none left to fight the main enemy air fleet when it comes. And my own Irish rising, I said it was men like him who had caused our fleet to be separated, and why the hell didn't he leave the fighting orders to the men who were doing the fighting? I said he was talking loud here, but why didn't he get into the army himself? This was a fool statement as since the draft law passed there is no volunteer enlistment and all the units are selected.

But it was the signal. This debate, mind you, was going on before an open microphone, as the idea was to convince not only Boston but the rest of the country that this mass hysteria must cease.

Well, the microphone certainly heard something then it had never heard before; it heard the squashing of a rotten egg that hit me as square on the chest as if the fellow who threw it had fired a rifle. Then came a deluge of them.

Only at that moment did I realize what had happened: these men were propagandists of Hannibal's Steel Fists sent to the meeting to create panic.

I only had a water pitcher, a gavel and a glass handy. But I did some damage with them by simply climbing down off

the platform with the pitcher in one hand and the glass and gavel in the other and picking out these birds. I laid around me right smartly until the cops came to bust up the affair.

I tell you this only that you may see how Hannibal is managing to disrupt our effort at war. Of course, the semi-dictatorship that the president has established will enable the president to ignore such protests from now on (unless there is a revolt) which I doubt, though it might come if we begin to lose the war.

Well, enough of me. Kay Carstairs is with us in Washington. She was prisoner of Hannibal, but escaped and has given valuable information to Farnham. Incidentally, Farnham is proving to be a powerful leader. He has a genius for organization. And, by the way, I think he is in love with Kay. More competition for you and me and O'Hara and a half dozen others in the same condition.

This letter is to get your opinion of the fighting possibilities in the Atlantic. I've been reading Janes' *Fighting Ships of the World*, and you are outnumbered and outgunned. But Dunning is a cagy admiral, and he knows more about handling naval air war than anybody we've got.

Miles read the big scrawled signature. He thought about Kay for a moment, but then as twilight fell he saw that the wake of the *Concord* ahead was veering to port. The fleet was turning. Instantly all else was swept from his mind.

As he turned back to the ward room he saw sailors dashing about to get the planes above decks. What did this mean?

ON BOARD THE *New York*, where he raised his flag, Rear Admiral Dunning paced back and forth in his spacious quarters in the stern of the battleship. He had given the order for all ships to turn six points to port. And on his face was the realization of the importance of the order.

Dunning's teeth bit hard on the stem of an empty pipe. He knew now what Lord Jellicoe must have felt that afternoon at Jutland in 1915 when Von Scheer launched his torpedo boat attack. What Jellicoe must have felt when he saw his own fleet outmaneuvered and outshot. Jellicoe, who as had often been said, was the only man in the world who could have lost the World War in a single afternoon.

Could Dunning lose this war now on the basis of the decision he must make when he located the Italo-German fleet? Should he turn away, avoid battle, take refuge in Chesapeake Bay under coast defense guns?

That was what the German fleet had done in 1914, gone behind Heligoland, and thus surrendered the supremacy of the seas to England. But the fact that the German fleet was there behind its mine fields—"A fleet in being"—had prevented England from landing an expeditionary force on German soil and taking the German armies in the rear.

If he retreated now, the Italo-German fleet could range the coast, shelling and creating a reign of terror. But if the Germans and the Italians intended to move troops, they would not dare put transports to sea as long as he, Dunning, could dart out and sink the supply ships. But what would the American people say? With Boston and New York, Philadelphia and Baltimore, Charleston and Savannah already seeing spooks by night. Already yelling for the Navy to do something.

The people whose protests had already weakened the Pacific fleet without strengthening his enough—in their frenzy they would brand him a coward.

But suppose he offered battle now, and steamed in for broadsides. He was outgunned. He had not sufficient planes to retain command of the air. Suppose his fighters, his bombers, his spotters were shot down. Blindly he'd have to retreat while the enemy, locating him by their planes, blew his fleet to destruction.

On the other hand, if by surprise he could get command of the air, the ship odds now against him would not mean so much. It would be the enemy who were blind and he could see. He knew his gunnery records and in maneuvering he had the reputation of being wily, clever and daring. He stared out at the squat gray warships that steamed in perfect formation.

It all depended, he told himself, on whether he could gain command of the air. Suppose he risked an attack. In case the air attack failed, would there still be time to break off the battle and save the fleet? How many "flying deck" cruisers had the enemy? How many fighting and bombing planes could they muster? He could only guess at this; his guess based on peacetime Intelligence reports.

His mind turned to another angle. Suppose he could draw off, pretend to flee, and pull the enemy fleet in pursuit until he was close enough to call upon shore airdromes for air reinforcements enough to insure his command of the air.

His mouth twitched. He could see it all plainly, presuming he had the air power. The first contact; the destruction of enemy aircraft carriers, the dispersal of the enemy planes; his destroyers laying a smoke screen behind which he could maneuver to cross the enemy's T. His deadly broadsides bringing the odds rapidly down until he could boldly strive for victory.

A door opened behind him and a fleet aide hurried in. His face was bright, his eyes sparkling.

"They've located the enemy fleet, sir."

Admiral Dunning removed his pipe. He frowned. In his fleet, even in excitement, men did not talk so vaguely.

"Who are 'they?'" he rapped. "Who found the fleet?"

"Gregson, sir, reconnaissance pilot of Admiral Nixon's flagship. The information was blinkered to us. Gregson is on his way. The enemy is only one hundred and fifty miles away. Here's the position, sir."

He gave Admiral Dunning the latitude and longitude. South of the Grand Banks, steaming fifteen knots south by southeast. And there was the total of the enemy battleships sighted. Dunning scanned the figures closely.

Twenty Class A cruisers. Nine battleships which did not include the so-called "pocket battleships" of the German *Deutschland* type. There were three of these, powerful, terrible engines of war. Forty destroyers grouped with the fleet in a screen. Probably thirty more elsewhere.

Four aircraft carriers; total of fighting, bombing and torpedo planes carried estimated at six hundred and eighty.

Nearly one hundred and fifty fighting planes, Dunning thought—more than he could muster.

Rapidly he counted the rest, the sloops, the submarines, the torpedo boats, the minelayers. But he knew the answer long before he reached the end. He was outgunned thirty-five percent, by huge sixteen-inch weapons that would throw more than a ton of shell. The enemy was steaming south by south east. He could still avoid them if he wished.

Dunning knew that the moment of high decision had come. He could fight or run, but he had to do one or the other quickly.

Always, as he pondered, he was aware of the one unknown factor in modern naval warfare; the use of the airplane as a weapon of offense. He himself had been at loggerheads with higher officers over its efficacy. Not that he belonged to the foolish school who believed airplanes would sink battleships. But in blinding the enemy, disrupting its destroyer screen, attacking its submarines—he pulled his thoughts back to the specific problem.

Should he fight or run?

He sent for Gregson, the pilot who had discovered the enemy fleet, questioned him exhaustively. Then, when he was done with gathering facts, when he had digested the material, when he had checked his line of retreat, he made his decision. He would risk an air encounter, a surprise attack on the enemy aircraft carriers. If he succeeded in gaining air control he would risk full naval action. If the air attack failed, he would break off and retreat.

He gave the order, "Turn six points to port—all ships."

And ordered away his carriers under escort for a dawn surprise attack.

11

THE ENEMY GUNS

LIEUTENANT BURTON MILES met the dawn at fifteen thousand feet. As flight commander, he flew at the point of a wedge-shaped V of Curtis fighting Hawks. Behind him, ahead of him, on both sides of him flew other wedges. Three hundred and twenty planes in all. The order read, "Your mission is to escort bombers to bomb and destroy flying decks of enemy aircraft carriers. You will then engage enemy fighting planes and destroy them."

That was the mission of Miles' squadron. Other echelons of fighting planes were held in reserve to escort and protect the torpedo planes. These last, each carrying from one to three Whitehead torpedoes, would make a mass attack on the enemy's main fleet. What would result was still unknown. That is to say, modern warfare had not yet tested whether a plane, flying low and straight and slowly to launch a torpedo, could survive destruction long enough to get its missiles launched.

There were other aircraft in reserve to drive off any enemy bombers who might wriggle through to bomb the flying decks of the American aircraft carriers. Miles was thinking of this last possibility as he looked down at the gray, ridged sea. He was flying a land plane. He had fuel supply for three hours. When that was exhausted (and if he had not been shot down), where would he land if the aircraft carriers had no decks?

There was nothing but the vast sea in which he would instantly swamp, and after that, if he was not stunned and drowned, he would float in his life preserver and hope to be picked up. He weighed it all coolly; he had thought of the risks long ago.

Watching the squadron leader's pennons, he turned his mind to the probabilities of victory. Miles was no fool; he had made a stiff study of naval tactics and he was aware that today's battle would make naval history; victory or defeat, the tactics displayed, the use of each naval weapon would be closely studied by admirals for years to come. Questions of aircraft value in naval conflict that had been hotly argued for years would be answered now. Could a naval bomber disable a battleship or cruiser sufficiently to take its broadsides out of the final smash of sixteen-inch guns?

He knew Dunning had made a life study of aircraft as an auxiliary weapon of maneuver and offense. Miles had known that since he had studied under Dunning at the naval college. He winced to remember that, studying how a clever commander would toss in his air force at the precise moment, he had thought of it as a sort of chess problem. Not as a combat in which men would die.

The mist deepened into clouds that hid the earth from his view, and he could only follow in his position and watch the compass and wait. At two hundred and thirty miles an hour, the wait would not be long. He looked at his guns, felt at the toggles of his light bombs, and did a dozen other jobs of checking. He thought, as many a man before him had thought, that the waiting in wartime was the most intolerable suffering. The chill of the high altitude struck through him.

Then, on a sudden, the signal came. He never knew what had caused it; he was only aware that the air suddenly swarmed with planes. The thing he had visualized, imagined, was here. And all the things he had promised himself he would do, he did not do.

All he could see was a flight of planes with Iron Crosses on their wings, and at the signal he waggled his wings, threw over the stick and then out, and the Hawk turned on her right wing, nosed down, and with the throttle wide open he dove a thousand feet.

He had picked his target, a green plane, at the moment doing a half-roll. At a hundred yards Miles tripped his guns. Four Brownings, their fire converging at the rate of twenty-four hundred bullets a minute. Two mounted on the wings, two firing through the propeller. At the speed he was going he was past his target before he saw the effects of the fire. He only knew that his flight formation was broken up and signaled, each man for himself. Making a pivot turn, he nosed up at a gray undercarriage centered between two Iron Crosses that hung almost over his head.

He knew he had shot down this plane—but it was the last he knew of the fight. He saw his tracer stream rake the gray plane, breaking the propeller first. The motor of the German caught fire and as Miles leveled off, he saw the pilot spring outward and go hurtling down, pulling frantically at the parachute strapped to him.

MILES SAW NO more than that. He didn't even see the enemy plane that must have curved in on his tail. He only knew a few bright sparks flashed past his head. The cyclone motor ahead of him sent back a blast of black smoke and then a sheet of fire. A few sparks spattered off his guns. He turned, felt his head and found he had no goggles and hardly any helmet. His hand must have reached out to the throttle because the flames continued but the motor did not explode.

He kept saying to himself, "I'd better bail out."

There were no more bullets flying past him. Within him was the sudden urge to take his ship down. Below he could see other planes massing and milling, and he should take his plane through them. The fire-wall was keeping the flames away from his legs. He could go down a little way anyway.

He nosed the ship steeply until the controls were sensitive, aware now of a dreadful numbness in one side of his head and a great lethargy that made him want to close his eyes just for a moment. He must have shut them, for when he looked again, the water was plainly in sight and there were no planes around.

Indeed, there was nothing in sight save the battle ships below that were drawn up in severe lines, the bow of each following in the wake of the other. Possibly this was the fleet; he could sit down and be picked up.

The flames were hotter, eating at the wings so swiftly that the whole plane would be blazing in a few seconds. No chance of side-slipping in now.

He unbuckled his safety belt. It was time to shove off. The altitude must be, he thought, about eight thousand, maybe a little more. The altimeter was no good—the instrument board was useless.

He climbed up against the wind pull and tensed his feet against the side of the cockpit. He jumped up and out in a jack-knife dive. As he went out and away from the plane he suddenly thought, "I've been shot down. I'm out of it. I'm—"

His right hand had caught the rip-cord grip, and as he suddenly found himself on his belly looking down at the sky, he pulled it. The chute made him do a quick flop, jerking him upright with a speed that snapped his neck against his shoulders.

He was now in a soft, complete silence, swaying at the end of the cordage, being blown, he noticed, in the same direction the ships were moving down there. He stared at them.

The truth finally dawned on him. "They're not American ships."

Memory of the days in college, studying silhouette recognition, flowed easily back. The *Cavour* and her type, Italian battleships; the *Von Scheer*—she's a thirty-six thousand tonner—sixteen inch guns. Hard hitter. German.

But what were they all doing here? Smoke and dashing destroyers, and tiny little chips which must be those torpedo boats—forty-mile-an-hour motor boats of the Italians, carrying two torpedoes.

His eyes got heavy, but he fought off his weariness. He'd have to be ready when he got down to the water or drown under the smother of his chute. No sense in being drowned under a chute and cordage. He'd better find his knife and cut loose about fifteen or twenty feet above and be ready to swim.

He had out his knife and got the blade open. He looked

above, but the sweep of the chute blotted out what was going on. He could see wreckage dotting the water below. Fifteen or twenty planes. He wasn't the only one shot down.

Shot down! The words cleared his mind abruptly. He who was never to be shot down, who was to rage across the skies behind four blazing guns and clear all before him. He had been shot down in his first combat.

The sea rose rapidly now to receive him. The utter silence of height was gone. He could hear dull rumbling and feel a sort of concussion.

The big battlewagons were at it now—this time for keeps. He looked down. The water was less than a hundred feet below. He got a grip on the cordage with his left hand and slashed his harness. Careful now. He had seemed to be floating for so long and now he was falling fast. The wind sent him skimming over the waves. A swell, larger than the others, was forming ahead. He let go with a swing that threw him to the right. He tried to hit the water feet first but the swing sent him sprawling. He struck almost on his back.

His life jacket brought him bobbing to the surface. The wind had pulled the chute along, was still dragging it, so he was clear. And for a moment he was strangely relaxed. The chill water hadn't struck through his padded suit; only his hands and face had felt the iciness of it. So he told himself he was down and he was alive. After the first shock of the water he looked up.

Perhaps sixty planes or so were in sight under the clouds, milling around, apparently senselessly. The rest of the fight was out of sight. How was it going?

Then suddenly he realized the expedition had failed. Its purpose had been to destroy the enemy aircraft carriers. But the American planes had never reached their objective. Even here, rising and falling on the waves, he could see the enemy aircraft-carriers, faint gray shapes moving in the distance. And moving fast, as he could see.

He could hear the concussion of guns, but whether it meant cruiser skirmishes or actual battleship broadsides he could not tell. He thought to himself grimly that the fate of the battle settled his own future. If Dunning won he would be picked up; if the Americans lost…

AT TEN O'CLOCK Admiral Dunning knew his attempt to command the air had failed. Outnumbered nearly two to one, his attack planes had not only been unable to break through the enemy screen but, worse yet, had failed to hold a sudden bombing attack launched on a long flank turn that crippled the flying decks of his own *Curtis* and *Concord.* Nor had he expected from the Italians the bold maneuver that cost him the *Lexington.* Five of the tiny torpedo boats of the Italians—merely motorboats with terrific engine power—had swept in apparently from nowhere. The first two, traveling close to sixty miles an hour, struck the *Lexington's* steel torpedo nets and the resulting explosions tore them to bits. The other three, charging straight in, never launched torpedoes. They simply struck the thin-skinned hull of the *Lexington* and the war-head torpedoes did the rest.

Every man aboard the Italian mosquito ships was blown to bits. A hole forty feet in diameter was torn in the *Lexington* at the water line. She was down by the head in ten minutes and sank at four o'clock.

Dunning kept his spotters aloft until the last, and it was well he did. For, harried by air attack, trying to retreat, he found that the enemy had the legs of him. The enemy cruisers swept around his flank and engaged Admiral Hood's scouting squadron. He had no choice now but to turn and fight, for destruction at the enemy's choosing lay ahead.

He fought as a wolf in a trap might fight; desperately, cunningly. And by a ship's right-about, quickly executed in the face of odds, he outmaneuvered the coalition fleet and actually crossed the enemy's T. He brought his broadsides to bear, first on the *Von Scheer*. The American gunnery had never been higher. Three salvos brought his guns on the target at twenty-six thousand yards and with no dispersion the third salvo was home.

Seventy-two enormous steel tubes, each throwing a ton of armor-piercing steel, blasted in explosions so terrific that the vast American steel fortresses rolled to the gun recoil. Over the horizon, where the spotting plane was now fighting desperately against death, the huge shells soared. The *Von Scheer's* bow and quarter vanished in a cloud of smoke and flame. The low-hung gray vessel shuddered, stood still, heaved upward as if in agony. When the brown smoke had vanished, the man-of-war was half-submerged, drifting dangerously in the path of sister ships.

But to cross the T Admiral Dunning had to turn ninety degrees and this to the north. Then his spotting planes were shot down. Blind, he had to turn without even a slight mist to protect him. And in turning to run, he had to face the broadsides of the main coalition fleet.

His cruisers were beaten in detail by the *Deutschland* and her sister battle cruisers. His own broadsides were no longer on the target. The enemy's marksmanship was as excellent as his had been.

First the *Utah* heeled out of line, her protective blisters pierced by shell. Then under the impact of two hundred thousand tons of shells, the *Wyoming* seemed to melt away.

The *New Mexico* was disabled by six waterline shots, and as she yawned in the sea, alone and abandoned save by her crew, a dashing torpedo-boat-attack left her sinking. From now on what had been a battle became a rout. Dunning had no recourse but to run. But the *Cavour,* the Roma, the *Von Hindenberg* and the *Mayence* had the speed of him. They came into range at 2 P.M. with spotters up and beyond AA reach. The *New York* was last to feel the enemy's fury.

But come it did. Dunning had known it was coming, and he left the plotting room in the bowels of the *New York.* Some inner urge dragged him to the tiny quarterdeck to meet his death.

The enemy ships lay below the horizon. The *New York's* sleek powder-grimed guns were no use now. He had OBS officers and they had fired four broadsides but without knowledge as to the results. Dunning ordered the sea cocks opened and the *New York* abandoned by the crew.

He chose to stay aboard. No fault of his that the vessels had sunk, that men had died. But the blame would fall upon him. He was old, and he was suddenly tired and the thought of being a prisoner or coming into New York as the man who had lost the war sickened him.

The *New York* was abandoned under a broadside impact that wrecked three boats and smashed her port blisters so that she heeled until her guns nosed into the water.

She was hulled by five o'clock. By a miracle the blast

of steel spared Dunning. He stood with his unfilled pipe clinched between his lips. And as the *New York* turned turtle, he went under with her.

Save for a few submarines and a minelayer, the entire American Atlantic fleet was destroyed. The minelayer was caught at dawn by a fast cruiser and blown to bits without being able to fire a decent return shot. The American submarines escaped a circling destroyer net.

Thirty thousand men died that day, and the Atlantic Ocean was commanded by the enemy. The United States could offer no sea defense worthy of the name....

Lieutenant Burton Miles saw the *New York* turn turtle. In the late afternoon of that day, carried on the long swell of the waves, he saw the war lost. The enemy fleet went on and he was alone on the ocean. He floated there a while, his teeth chattering, too cold even to think. But at last with struggling movement he got out his automatic pistol and looked at it. Then, swiftly, he put the muzzle to his temple and pulled the trigger once—twice—without result. But the third shell was good.

12

THE MEN IN GREEN

THE ANNOUNCER'S VOICE cracked; he paused a second, swallowed hard and said, "Ladies and gentlemen of the radio audience, we interrupt this broadcast of the Goodies variety show, to permit your friend and mine, the ever popular Spike Brenn, to bring you important news of the war."

Spike let his eyes sweep the circle of suddenly silent radio artists. He looked beyond them to where perhaps half a house of spectators watched. Then he nodded to the announcer and stepped to the microphone. He wet his lips, forced himself to speak distinctly—even slowly.

"Friends," he said, "you must prepare yourselves for bad news; you will need all the courage in you to bear what I have to say.

"The American Atlantic Scouting Fleet has been defeated. More, it has been, except for fifteen submarines, completely destroyed. The battle took place day before yesterday at dawn and by dusk the American flag had disappeared from the sea and the sun.

"To those of you who had sons aboard the battleships, I can only say that there still exists hope that many were picked up by enemy vessels and are now being held as prisoners of war. Yours may be among them, so do not lose all hope yet. Others—many—too many, God help us"—his voice cracked but he got control immediately—"have given their lives for the nation, for democracy, for you. May God have mercy on their souls and may He receive them as heroes who died for the liberty of our people.

"Few details of the battle are known, as the submarine flotilla from whence comes our information retreated early from the main conflict and can tell us little save that enemy destroyers pursued them as far as Nantucket Lightship. Intercepted enemy radio messages announce their complete victory.

"In this hour of our distress, I ask you to have courage and to hope. The Japanese fleet is being held beyond the Hawaiians. The country is mobilizing swiftly, and despite this setback, ultimate victory must rest with American arms which have never known final surrender and defeat."

He ceased to speak and stepped back from the microphone. He had other news, an intercepted radio that meant but one thing: invasion of America. But this he could not tell nor would have told had he been able to. He went back to his office intending to call Farnham. More and more he was coming to depend on Farnham in these times. As he entered Kay came to him.

"You should go and rest," she said. "You're—you look badly, Spike."

"Rest," he said, looking at the telephone. "I wonder if I'll ever rest again." He leaned back, waiting for his call to go through.

"How are the people going to take it?" he muttered. "How badly have they been poisoned by the Steel Fists?"

He was thinking of the sullen opposition of the Steel Fists. Already, since the president had forbidden open meeting, there had been conflicts between them and the police, conflicts in which the police had not always come off best. There was, Spike knew, propaganda secretly put out by the Steel Fists; how far had its defeatist tone undermined the American will to resist?

His fan correspondence, scores of letters and telegrams each day, gave him some idea, and he groaned as he read it.

Here was a telegram from Akron, Ohio.

> MY BOY WAS ON THE NEW YORK STOP YOU BUTCHERS HAVE MURDERED HIM STOP LET THIS SLAUGHTER CEASE AT ONCE.

Another envelope contained a "throw-around" sheet, cheaply printed.

> The intrenched rich are murdering your sons to protect themselves. You can stop this war by refusing to fight, by refusing to support it with your money. The oligarchy of America must fall. Are you going to fight the wars of the rich? Are you going on starving without work, without hope to support a regime that slaughters your youth? A New Era will dawn for America if you will demand peace. The Italians and the Germans do not make war on the American people; they make war on the leaders who would keep you in slave subjection. They come to help you, and not with any thought of conquest. Refuse to fight. THE STEEL FISTS.

Spike swore and hurled the paper on his desk. What

could the future hold for a country besieged from without, torn within.

As for the inarticulate majority, the people of America who write no letters and do not express themselves other than to their friends, a curious state of mind came into being. A strange silence that was broken only by sudden savage outbursts such as occurred in Indianapolis. There a man who had been found lurking around the airport where a squadron of military planes had landed, was seized and charged with espionage. The police were taking him to jail pending an inquiry when the gathering crowd, at first curious, suddenly went berserk. The man was seized and hung to a lamppost.

There were four other such outbursts. It was hysteria and the action of people squirming in the grip of intolerable suspense. But for the most part they bore the suspense silently. Even the newspapers were subdued; the *Sphere* broke the rules of its front page in reporting the defeat of the Battle of the Grand Banks.

"For two centuries," said this newspaper, "Americans have lived in the richness of plenty. Not since 1812 have we been invaded; nor have our people been called upon to show those traits of courage, and of endurance that made this nation great.

"But we must reveal our courage now; we must sacrifice, we must stand on our feet with our backs to the wall and fight now to the last to save for our posterity the great heritage that was handed to us."

It was the first hint that there would be invasion. Spike wondered where the information came from. He made his noon broadcast and prepared to catch the three o'clock plane for Washington to investigate.

IN A PENTHOUSE atop the Crystal Building's thirty-seven stories, John Hannibal listened to Spike's noon broadcast. Since Spike had become a government propagandist, he could be depended upon to reveal the government attitude. The government was jittery; that was plain.

Dorsey came in accompanied by the Council of Eight. Their eyes were eager.

"It's come," said Dorsey, holding out a decoded telegram. Hannibal took it, read it at a glance.

> TRANSPORTS SAILING TONIGHT AT MIDNIGHT STOP WE SHALL HARASS COAST AS ORDERED

Hannibal smiled harshly. Now that the final moment had come, he felt no exaltation. It was as if something foreseen, inevitable, unstoppable, had come to pass. His blazing blue eyes studied the eight faces ranged in front of him. The men who had carried out his every order. They spoke of patriotism but he knew what drove them—personal greed and ambition. Just as greed and ambition drove Italy and Germany to play his game.

"Your sectors are ready?" he asked the eight men.

"Yes, sir," they chorused.

Hannibal nodded. He had known the fact; he wanted to watch their expressions.

"Send the order," he said.

Dorsey ran to the next room where a powerful short

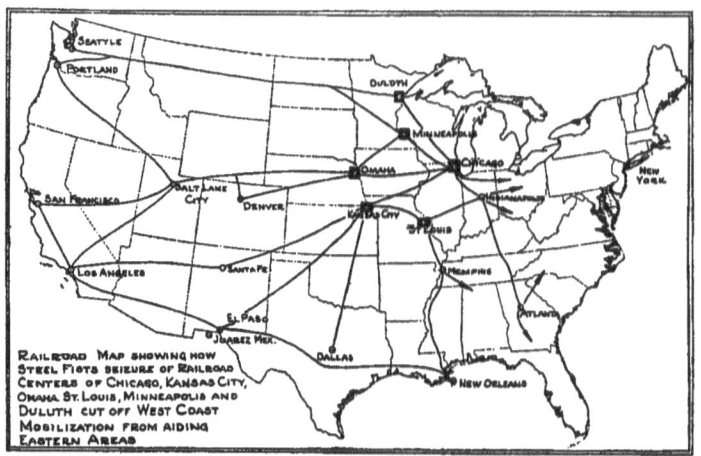

RAILROAD MAP SHOWING HOW STEEL FIST'S SEIZURE OF RAILROAD CENTERS OF CHICAGO, KANSAS CITY, OMAHA, ST. LOUIS, MINNEAPOLIS AND DULUTH CUT OFF WEST COAST MOBILIZATION FROM AIDING EASTERN AREAS

wave radio had been set up. "Send Code order six," he yelled.

Hannibal said to the Council of Eight. "You have been rehearsed in the plan. You know every detail that must be accomplished in the next forty-eight hours. You are now Lictors, each supreme in your sector with the authority delegated to you by me." He paused. "I need not add that we rise or fall together; that five years of planning depend on what you do in the next forty-eight hours."

They stiffened to attention, slapped clenched right fist over their hearts.

"You can depend on us, Seneschal," said one.

Hannibal relaxed and shook hands with each one. "Your planes are waiting. So I won't hold you. Use the short wave and the 'A' code for all communications."

They were gone, then, and Hannibal was alone. He sat down, aware now for the first time, of a sense of helplessness. He had planned for six years; he had tested every thread of the woof; he had carried the reins of authority. But now that authority had passed to others. Like a general who has committed his army to battle, he could no longer change one single fact. He could do nothing but sit back and wait for success or failure to come. Some World War general—he thought it was Bullard—in commenting on this sense of helplessness, after his division was committed to battle, declared that he used to play solitaire to keep from brooding and worrying until the first reports came in. Hannibal took out a deck of cards and laid them out. It wouldn't be long now.

Yet he could not forebear an occasional glance at the wall map of the United States above his head. On the map thirty-four key cities were ringed. On the map the communications system of the country was sketched in with blue pencil. Everything depended upon swift, unhesitating action. Would such action take place? In his preoccupation he played a spade jack on a club queen. He gave up and went in to talk to his son Stephen.

It was exactly 1:20 P.M.

AT TWO O'CLOCK Spike said, "We'll save time by taking the subway to the Penn station. Hurry up, darling."

He seized Kay's suitcase and they went down to the curb and took a taxicab to Fiftieth Street where there was a kiosk to the West Side subway. Getting out, Spike noticed a lot of people standing around, but since this is a phenomenon encountered in New York at almost any time of the day or night, he paid no attention. His huge body elbowed a passage through for himself and Kay and he reached the platform. A five-car local train stood there, dark. Spike thrust a quarter through the opening in the change window.

"Five nickels, please," he said.

The subway employee thrust the quarter back. "You'd better try somewhere else, brother. The power's off. The trains ain't running."

"Power off," Spike repeated. "That's impossible."

He had, years ago as a reporter, made a study of New York's problem of supplying electricity; because the city lived on electric power. And with underground conduits and secondary hookups, he knew that it was impossible for the subway system to be without power, save in a brief interval when a wreck or other accident happened, and even then, the power was only off in a particular segment. But he had no time to argue the point.

It took forty-five minutes to reach the Newark airport and he wanted to make the three o'clock plane. He hurried back to the street and found a taxicab.

"Eastern Air Lines office and step on it," he ordered.

He saw nothing untoward on the trip downtown save the unusual number of people milling around. But Kay, listening during a traffic stall, said, "Did you hear that?"

"Hear what?"

"The electricity is off. Those people can't get back to work because the elevators aren't running, and there are no lights."

Spike grunted. New Yorkers depended on elevators as some people depend on trains; they could have walked up, he reflected. But lights; that was serious. One-third of the offices in New York require artificial light during the day, due to the high buildings. He wondered what sort of accident had happened to the New York Edison Company.

He thrust Kay into the Eastern Air Lines bus a minute before it was scheduled to shove off. And on the trip he encountered other phenomena. Surface cars were stalled; there were no illuminators in the Holland Tunnel. People were clustered in knots, talking. But what gave him a sudden shock of alarm was that when the bus emerged on the Jersey City side he saw surface cars stalled there, and electric signs that blink their messages day and night, dark and dirty-looking.

"I can understand maybe there was an accident in New York," he muttered. "But why is Jersey City tied up, too?"

The bus driver surmised there had been one hell of an accident somewhere. A passenger said darkly, "Probably some damned Italian or German spy sabotaging."

Kay and Spike exchanged glances. They arrived at the airport and went in for the weigh-in and ticket-check. As they entered Spike saw the new uniforms. He reached out a hand and stopped Kay.

"Look!" he muttered.

THE ROOM HELD fifty or more men in uniforms of a type that neither she nor Spike had ever seen before. These men wore dark olive green breeches and green wrapped leggins; green jersey sweaters of the turtle neck variety. On the chest of the sweater, over the heart, was a large silver Steel Fist. These were the privates.

The non-commissioned officers wore V chevrons of silver on each arm, one for lance-corporal, two for corporal, three for sergeant and a silver diamond under the chevrons for top-sergeant. Silver overseas caps of 1918 shape and style were on their heads.

The officers wore the same uniform except that besides Sam Browne belts they had donned silver-belted trench coats with a green Steel Fist on the chest. On their shoul-

der straps were one, two and three tiny replicas of the Steel
Fists, according to their rank.

The soldiers carried rifles, Springfields as Spike was
quick to see; the officers had heavy automatic pistols belted
to their right hips.

One of the officers, wearing three Steel Fists on his
shoulder straps, was turning away from a man, apparently
the manager of the airport.

"But, Centurion," said the manager, "we've got schedules
to make, mails to carry. We can lose our contract. You've—"

"You give me any more argument," said the Centurion, "and I'll throw you in the can. I'm running this place,
and no plane takes off. Get that?" He turned to face the
groups of passengers who had huddled where Spike and
Kay stood.

"You people might just as well go home and sit," he said.
"The Steel Fists have taken over this country and we're
running it. No planes leave today." He turned to what
was apparently a first sergeant. "Decurion, clear this place.
Drive all these people out."

A U.S. Army major, standing not five paces from Spike,
had been getting redder and redder. Now, as a private came
at him with rifle at port, he sprang forward.

"Damn you for a traitorous swine," he said, "do you realize this country is at war?"

"Now, shut up, play-soldier," said the Centurion, "or I'll
get rough."

"Rough! Damn you, I'll see you shot."

"Carter," said the Centurion, "take this out and pour a
little Mickey Finn into it."

A squad rushed the major and by the time they had him

out the door he was nearly naked. Gun butts had laid red bruises on his back.

Spike felt Kay trembling violently.

Outside as he sought a conveyance back to New York, Kay whispered, "What does it mean, Spike?"

"It means," he said quietly, "that Hannibal has worked out the only way he could get power in this country. With the nation at war in the east and the west, he has begun a revolt and seized communications and key centers. God help us all now."

13

NEW ERA

WHEN MEN LATER were able to piece together what had happened on that historic day of October 21st, it was amazing to see how simple Hannibal's plan was and how brilliantly it was executed. In New York, for example, fifty thousand uniformed Steel Fists were in motion to prearranged objectives by two P.M. The first and biggest raid was on the plants of the New York Edison Company.

Policemen, seeing the marching men in odd uniforms, put in a call to headquarters in Centre Street. But there were no reserves to come. They were already out on other emergencies. After all, there are only twenty-six thousand police in New York.

The Steel Fists formed with military precision. The policemen, used to disorderly mobs of New York, were aghast at the swift efficiency of the formations. They were more amazed at the automatic rifles and musette bags of extra clips. To each company, one cop later said, were attached two light machine guns in teams, a loader and a gunner.

A motor truck without license drew up close to a Steel Fist officer wearing a silver overseas cap with a star, and received an order. Hastily a squad of Steel Fists leaped at the truck and before the policemen's eyes, six heavy duty Browning machine guns were unloaded and two other squads of men fell upon them and began assembling them for use.

Over all, then, suddenly, came the yell, "First battalion—power houses!"

It had been rehearsed, that move, by men who must have studied every inch of the vast edifice in which was generated the power that kept New York alight and moving.

The heavy tramp of feet, running at the double quick, resounded through the streets. Another battalion appeared, and out of nowhere came a fleet of fifty trucks into which these men piled at a sharp order.

The man in the silver overseas cap went into the control room of the electric company. He had an automatic pistol in his hand which he waved to emphasize his orders.

"Pull the main controls," he ordered.

The chief engineer stared at him, gaping. "But those shut off every volt of power in the city," he protested.

"Pull the controls," repeated the officer. His hand steadied and the gun muzzle stared into the engineer's stomach. The engineer gulped; his face slowly turned green. He looked beyond the officer and saw a dozen men with automatic rifles. He looked at his assistants and they seemed like men turned to stone.

The officer with the silver cap fired his pistol. The wind of the bullet whickered past the engineer's head. "I won't miss again," said the officer.

The engineer shivered once. "Off controls," he said huskily, and started pulling the great switches.

The subways stopped. The electrified railroads to

Harmon stopped. The elevators shooting up and down within the gigantic skyscrapers stopped. Electric lights blinked out and surface cars stalled where they were. Motion picture theaters went dark; refrigeration plants, upon which New York depended for its main reserve of foodstuffs, began to grow warm and soon the food within would begin to rot. Newspaper presses ceased to turn. Broadcasting stations were burked as if a gigantic hand had squeezed the throats of the singers and entertainers within Radio City.

Short wave length amateur broadcasters could not dispatch one word. Telephones went dead.

In private homes and apartments starvation loomed. The electric ranges did not cook, and the gas company, dependent upon electricity to push the cooking gas through the vast pipes by pressure, could no longer furnish gas. There was no fire, no heat.

In New York, at that moment, a man could not ride, he could not cook, he could not eat. He could not drink water because the great electric pumps that supplied the pressure did not function. In the area of greater Manhattan, embracing a circle with a diameter of twenty miles, a population of six million people was suddenly as helpless as if stranded on a desert island without food or water.

IN THE CENTRAL telegraph control offices a company of Steel Fists took complete authority. No messages went out. In the telephone exchange, no telephone call was completed. A company of Steel Fists invaded the National Broadcasting Company's offices in Radio City. Another occupied the Columbia Broadcasting offices. Over in Newark a third company of Steel Fists dynamited

the plant of the Bamberger Broadcasting Service. As for
the minor broadcasting plants in New York, these were
smashed beyond repair by still other companies.

Police reserves hastily summoned were greeted by a
hail of rifle and machine gun fire that swept the streets
clear of them in five minutes. A police river boat patrol
was dispatched to Governor's Island where two thousand
troops made up the headquarters of the Second Corps
Area comprising the First and Second regular divisions.

The boat was sunk halfway across the river by machine
guns equipped to fire fifty calibre or half-inch slugs. More
of the same machine guns were trained on the East River at
this point so that any sally by the military from Governor's
Island could be resisted. From somewhere, probably only
John Hannibal actually knew where, three one-pounder
rapid-fire guns were emplaced together with a German-
type trench mortar that could lob flaming thermite shells
on any vessel dispatched from Governor's Island.

At five o'clock as the gray day was drawing to a close, a
battalion of Steel Fists accompanying a group of officers
wearing silver overseas caps and silver trench coats strode
into the lobby of the Waldorf Astoria on Park Avenue.

Even as they entered, military runners from the outlying
Steel Fists battalions began to race up with reports. John
Hannibal's chief of staff and his G-2 and G-3 received the
messages. John Hannibal himself listened, but paid little
heed. Dorsey would handle these details. Hannibal must
plan the events to come.

He turned to General Von Schlieffen. "Send a runner
to Miklas in the NBC. Also one to Powers at the electric

plant. I want electric power turned on for one hour. I'll broadcast a message in that time."

"Aye, aye, Seneschal," snapped the staff general.

The runners were dispatched. Dorsey said to the manager of the hotel, "The American Steel Fists have taken this hotel for headquarters. You will immediately evacuate all your guests and all your personnel, including yourself. You have precisely twenty minutes to do it in to save yourself grief."

That night Spike tried to rent a car to drive him and Kay to Washington. The garage proprietor shrugged. "I can rent you the car. But they ain't no gasoline, guy, and no way to get any. My pumps is dry and these here Steel Fists have stopped the tank cars from coming around."

No trains were running. After the electricity went out the Pennsylvania and New York Central, electrified, tried to bring in steam engines to move trains. The Steel Fists took possession of the yards and the stations. And did the same in Hoboken and Jersey City.

Spike heard one harassed, outraged railroad official cry, "You fools! Do you want a panic and starvation? New York only has seventy-two hours reserve of food."

"Shut your face and leave that worry to us," said the Steel Fist.

Elsewhere in the nation, though of course Spike could only guess at it, the same situation existed. From Seattle and Portland to New Orleans and Birmingham; from Minneapolis and Chicago to Detroit and Boston, the Steel Fists seemed to spring, armed and uniformed, from the earth. In thirty-four key cities they seized communications, transportation—authority. There were deaths, hundreds of them. But a mobile, disciplined and armed force, acting on a pre-conceived plan, overbore all sporadic confused attempts to resist.

The seizure of the railroad centers cut the nation to-bits. The northwest and the west were isolated from southwest and the south. The east and the northeast were entirely cut off. The mobilized army corps around San Francisco and Los Angeles managed to stop complete surrender of the local authority. But no railroads were running and they could not get east to prevent the uprising there.

On the night of October 29th, the United States was a paralyzed, inert mass of one hundred and twenty millions of people controlled and dominated by eight hundred thousand unemployed, savage, bitter men. Hannibal reigned supreme.

SPIKE AND KAY were in their rooms at the Metropolis Hotel when the lights suddenly flashed on. They stared at one another. In the cold dark city it had seemed that the lights would never glow again. At the same moment a crackling came out of the wall radio, hooked up to a central control downstairs.

Kay said, "What on earth—"

"Hush!" said Spike, walking to the wall loudspeaker.

"John Hannibal," Spike said, as a voice spoke.

"Men and women," came John Hannibal's voice over the radio, "those of you who had your radio tuned in when the power was cut off, please notify your neighbors to tune in on WEAF. I will allow exactly ten minutes for this purpose. Listen in, then, because there will be news for every one of great importance."

The radio went dead.

In the faint light Kay stared at Spike. "What does it mean?"

Spike shrugged. "The occupation and control of a city of six million requires some manipulation. We will probably hear in a few minutes how he intends to maintain control."

At the end of ten minutes to the second the radio crackled again and then came John Hannibal's voice.

"Men and women of metropolitan New York," he said, "listen carefully to what I am about to say, because your lives and your future depend upon it. By now you have some realization of discomfort; but you do not know what can happen to you unless you obey implicitly what orders I am about to give. Let me tell you of what may befall.

"Do you know that in the warehouses of New York there is only reserve food supplies for seventy-two hours? That if trains cease to bring food supplies into New York, you will feel hunger? Recall in your own minds the discomfort and inconveniences caused by a heavy snowfall. When your milk doesn't come? When the corner grocery store has no fresh foods, only canned ones?

"I control the railroad entrances and exits to New York. I control the electricity. I can deprive you of water, the lack of which will bring hardship in less than seventy-two hours. I can prevent you from going to work. By running trains out of New York and permitting none to come in, I can force you to migrate elsewhere. I can depopulate this city in four days time. Or starve you to death.

"Do you understand that? Now, listen to me carefully. I have no intention of bringing hardship to you. But I do intend to have your immediate and final obedience to the totalitarian state which I now, for the first time, proclaim to exist in the United States with myself, John Hannibal, as its head, its leader, its Seneschal.

"You have been preyed upon by the top and the bottom, the rich and the poor. You have worked hard for nothing, you have not even the guarantee of security in your old age. The resources which you, as Americans have inherited from ancestors, are being dissipated, stolen and wasted by inefficient stupidity upon the part of men who pretend to be your leaders, congressmen and government officials, who are not fit to handle the smallest fraction of the power you so carelessly entrusted to them. Over them, dominating them, are the rich and the incompetent whose greed has made you slaves.

"This country has been failing, not only abroad, but at home. Particularly in this country we are seeing our West converted to a desert; we are seeing men and women suffer privation because the system of distribution of national wealth has failed. Failed because of the greedy stupidities at the top, and the envious hatred of the bottom, that ignorant, dreaming riff-raff who call themselves Communists.

"The capitalistic system in this country has failed. The Communists offer impractical theories and dreams that cannot ever reach fruition. What is needed is a strong, resolute head with practical aims, and complete and final authority to adjust this country so that any competent man may have work to do, and he shall gain from that work an abundant living and insurance of security in his old age. The nation's resources must be conserved. The staggering cost of inefficient government foisted upon *you* must be abolished.

"Listen to me and go forward to new heights.

"Here is my program. The abolishment of stupid costly state governments which merely inflict their costs upon you. The abolishment of county governments which are archaic and belong no more in our scheme of things.

"In place I submit a central, positive government which maintains control of industry and agriculture, the two hands that make wealth. We abolish the mighty rich; we abolish the envious greedy dreamers who recruit from the lazy and the incompetent. My government shall be of the middle class; the people who produce wealth and need a firm government to prevent that wealth from being wasted or stolen.

"So intrenched has been the oligarchy of the rich that it has taken a war to shake their hold. Even now, the armed forces would crush me at their command if I did not control the national communications system.

"But I have called upon the Steel Fist governments of Germany and Italy to aid me. They are sending troops, not to make war but to help me establish a New Era for all Americans. When my government has been approved by you in plebiscite, the armed forces of Italy and Germany will withdraw.

"And I say to you now, and to the world, that all who oppose the landing of the Italian and German allies and their aid to the Steel Fists are branded enemies of the New Era state and shall be dealt with as traitors and be tried for their lives by my courts.

"I offer you hope, a new life, a freedom from the burden of taxation that has bowed you down. I offer you opportunity and work, and a just share of the wealth your hands create. I offer peace and tranquility and a new and greater nation which shall forge to new heights of security and peace for us all.

"Ponder this message. Stay in your homes. Tomorrow I shall give you light and water. The trains will run in and food will be had at no increase in price. Those caught trying to profiteer during this emergency will be shot without recourse to trial. Martial law prevails but only long enough to establish the new government.

"That is all for now. I shall address you later from time to time when I think you should be acquainted with the problems that I am meeting and effacing."

THE VOICE CEASED to speak. Spike and Kay had insensibly taken hold of each other's hands while they listened to the charming, sincere voice that brought, somehow, a tremendous conviction to the words they had just heard spoken.

"He can't do it," cried Kay suddenly. "It's incredible. Impossible. What of Washington? Of the president? The Army? The man is insane—utterly mad!"

"He has charm and persuasion," said Spike. "He has the country in his grip—with invasion threatened. A lot of people besides his own will believe in him."

"But not enough. Out of all the millions—"

Spike shrugged wearily. "History is full of stories of the disciplined efficient few who have conquered a nation. Take Franco's march through three-quarters of Spain. Take Napoleon's whiff of grape shot against the Parisians."

He paused. Then: "Don't you see? This man has planned. He knows just what to do and how to do it. He's opposed by mere bulk. The army can't even get mobilized against a foreign enemy without great loss of time. And every twenty-four hours will concentrate this man's hold."

He turned toward the window. "He's recruited behind him *youth*. Youth who came into a depression world to find no place for them, no work. Youth with an empty belly will listen even to this insanity if it promises food, work, a future."

He broke off sharply. Kay gasped. The rapping at the door resounded again.

"Open in the name of the New Era."

Spike's hand went to his gun. A gun roared outside and the lock on the door flew to bits. A boot kicked the door open. A man in the silvery trench coat of a Steel Fist officer entered. Behind him were several men.

The officer dangled a heavy automatic pistol by his side.

"Are you Spike Brenn?" he asked. His sullen eyes shifted to Kay.

"You know I am or you wouldn't be here."

"Smart guy," sneered the officer. His eyes were still on Kay. He licked his lips and then turned to Spike.

"You're under protective arrest," he grinned. "Come along easy and it will only be detention camp. Resist and I'll be delighted to shoot you."

The Steel Fists came into the room behind their leader. Spike was unarmed.

"Shall we give him a Mickey Finn?" asked the corporal.

"No. Handcuff him. Enemy of the State."

Spike looked at Kay. He was thinking, "It's happened and I can't stop it."

The corporal clicked handcuffs on his wrists.

14

DETENTION CAMP

IT WAS JOHN HANNIBAL'S chief characteristic to be cool when other men became flustered; to remain calm when others verged on panic. He told himself that this was because dire news made his head ache the worse and thus enabled him to think clearly.

He was thinking clearly now, and in front of him were dispatches and news reports that had even paled Dorsey's swarthy cheeks.

The Twenty-sixth, Twenty-seventh and Twenty-eighth National Guard divisions, of Massachusetts, New York and Pennsylvania, were fifty percent mobilized according to his Lictor in Philadelphia and Boston, and were preparing, regardless of equipment, to march against him and drive him out of New York.

The First and Second regular army divisions, completely mobilized, were preparing to move from their concentration areas in southern New Jersey, Maryland and Virginia and lay siege. This despite the fact that Hannibal had publicly announced he would starve New York until the troops were ordered elsewhere.

So Hannibal had radioed General Grunhauf on the transports and ordered an immediate landing. At this moment the transports were steaming toward the American coast under cover of the guns of the coalition fleet.

Hannibal had said to Dorsey, "Don't fret over something that has not happened. Mark my words, Washington will order these corps troops to oppose the landing of the Italo-German troops, thinking to stop them first and take care of me later. Trust Washington to be stupid."

But the fact that there was resistance to his regime demanded attention. So presently he summoned Dorsey. Dorsey was complete in his uniform of bright silver with an olive-green Steel First on his chest and gold stars on his shoulder straps. He was Shock Troop Commander, ranking next to Hannibal.

"Get Brenn out of the detention camp and have him brought here."

"Going to shoot him?" Dorsey asked.

"No. I'm going to try and win him to our side. We need propaganda—on the radio particularly, and someone to watch over the newspapers. We haven't dared to let them be printed. And we must get our campaign of education going at once."

"Of course," growled Dorsey. "But why pick Brenn? He'll never see our side of things, and he's damned dangerous. He and Farnham are the two men who ought to be liquidated at once."

Hannibal stood up, his face suddenly harsh. "You're altogether too damned quick with the shooting squad," he said.

Dorsey shot him a glance of anger. "A purge now is the way to strengthen our hold."

"You've been studying Lenin and Stalin," said Hannibal

dryly. "I'll be the judge of when a purge is necessary. Have Brenn brought to me."

Dorsey shrugged in resignation. "About the girl—are you still going to mix her with your affairs when they're critical?"

Hannibal fixed Dorsey with a cold look. "You have all the characteristics of a swine, Dorsey; arrogant in victory, whining in danger." He paused: "Go bring Brenn here."

Dorsey went out, his mouth quivering with repressed fury. He sent an aide with the order to get Brenn out of the detention pen. Dorsey himself sat down, took out a notebook with a clasp and key on it, unlocked it and made a few entries. They represented his private report to Volpi and Von Eitel.

"There is no questioning Hannibal's planning genius," he wrote, "nor his uncanny sense of timing. He has a persuasive manner and his mad conviction in his own rightness has visibly impressed most of America. But he is making the same mistake so many revolutionists before him have made; he is afraid to use death generously as a solution.

"As I have written to Your Excellencies before, it seems to me that revolution such as we have brought about here is a multiphased affair. Without Hannibal, it would not be possible. But after its success, there will be another phase when our grip on the country will need strengthening. The leader must then be firm and ruthless. I do not think—due to his inherent terror at sight of blood—that he has the strength to be ruthless."

THE DETENTION PEN was the 79th Armory on lower Park Avenue, a brown-stoned gloomy building with thick bars over the small windows and inside a sort of eternal twilight so that in the middle of the day you weren't sure that the sun was shining. It was packed full of humanity; and the smell was nauseating until you became used to it.

Spike Brenn was used to it. Now, leaning against a wall, he carefully took three-quarters of an inch of cigarette from behind his ear, lit the charred end with a match and allowed himself the luxury of three inhales.

But an instant later he remembered the reports that the Steel Fist guards had spread; that the Italian-German troops were landing. He had no doubt that it was true. Rumors have a way of invading even the thickest prison walls, and for two days he had heard of bombing raids by enemy airplanes along the Atlantic coast. Savannah, Charleston, Boston, Philadelphia had been scourged. The loss of life had not been great but the destruction of property and the terror had been enormous. These had been followed by bombardments of places like Nantucket, New

Bedford, Montauk and Myrtle Beach in North Carolina. Here, too, the loss of life was relatively small.

To Spike, old hand at war, this meant but one thing; the enemy was making feints to hide the real landing place. Feints that would keep the partly mobilized First and Second Army Corps shuttling up and down the coast. And now, with confusion everywhere, the Italo-German army had landed on the New Jersey coast.

Enemy troops on American soil. For the first time since 1812. Spike grimaced. What could be done to stop the inevitable? His glance swerved around the vast drill chamber crowded with men either standing or sitting on the floor. What, indeed, could be done, with the leaders of America—in New York at least—crammed helplessly into this stinking black pit?

There was the mayor of New York, five days of black bristle on his cheeks; his clothes baggy and stained, his hair ragged and uncombed. As Spike came up the mayor glanced at him anxiously.

"How do you suppose my wife and three kids are?" he asked. "You don't suppose—"

"They're okay," Spike cut in gently. "They're bound to be."

He passed on quickly because the look in the mayor's eyes made him a little sick inside. He elbowed past brokers and bankers and investment experts; presidents of vast corporations that extended their tentacles to the smallest village in America. He thought, "There must be a couple of billion dollars worth of wealth represented here."

But whose wealth now? And what would they give of that wealth for a two-inch steak nicely broiled, after trying to eat the filth that passed for food in this place?

He heard snatches of talk: "Hannibal is going to confiscate the wealth of the nation—""If you shout for him he'll let you work for him—""What's the matter with the army that they don't kill these swine—"

Spike turned back as his name was shouted. He saw a Steel Fist corporal, dapper and with his face screwed against the smell, forcing a passage with his rifle toward him.

"Okay, Brenn," said the guard. "Come on. I guess they want a little target practice on you."

"You think of the nicest things to say," Brenn growled.

He had seen the startled, fear-struck expressions that swept the faces of those near enough to hear. The guard thumped them aside with his gun, sending them sprawling. A white-haired old man who, somehow, had managed to keep himself clean in that place, picked himself up slowly. He stared at the guard.

"Five weeks ago," he murmured, "he would have kissed my shoe for twenty-five cents."

The guard said, "Why, you—"

He swung the rifle and the old man did not attempt to duck; he did not seem to care. The rifle butt smashed against the side of his skull. He went down as if pole-axed.

"Me, kiss his shoe for twenty-five cents," said the guard. "The rest of you had better watch how you talk or I'll have to get rough." He paused long enough to add, "Take the old buzzard out of the way and one of you wipe up the blood."

"No use taking him anywhere," said a man, raising from a kneeling position. "He's dead."

"DEAD?" THE GUARD looked a little startled. Then he

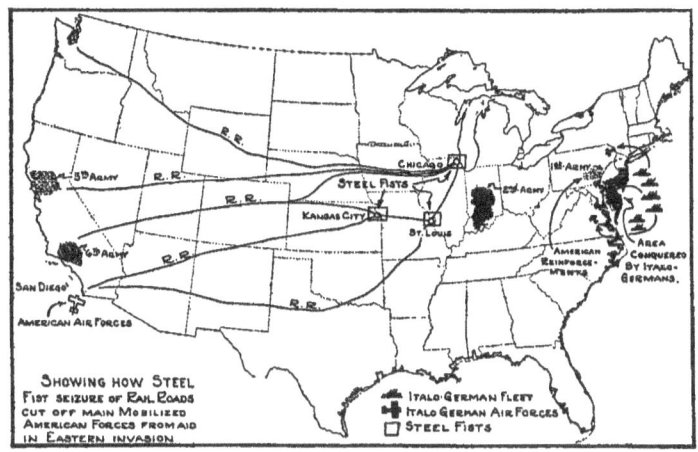

laughed. "Well, what of it?" He turned to Spike. "Come on, you."

More guards surrounded Spike; a car waited into which he was thrust. Only one person spoke during the ride, a guard. He wrinkled his nose and said, "Somebody oughta give this coot a bath. He's ripe enough to rot."

In the anteroom to Hannibal's general staff room Dorsey also wrinkled his nose. "Get him a bath, somebody, before he goes in to the Seneschal."

So Spike had the chance to strip his huge body and gasp in ecstasy under the tingling smash of an ice-cold shower. He was supplied with clean linen, much too small, but when he finally emerged he felt again human. Again he passed through a half-dozen rooms, swarming with Steel Fist officers. And then into the utter quiet of Hannibal's sound-proofed office.

He stood straight, cold-eyed before the desk. Hannibal's blazing blue eyes swept over him.

"Sit down, Brenn," he said.

"Why?"

Hannibal shrugged. "Suit yourself. I've quite a little to say, and then a question to put to which I want your final answer."

"You have it now," said Spike. "It's no."

Hannibal lit a cigarette, passed the case to Spike. Spike fished out the half-inch butt he had saved and lit it. Nothing was said for a moment.

Hannibal said, "You think of me as a traitor, don't you?"

"You're worse than a traitor; you're a mass murderer of your own people."

"What would you say if I told you that I loved my country even more than you do?"

Spike pinched his fingers down on the cigarette butt. "You're mad; you don't love anything but power."

"You're wrong." Hannibal leaned forward. "I love this country. And I think I proved in 1918 that I loved it well enough to fight for it then."

"And yet you bring this madness upon it."

"I fought for the Nation in 1918—and I'm fighting for the nation now. Then I merely thought I was fighting for the country; it was someone else's battle."

"Cut out the guff," snarled Spike. "You deliberately brought on a war with Japan. Not that Japan wasn't ready—you made the excuse. You brought on a war with Italy and Germany. And just when, like a man snarled in rope, we were trying to extricate ourselves, you start an internal revolt that insures defeat abroad, confusion, chaos, at home. Don't talk such bloody rot."

"Superficial observations," said Hannibal, leaning back. "True, I did all you say I have done, war with Japan, Italy, Germany, and an internal revolt. But can't you see that to put in my new regime, to oust the old—the only way I could have done it was the way I did. Geographically and otherwise, America is strong. I most certainly believe the war with Japan would have ended in stalemate with our loss of the Philippines, but without exhausting the country's resources. But for my intervention, Italy's and Germany's combined fleets could not have dominated the Atlantic. And without my revolution—for revolution it is, Brenn—no expeditionary force could have landed and survived."

"Why do you tell me all this?"

"To lead up to my program. I've thrown out the old capitalism, and I have more people thinking my way than you know. I've got a new program—the chief plank of which is to give the country back to the people who create its wealth."

"The best thing for those people that could happen would be for someone to shoot you."

HANNIBAL IGNORED THE deliberate savagery of Spike's tone. "Listen to my program," he said, and he was using now the soft persuasiveness of his radio voice. "I'm going to do away with overlapping governments, from state down through county, that eat up forty percent of the national wealth to keep stupid politicians in soft sinecures. I'm going to nationalize the bank, take away from a few private individuals the control of the nation's credit; I'm going to nationalize the water power, the railroads, increase wages, set up an absolute old-age security that a man can depend upon. I'm going to nationalize big corporations and see to it that production goes up by keeping prices down. Instead of working for himself, the worker is going to work for the nation and take his just share of his earnings for decent living and assured future. I'm going to abolish the national debt—wipe it out."

Spike yawned wearily. "You've just lifted the Fascist, Nazi, Socialist, Communist programs bodily. The things you outline are good, and they will come, but in time, by evolution, not by turning the country over to be looted by foreign soldiers and the riff-raff of our own nation."

"You think my plan is impossible?" Hannibal said, strangely cold.

"I don't think it, I know it. Progress can't be hurried. You can't rush people into Utopia, as the French found out in 1795 and the Russians in 1920. But you didn't bring me here to—"

"If you think my plan will fail, what is your alternative?" cut in Hannibal softly.

"My alternative," Spike leaned back and laughed. "My alternative is that you disband your Steel Fists. Drop your control of our transportation system that is leaving the country open to the invader. Hop a ship and hide some place, or take a gun and—but you wouldn't have nerve enough to kill yourself."

"You think so?"

"I know it." Spike regretfully dropped the cigarette butt, of which less than a quarter of an inch remained. "Your kind squiggle at the last moment."

"You wouldn't believe that I'd kill myself at this moment if it would help the country?"

"No."

Hannibal nodded thoughtfully. "Then it would do no good to ask you to become the minister of propaganda, to broadcast and soothe the country so I can hurry the evacuation of the Italian and German troops."

Spike looked at Hannibal a while silently; then he laughed. "You thought I'd do that?"

"I don't know," replied Hannibal. "I thought you brilliant, a man keen on his country's manifest destiny, I thought you could see my way was best." He paused, and added curiously, "On a choice between the firing squad and the job I offered, your choice would already be made."

Spike partly turned away. "You don't have to play with me. I can take it."

Hannibal had apparently pressed a buzzer. An aide entered and Hannibal said, "Take him away."

Spike turned. He wanted desperately to ask about Kay, but he did not. He walked out of the room. There was a little delay while his two guards were summoned and he got the notion they were going through the gestures of issuing a death decree. He shrugged; silly nonsense going through the formality of legalizing murder. To his amazement Kay Carstairs came through the office, accompanied by two guards; they were headed for Hannibal's office.

Forgetting himself, Spike strode to her. "I was wondering—" he began.

"I'm all right," she interposed swiftly. "But you—"

"Okay," said Spike. She couldn't hear until later what was to happen.

"The government's fled from Washington," she said. "I just heard it. Capitol was bombed, and the Germans and Italians are inland, going toward Philadelphia and the Potomac."

"Can you get away?" Spike lowered his voice.

"Hey, cut that," said the guard. "Hey, who's looking after this big guy? What's the idea of lettin' him wander around loose?"

She was gone, then, and his two guards, everything apparently regular, fell in beside him and led him down to the street where the car was.

"Step on it," said one guard.

SPIKE LEANED BACK carefully in the seat. He became aware, with a start, that they had not put back the handcuffs. He sat for a space while the car sped swiftly through the night, thinking about this. Funny, two hundred and twenty pounds of him, six feet five of him, turned into crow-bait. Leaning against a wall, trying to look into twelve steel tubes without flinching. A hell of a way to die; like standing and letting a motor car hit you.

Something came alive in Spike Brenn then. He didn't think a lot more about what was to happen; he simply knew that if it was to happen this was the way he wanted to go out.

He turned, lifted his hand. "Got a match?" he asked.

The guard started to fish for one. Spike said to the other, "What time is it?" Automatically, without thinking, the man turned up his wrist and started to thrust back his sleeve.

Spike hit him on the skull with a huge ham-like fist that seemed like a piledriver. The man screamed.

The guard who was looking for a match straightened and said, "Hey—" and then Spike hit him in the face.

The chauffeur drew an automatic pistol and fired back at Spike. But he was trying to steer the car at the same time, and he couldn't turn far enough and the bullet thudded

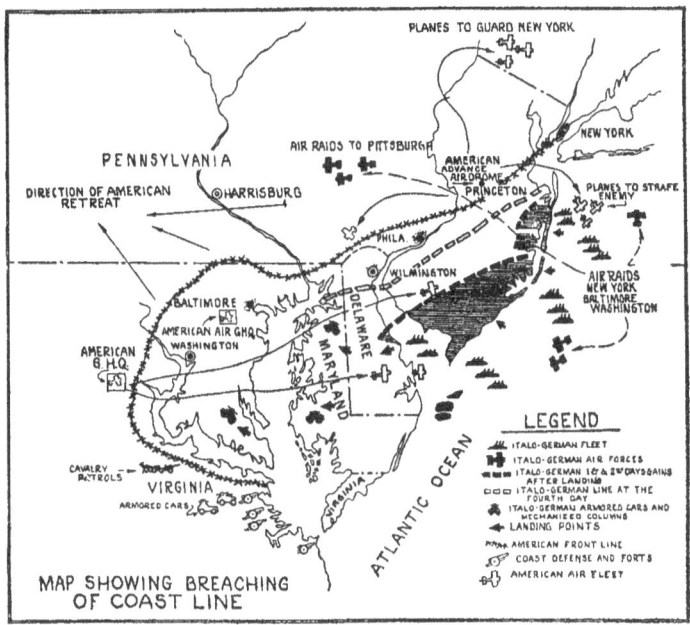

PLANES TO GUARD NEW YORK

NEW YORK

AIR RAIDS TO PITTSBURGH

PENNSYLVANIA

AMERICAN ADVANCE AIRDROME

DIRECTION OF AMERICAN RETREAT   HARRISBURG

PRINCETON   PLANES TO STRAFE ENEMY

PHILA.

WILMINGTON

BALTIMORE

AMERICAN AIR GHQ.

AMERICAN G.H.Q.   WASHINGTON

AIR RAIDS NEW YORK BALTIMORE WASHINGTON

MARYLAND

DELAWARE

VIRGINIA

CAVALRY PATROLS

VIRGINIA

ARMORED CARS

ATLANTIC OCEAN

LEGEND
- ITALO-GERMAN FLEET
- ITALO-GERMAN AIR FORCES
- ITALO-GERMAN 1st & 2nd DAYS GAINS AFTER LANDING
- ITALO-GERMAN LINE AT THE FOURTH DAY
- ITALO-GERMAN ARMORED CARS AND MECHANIZED COLUMNS
- LANDING POINTS
- AMERICAN FRONT LINE
- COAST DEFENSE AND FORTS
- AMERICAN AIR FLEET

MAP SHOWING BREACHING
OF COAST LINE

into the upholstery. Spike seized one of the guard's rifles, and jabbed it, butt first, into the base of the chauffeur's neck. He heard the crack distinctly as the man's spinal cord broke. The car, already slowed down, held a straight course for a second and then veered toward the curb. Spike straightened it, cut the ignition. One of the guards behind him moved, and he kicked back with his right leg and silence followed.

Then the car was stopped at the curb. Two of the men were dying, and one was totally senseless, his face a mass of bruised flesh. Spike looked at all three of them. He looked out at Park Avenue. Once a busy hive of swarming taxis and private cars, it was strangely desolate.

Then Spike flung back his head and laughed silently. As easy as that. And he was going to let them shoot him like a decoy duck.

He fished in the guard's pocket and found cigarettes, took one from the package and lit it. A deep inhale shook him to his heels, and he knew his heart was thudding.

"As easy as that," he repeated. "If we could get a counter organization, we could smash Hannibal and all his swine— as easy as I did that."

And here was a car. An official car that might get him gasoline for part of the trip. Swiftly he tumbled the dead chauffeur into the gutter. He tried on the man's silver overseas' cap, but it was too small. The dead guard's fitted better. He flung out the other two, took the rifles and the bandoleers of cartridges. He got behind the wheel.

"No," he muttered. "This isn't over. It's just begun."

15

TECHNIQUE OF INVASION

COMMENCING SOUTH OF Fort Hancock and stretching for hundreds of miles toward Chesapeake Bay, the coastline of New Jersey is very flat and sandy, and because of this fact has many resorts where the city people flock in the heat of summer. Long Branch, Deal Beach, Asbury Park, Bradley Beach, Atlantic City—the resorts are numberless, the firm sand going shallowly into the sea so that swimmers may wade out some yards before going over their depth. Militarily speaking, such beaches also make ideal landing places, because troops may leap from beetle-boats into the shallow surf and race ashore to take cover under the huge grass-grown dunes.

On a morning in late October while a light mist lay over the land and the sea, squat grim men-of-war, their gray shapes almost invisible in the dull gray of the dawn, ranging themselves in single file, steamed south under bare steerage way. Inside their protecting lengths were other ships, forty of them, each what is known in transatlantic travel as a "monster" liner; that is to say, passenger vessels of sixty thousand tons displacement. Each was loaded to the plimsol line with troops.

The weather was very calm, and presently the sun would burn off the mist to bring a crisp bright October day.

All night launches had been scurrying among the huge transports, towing additional beetle-boats—huge round-bottomed barges especially constructed to carry a hundred soldiers with equipment at a single load. These extras had been brought from the still-unfinished aircraft carrier *Munich* whose special davits were still swinging others outboard and lowering them.

Already, on several of the transports, troops, warned to utter silence, were filing down Jacob's ladders to take their places in the beetle-boats. They were loading by companies. Some of these transports, swinging into the tide and wind, stood ten miles off Seabright, Long Branch, Ocean Grove. Others lay off Seaside Park and Barnegat City. There was a final group off Atlantic City and Brigantine Beach. And last—and the smallest group of all—four transports stood in toward Rehoboth Beach.

The aircraft carriers of the coalition fleet of Germans and Italians had their planes out, but none would fly until visibility was better. Although for the past three days fast speeding cruisers and bombers and attack planes had shelled and bombed the American Coast from Boston to Savannah, Georgia, no shot was fired here as yet. Reconnaissance planes for two days had flown over the littoral, taking photographs—that was all.

But the results of those photographs, now reduced to targets on maps with proper deflection and elevation marked, were in the hands of the gunnery officers of the fleet guns. These guns, their turrets swung, leveled their broadsides at the shore, now invisible in the mist.

On board the battle cruiser *Deutschland*, set aside for his post of command, General von Blutcher, commander-in-chief of the Italo-German army, said to his Italian subordinate, General Della Gravi, "We have covered everything, I think."

The Italian looked over the order of battle.

At five-fifty the guns of the Allied Fleet would commence firing. From sixteen-inch guns that would bombard the coast to a depth of twelve miles to the light destroyer four-inch rifles that would comb the sand dunes, a protective barrage would be put down to smother and silence any enemy fire. Not that von Blutcher expected much; the days of feinting, first along Long Island, then the Massachusetts and Rhode Island shore, then south of here, he had forced the Americans to spread their resources of defense thin. There were a few trench emplacements marked by newly turned earth; he would have some losses. That was to be expected; but nothing out of proportion and, indeed, there would be many less than the British had had at Gallipoli, the last sea landing under fire comparable to this operation.

DELLA GRAVI SAID, "Perhaps your first day's objectives are too advanced. Can we drive to such depth?" Von Blutcher nodded his head vigorously. He had worked out those first day's objectives with great care. He told Della Gravi that beach heads in depth must be consolidated so that later troop landings could be made without loss or delay.

The black Arrow division to the north, certainly could strike inland to Red Bank and Freehold. The covering barrage should make such an operation simple. The Prussian Guard corps should have no trouble in reaching Lakewood and Lakehurst to secure the main roads inland to Camden; two of these roads would be precious for the mechanized forces to overrun the country to the north and west of Philadelphia.

As for the troops between Cape May and Atlantic City, these were shock divisions and they must drive fast and powerfully with motorized troops to seize the Bridgeton-Egg Harbor line the first day. That was vital.

"We pivot there to swing toward Baltimore," Von Blutcher said, "and the depth of the first day's drive enables us to make further landings to the south and seize everything north and east of Chesapeake Bay."

In that way, as Della Gravi could see, Washington was outflanked. And Washington must be seized—that was Hannibal's order.

"After that," said von Blutcher, "we shall have no definite objectives until we encounter stronger resistance. We shall drive toward Pittsburgh. If we seize the New England states which the north end of the landing cuts off, and invade Pittsburgh and the steel and coal regions, nothing can dislodge us before winter puts an end to campaigning. And who knows? Hannibal should be in a position to negotiate with authority for an armistice."

Della Gravi smiled; he had already seen the terms of that armistice.

The two officers smoked and talked, more to pass away the time than anything else. The plans were drawn, the orders issued, the situation out of their hands until such a time as the fighting ashore began and there should come demands for reinforcements and use of aircraft and gunfire to put down such resistance.

Both men were abstemious, but as the second hand reached five-fifty and the thudding concussions of the combined fleet fire suddenly shook them in their seats, Della Gravi poured out two thin, small glasses full of Strega and they drank them silently without clinking the glasses.

The barrage lasted for only fifty minutes, but in that time it was terrific and awesome. Eighty warships with guns ranging from sixteen-inch broadsides to three-inch rapid fire, pounded the shores inland, the waves of shells moving forward and backward like a comb through the hair.

Between the transports and the shore, destroyers raced up and down, their squat funnels emitting torrents of greasy black smoke that spread an impenetrable veil that drifted slowly toward the shore under the influence of the light wind. Launches manned by sailors in steel helmets took in tow the beetle-boats, crowded to the gunwhales with soldiers in full fighting equipment.

At seven o'clock the gigantic roar that had rolled in from the sea ceased for a brief moment and the consequent silence hurt the ear after such turmoil.

The barrage took up again in a steady rhythmic thunder as if a giant were playing the bass of an incredibly big organ. The launches dashed for shore, towing their cargoes of human freight....

AT QUARTER TO six Major Glen O'Hara of Intelligence was whirled in a staff car along the concrete ribbon of road that led from Lakewood to Point Pleasant. He was slouched in the rear seat, weary as only two sleepless days can crush a man's vitality, but he could not even doze.

His mind still turned over the sickening news that Spike

Brenn had brought from New York. It was impossible almost to believe that Spike Brenn, star of the radio, had been arrested, condemned to death, and had escaped only to be forced to take refuge with the First Division to save himself from death. And what news Spike had brought. Combined with what O'Hara already knew, the situation made him writhe.

New York bowing down to this Hannibal! The people already beginning to shout, "Salute, Seneschal!"

And the rest of the country in turmoil, strife and revolt. Yet despite the intolerable activities of the Steel Fists, the bewilderment of the people, Washington somehow expected the army to fight off an invader and turn swiftly to quell this Steel Fist uprising. What the hell did they expect anyway?

He had been at the First Army headquarters that morning and himself had seen the impossible conditions under which the army was trying to mobilize and function. Mobilizing fighting men into an army is not a simple thing to do even under favorable conditions.

The gathering of even twenty-thousand men needs transportation carefully timed to mobilization areas, and the vast number of men must be fed, housed, kept clean; they must have munitions and armaments of all kinds. And in the modern mechanized armies where one man with an automatic rifle can fire three or four hundred rounds of cartridges in an action, the job of munitioning them is terrific. Then there is sanitation, ambulance and hospital and field dressing station service. And a continuing supply of food, equipment, ammunition. It takes the work of six men to keep one man fighting.

All this must be carefully planned in advance, not for merely twenty thousand men, but for two army corps of two hundred thousand men.

Nor did the problem, as O'Hara well knew, cease with the mere gathering, provisioning and arming of men. In modern times armies are specialized instruments wherein each man and each unit has a special task to do, and unless this task is well done, the whole army does not function properly.

Two hundred thousand men cannot go charging blindly around the country; so the information service must be prompt, accurate and revealing; the communications lines must be protected and kept open to supply battle losses; a plan of defense and attack must be worked out and the troops deployed properly to defend or attack on that plan.

Under the best conditions this requires time and care; with revolt within the country, with communications broken, with troop trains not moving, with endless freight cars full of food and munitions rusting on sidings, the problem was well nigh insuperable.

As O'Hara bitterly admitted, the First and Second Army Corps were but fifty percent mobilized; indeed, right now, with the landing liable to come at any moment, the First Division of regulars, ten thousand men with auxiliary troops attached, was the only complete fighting unit able to take the field. It would take days more to round out the corps. And with sabotage in munitions factories, with the railroads in the hands of the Steel Fists—how would supplies come to the battlefront? Artillery shells? Thousands of them? Replacements? Particularly, after the present reserve was gone, how would more supplies of gasoline get from Texas and elsewhere to keep planes in the air, tanks in action, mechanized columns moving? O'Hara had heard General Marley say, "We'll do our duty." Marley would fight with what he had.

But O'Hara knew that already preparations were under way to abandon Baltimore, Philadelphia, Washington and New York, and make the first offensive stand in the Allegheny ridges. Delaying actions would be fought, but a combination of time and terrain and reinforcements would be needed for the American Army to take the offensive and stop the invasion. But could the invasion be stopped by an army working without the nation's support? The rank and file of the people were stunned, apathetic. Hannibal's pounding propaganda via the radio was making converts to the New Era; the draft to fill out the reserve was meeting active opposition.

For instance, five squadrons of huge Boeing bombers were held helpless at Oklahoma City, prevented from flying to reinforce the air arm in the East, because they could not get the high octane gasoline necessary.

Confusion existed in the War Department which was pulled one way one moment (orders to put down the Steel Fists) and then told to resist the invader at all costs. Hannibal's strength was growing hourly as his Steel Fists bloodily put down riots and strikes against their own power but encouraged strikes and sabotage in munition factories. Even Farnham, genius though he was, could not keep war production to the peak necessary.

The sudden stopping of the staff car aroused him from his black thoughts.

"Here's the battalion C.P., sir."

O'Hara opened the door, got one booted leg to the ground. He froze like a pointer, his head cocked. Out of the air over his head came a series of sighs, hisses, whistles and, closer, a shriek.

"Shells!" he yelled and hurled himself flat. The chauffeur hit the ground beside him.

The barrage roared down upon them and in a series of blazing red flashes the earth was torn apart.

16

AN ARMY WITHOUT A COUNTRY

THERE WAS AN officer there and men around the breeches of two machine guns, now silent. O'Hara scrambled up the bank beside the embrasure and fell panting into the pit. He was blackened and dirty, and there was a long gash from a shell fragment on his left arm which he had hastily bound with the tail of his shirt.

The officer lowered his automatic pistol and said, "How's it going elsewhere?"

O'Hara picked up a spare canteen and, unscrewing the cap, took a long drink. He was hot and weary and it was now noon and he hadn't had food or drink since the night before.

"Lousy," he said, exhaling. "There are a lot of enemy stiffs rolling in the surf but they've effected a landing in depth. Between here and Sea Isle City anyway, which is as far as I checked."

The officer cast a wary eye at the sky, now clear. Distantly came the rumble of gunfire.

"We knocked off a lot," he said casually. "We kept silent until after the barrage had rolled by, and then when the beetle-boats showed up, we began to uncork." He licked his lips. "Swellest targets you'll ever see. Boatloads of them.

We did fine until they got a portable radio set ashore and the mist burned off. Then a plane spotted us."

He paused, then added, "I lost the whole outfit except those two guns."

"What are your orders now?" O'Hara asked.

"To cover the road out of Lakewood until I pull out."

"Tanks or anything big ashore?"

"Not last I saw." The officer shifted restlessly. "I'll be damned if I see why our planes can't stop those guys. We could take the rest of it; it's the lead rain on your back that raises hell."

The gunners muttered a low assent. O'Hara sighed; he didn't know why the American pilots had lost control of the air, but he could surmise.

"There must have been a lot of them," he observed, thinking of the aircraft carriers.

"A lot of them—the sky was lousy full. You couldn't see the sun sometimes, there were so many of them."

O'Hara got out his notebook. "How many enemy troops do you figure on your front?"

"Six battalions between Point Pleasant and Spring Lake Beach."

"See any prisoners?"

The officer nodded. "We didn't get any, but Captain Rainsford of the Fifty-second had four, three Germans and a wop. He said there were three divisions on our front, all shock troops."

O'Hara made an estimate of that and whistled softly. Three divisions with auxiliary troops meant around thirty-five thousand men. Not, of course, that all of those divisions were ashore yet. But the fact gave him a basis of calculation on the density of attack, and it didn't look so good.

He asked a few more questions—fighting quality of the enemy, endurance under fire. The officer paid grudging tribute.

"They took it on the chin. Two of the boats grounded badly after our guns peppered the boat crew—came in broadside and we couldn't miss. But they just jumped in the water and came ashore and dug fox-holes in the sand. Good troops."

A half-hour later as shells began to crump along the roadside, O'Hara started back to his car. He noticed that despite the fact that the barrage had steam-rolled here most of the morning, the surface of the road remained untouched. This proved two things; the enemy's maps were excellent, their marksmanship good; and second, that they intended to use these roads for mechanized troops and were saving the metaled surface.

HE FOUND THE chauffeur asleep in the back of the car, and hurried him to Willow Grove, outside Camden where the division C.P. was temporarily established.

He made his report—and learned the truly bad news. The enemy had breached the coast in three places; striking inland from Seabright and Highlands, Pemberton to Lakewood which O'Hara had reported, and from Sea Isle City to New Gretna. Motorized forces were landing and the American high command expected the Jersey peninsula to be overrun and was ordering tank traps and road surfaces to be destroyed to delay them. The First Division was preparing to harass the advance with a thin screen of troops, but to withdraw with the rest of the Second Corps which had established headquarters at Bethlehem, Pennsylvania.

O'Hara found out the reason for the enemy's command of the air. Shortly after six o'clock that morning a hundred planes, thirty percent heavy bombers, had been discovered flying toward New York. The temporary air-service headquarters at Princeton had been alerted. Two hundred planes, half of the American aviation on the front, were ordered aloft to destroy them.

The aerial fight had occurred just over lower New York City where the bombers had reached before the American pursuit pilots got into action. The bombers dropped their tailgates; and lower Manhattan between the Battery and Fourteenth Street had suffered most. Five fires had raged from thermite bombs, and something like three hundred were thought to be dead, another five hundred injured.

For this the enemy Heinkles and Savoia-Marchettis paid dearly. Of the hundred planes sent on the mission, only fourteen escaped; the rest were shot down or crashed. The Americans lost sixty planes.

But as against this enemy loss, the result had been achieved. The American air force, split, and half of it led off on another attack, was unable to punish adequately the enemy's landing. The sacrifice of eighty-six enemy planes could be considered reasonable since it saved troops landing.

Spike Brenn told O'Hara this. He had been talking with the C and C. He told O'Hara something else, too.

"The government has abandoned Washington and moved to Chicago."

O'Hara shrugged. "We couldn't save Washington anyway. Just as well."

"That's what you think," said Brenn grimly. "Only in Washington the troops from Fort Myers kept the Steel Fists out. Who's going to keep them out of Chicago which they run? Who's going to save the government from the Steel Fists?"

O'Hara whistled under his breath. At last he said, "It's insane. Who's going to run the organization?"

Brenn stepped to the portable radio and turned it on. After some preliminary crackling it warmed up, and Dorsey's voice, in the middle of a sentence, boomed into the room.

"… I repeat, Seneschal Hannibal does not make war against the people. The bombs dropped today were in lower New York which the moneyed class owns. The real people of America will not be harmed if they will but listen to the message of the New Era.

"The Italians and Germans do not come as conquerors; they come as friends to deliver us from the bond which we could not shake off alone. They will leave the country as soon as you acknowledge Seneschal Hannibal's leadership and you will be permitted to do that by plebiscite as soon as Hannibal is established in Washington. That, I believe, will be within a few days.

"Then a new Congress will be elected by you, based not on political or regional representation, but upon representation of working groups which is as it should be.

"You can end this invasion immediately; refuse to support the army; refuse to let your children be butchered by the rich who wish to keep you in subjection. Refuse

to work in munitions factories, refuse to transport munitions to the army. The war will end, then, and Italy and
Germany will withdraw. Japan will end the war tomorrow on the basis of us ceding the Philippine Islands. And
why shouldn't we? They mean nothing to us but continual
expense to you as taxpayers while the rich drain what cream
there is. They are too far away to defend, and we have no
business there.

"The war can end. Seneschal Hannibal will end it tomorrow if you speak the word. Think, my friends, and act at
once. There is chaos now, but there can be security, prosperity, peace and a New Era tomorrow."

The voice ceased; the radio went silent. Brenn looked
at O'Hara. "There's your answer; there's the man who will
run the government."

O'Hara laughed harshly. "An army without a country—
that's us."

At nine o'clock that night came the news that President Henderson, fearing for his life, had taken airplane
for Juarez, Mexico, just across the Rio Grande from Texas.
Before he left, however, he had issued orders that the army
fight the invader so long as sabotage and hindrance would
permit. He issued an order to all citizens to fight the Steel
Fists. But it was a helpless sort of gesture.

"Mexico," muttered Brenn. "That means the Steel Fists
have gained so much that he is no longer safe in his own
country."

"And," pointed out O'Hara, "neither are you if you leave
the protection of the army."

Brenn stared moodily. "It seems like the end of the
world."

HOPING AGAINST HOPE that the inadequate American troops could detain the enemy's advance, Spike Breen remained with the First Army headquarters. He bunked with O'Hara and thus he knew the details of the American defeat. It was not really a defeat, as O'Hara pointed out with the aid of a map.

"We've got roughly twenty-five thousand men opposing the thrust of two hundred and fifty thousand," O'Hara said. His voice was thick and hoarse and his eyes red from lack of sleep.

"We're mobilizing as fast as we can, but it isn't fast enough. The enemy know we need time and they don't intend to give us any. So all we can do is fight delaying actions, slow up their advance, and gain time to throw the First Army complete at them, and try and mobilize the Second Army around Columbus, Ohio."

"But you're not delaying them," said Spike.

"Twenty-four hours at a crack," said O'Hara. "We held Monday on the Dughill Ridge-Paris Ridge line, from Sugar Loaf Mountain to the Pennsylvania-Maryland line. They turned our left flank and we've got to pull back to the Monocacy River-York line."

Spike frowned. Looking at the map, it seemed incredible to him that in such few days the enemy had overrun New Jersey, out-flanked New York, captured Philadelphia, Baltimore, and forced the Americans to abandon Washington.

Pittsburgh and the coal and iron and steel resources lay ahead, and if this American army failed to hold in the Alleghenys, then the loss of Pittsburgh would badly cripple the American munitions system.

"We've slowed up their mechanized divisions," O'Hara

said, "we've blown up the roads, dug tank-traps, and destroyed the bridges. They can't advance until they bridge those. But their attack is gaining weight. We've got to stand on the Gettysburg battlefield, or fall back behind Harrisburg."

Spike looked out the window. Here at Chambersburg, the First Army GHQ, he could look across the Cumberland Valley to the hills of Gettysburg. There, once before, Americans with their backs to the wall had resisted Lee's conquering advance to take Washington. Had stayed Pickett's charge, and foiled Lee's genius and turned him back to preserve the union. He was remembering the speech of an American who had said there "We are gathered today on a battlefield of that war... to see if government of the people, by the people and for the people can long endure..."

Now, a second battle of Gettysburg loomed, and for the same reason; could government of the people, by the people, for the people continue to endure?

He came out of his abstraction to find O'Hara's red-rimmed eyes on him. "You weren't listening," O'Hara accused.

"I—no—I'm sorry, O'Hara," Spike apologized; "what was it?" He pulled out the pipe he had managed to get hold of and started to fill it.

O'Hara grunted in disgust. Then: "What I said, you zany, is that unless we can stand before Gettysburg, astride the Chambersburg Pike until reinforcements get through the Cashtown Pass, we're finished."

"Can you hold?"

O'Hara nodded to the door of General Selby's room. "That's up to Selby."

Hours seemed endless to Spike; filled with nothing but disaster. Military pilots reporting stronger gatherings of enemy troops; front-line runners panting in to battalion headquarters with reports that the enemy out-numbered them two to one, three to one; they couldn't hold on without artillery and reserves. And no reserves worthy of the name. Selby, harassed, feeding in few battalions of alleged fresh troops, using his artillery like a wizard, hanging on tenaciously to the Sixty-sixth Infantry and the Seventh Cavalry Brigade, his only mechanized force, to use as a last resort to achieve a turn in the tide or save a rout.

German Heinkles and Italian Fiats and Savoia-Marchetti planes winging to Boston, to Scranton, Wilkes-Barre, Detroit, Cleveland, Columbus, raining death from the sky.

A stream of wounded drifting back to be evacuated along U.S. 11.

But always the piling up of enemy pressure, the increase of suspense; troops arriving but not fast enough. And so on the fourth day, while Spike and O'Hara sat outside, General Myron Selby came to his final decision. He thrust a cigarette into a long holder, and sat alone, deciding the destinies of a continent.

Here was his problem: his right flank, protected by mustard gas in the valley, stood fast. His center, just south of Gettysburg, was being hammered but had not retreated. It was his left flank that had failed. A savage attack by the enemy's light tanks, followed by trained combat groups had broken his first line. A counterattack had not restored the situation; more bluntly, the counter-attack had failed with terrific losses. Enemy attack planes were strafing the holders of the second line.

But the worst, the crux of it was, that the enemy, having broken through and carried Wolf Hill, was now in a position to launch a new attack which would envelop his left, force him to flee or else be rolled back in disaster. That the enemy was furiously at work preparing for this new thrust at the weak left flank, his reconnaissance had told him.

He had one weapon upon which to rely; his Sixty-sixth infantry and Seventh Cavalry, the mechanized outfit which held a couple of world's records in speed of maneuver. He could launch these units from Carlton, drive into the enemy's exposed right flank, drive it in and thus get a chance to reorganize his limping left flank and hold until morning.

But suppose he did throw in the mechanized units; they would be destroyed, useless to him. And if he did throw them away, sacrifice them, and the reinforcements coming through Cashtown Pass did not arrive in time, he was done. He had shot his bolt. And would the reinforcements come? Men were doing herculean work to get the First Army ready; but battalions of troops were necessary to bring through a supply train because roads were blown up by Steel Fists, and railroad tracks torn up.

Yet if he did not stand, then the enemy would roll on and he would have to pull out and lose weeks in reorganization. He might be unable to make a stand this side of far-western Pennsylvania.

Selby knew the necessary strategy, but there was a greater problem—the problem of his duty. An army without a nation, he thought. And so thinking, he made his decision and called an aide to his side. He began to dictate the order that would launch the Sixty-sixth and the Seventh at two o'clock. "They are to go through to Cavalry Field and Towney," he concluded.

The aide sensed the vital character of the move. He clicked his heels, went out, and Selby bowed his head and stared at the blankness of his field desk. How would the dice fall? Had he saved the country, or had he lost a war?

17

IN LINCOLN'S ROOM

THE BOY, STEPHEN Hannibal, was on the floor when Kay entered, playing with his toy soldiers. He had hundreds of them, all green, and besides he had small tanks, toy cannon, and an air pistol. He would throw the tanks at the massed tin soldiers and watch them fall. Those that stayed up after such tank attacks, he shot with his BB pistol. He was very intent on a problem which apparently had to do with the destruction of the right wing of the toy army he was attacking.

Kay watched, noting the sun glints on his fair head, the excitement in his bright blue eyes. A sense of pity suffused her.

Every soft, human impulse of the boy was being stifled; every boyish enthusiasm save it was for war, was crushed. He would grow up a man and find out he had never been a boy. And what kind of a man? We are all, she reflected, victims of our environment; what we are told as children remains with us always, even though subconsciously, and we perform acts as grownups that have their basis in child-hood impressions. Stephen would be a cold, aloof martinet, a man without pity, a man without a soul.

Her heart protested that this should be. Impulsively she dropped to her knees beside him.

"Put them away," she cried, sweeping her arm at the soldiers; "haven't you ever wanted to run in the sun? Wade in a brook? Climb a tree? Haven't you ever wanted to play with other boys?"

He had scowled as she destroyed the orderly formation of his soldiers, but at her words the frown died away. He looked up into her face. A smile lifted his cheeks. Shyly he said, "I've often thought about it. But—but Father wouldn't like it. You see, I am to be a leader of men."

Again Kay acted impulsively. With an inarticulate sound she swept his slim body into her arms, and crushed him to her.

"Poor poor darling," she crooned.

His arms crept around her neck, and he snuggled his golden head against her cheek. For a moment there was silence. Then he said softly, "I love you."

Kay held him so until a sound behind her caused her to turn her head. John Hannibal stood there, arms folded, one of his eternal telegrams clinched in a fist. His blue eyes did not blaze so fiercely.

"Do you love him?" he asked quietly.

"I'm sorry for him."

"I love him; he's all I have." Hannibal spoke gently. "He needs what I just saw—you—a woman's affection, a woman's tenderness. I can make his brain and body. I can't make his soul."

Stephen tugged himself out of Kay's arms and came to rigid attention.

"Go get your things ready, son," Hannibal said, "we're leaving by plane in an hour."

"Very good, sir," said the boy. He about-faced, and ran to the door.

"He could be such a splendid boy," Kay said.

"And will be." Hannibal came closer to her. "You know how I feel. You know I love you—as much as it is my capacity to love any one. I need you, Kay, so does Stephen."

It was at times like this that Kay could no longer feel hatred for John Hannibal. She could only see him as a man, lashed on by the whips of his destiny. Not a master, but mastered by this which boiled and fumed in his brain. She thought for a moment that he was brilliant, he was fine, that influenced by some one—yes, herself—all that had been done might be undone. But she thrust the temptation from her. She remembered Norm, her brother whom this man had killed. Yet looking at him, the desire to tell him what he had done, fled from her. She knew that though Norm was dead and at Hannibal's command, Hannibal himself did not know he had caused that death, so she suddenly brought her thoughts to a jarring halt.

Hannibal had spoken about going away, taking Stephen with him. Where? She must know. "Where are you going?" she asked.

He accepted the temporary rebuff. "To Washington. To the White House."

She was staggered. "Impossible!"

"Why? Henderson has fled to Mexico. I have word here"—he waved the telegram—"that the Italo-German forces administered a crushing defeat to the Americans at Gettysburg. There is no longer any resistance worthy of the name."

ENEMY LAUNCHED MECHANIZED ATTACK YESTERDAY AT TWO O'CLOCK WHICH WAS SUCCESSFUL UNTIL THIS MORNING AT DAWN STOP WE THEN COUNTER-ATTACKED ON ENEMY'S LEFT FLANK AND PENETRATED TO THE DEPTH OF THREE MILES ENEMY RETREATED IN SOME DISORDER WE ARE EXPLOITING BREAK THROUGH WITH ALL MECHANIZED DIVISIONS AND HOPE FOR COMPLETE DESTRUCTION AS ENEMY'S REIN- FORCEMENTS DID NOT COME UP SUGGEST YOU OCCUPY WHITE HOUSE AND ISSUE YOUR MANIFESTO STOP WILL LIKELY BRING ABOUT END OF ALL RESISTANCE

VON BLUTCHER.

Kay quailed inwardly at the significance of the words. The American army defeated.

Hannibal saw her emotion. "Let's have it straight, Kay, you're against me, aren't you?"

"Yes," she blazed, "I think you're a—a monster, a traitor; you've brought ruin and disaster on your country."

"Would you change that if time proved I'm right?"

She shook her head, Hannibal nodded. "I see," he said, almost to himself. "Yet time will prove me right. And even if you are against me, Kay, I've got to have you. I want you with me—wherever I go, whatever I become." He paused, then added hesitantly, "One can be surrounded by people and be so alone."

"You will sit in the president's chair?" she half-whispered.

"I will be leader of this country—dictator if you like." He paused a moment, then went on: "Nothing can stop me. Admiral Evelyn in command of the Pacific Fleet is faced by the Japs and dare not return to America. He will base at the Hawaiian Islands until I gain his allegiance.

"I have captured the Chesapeake defenses. I could bring another million Italians and Germans to this country if needed. Farnham and Henderson and their ilk are in Juarez, fugitives, emigres, a price—my price—on their heads.

"My Steel Fists enlarge by the days. I am master of this nation; in another thirty days there will be none to dare deny that mastery."

He waited but she did not speak, standing there, white, shaken and ill. Gently he took her by the arm. "Come along. I want you there when I enter the White House."

As she followed him, through the opened window struck the deep powerful thrum of military planes. She clutched his arm.

"Then if you are master, you can stop the bombing of Detroit, Chicago, Indianapolis. You can stop all unnecessary slaughter."

"Yes," Hannibal said, "I can. The slaughter, I hope, is over with."

Dorsey, passing as Hannibal led her down the hall, heard this remark. His mouth opened, snapped shut.

JOHN HANNIBAL'S PRIVATE plane circled Washington,

accompanied by a squadron of Fiat and Heinkle pursuit planes. Kay looked out at the shambles of the public buildings, some burning even now though the Americans had deserted the capital three days ago. She looked across at Hannibal. He, too, looked down, his face impassive save for the blazing blue eyes that missed nothing. She thought bitterly, "Many times I've been here. Many times I've looked upon a beautiful city. But I never thought to be a prisoner here and to see a madman seated in the house of Washington."

Prisoner she was, although the guards treated her courteously, and Hannibal was all attention when she spoke. But she perceived that guards always stood between her and Hannibal, and she knew the very clothing she wore was searched each morning to make certain she carried no weapon. She knew Dorsey hated her.

The plane circled lower, crossed over the Mall, now torn with bomb holes, and glided across the branch of the Potomac into Hoover Airport. It landed lightly and taxied to the ramp. Hannibal helped her and the boy out while guards brought the baggage. The escort of Italian and German planes thundered low, then climbed and stunted in formation as if to salute the historic moment. Hannibal did not even look up.

In the ride across the city to the White House Kay saw better what damage had been wrought.

Italo-German bombers had bombed and gutted with fire. And in turn the Americans, holding the south bank, had burned and destroyed all that the bombs had left. Both sides, however, had spared the White House, the Capitol and most of the beautiful government buildings in the downtown section. Staff cards bearing the insignia of the Steel Fists escorted Hannibal's car and there were other cars, armored cars, out of which swarmed aides and leaders of the Steel Fists. So they paraded to the beautiful white building that had housed the presidents of the United States.

Dorsey, his lean, thin-lipped face showing as much exultation as it ever had, suddenly shouted, "Hurrah for the Chief! Long live the Chief!" The Steel Fists drawn up on the lawn in parade stiffened.

As Dorsey yelled he struck his left breast over his heart with his doubled fist. A hoarse terrible roar burst from the Steel Fists. The thud of their fists on their chests was like a monster drum.

Hannibal smiled. "Thanks, Dorsey," he said. "Is everything ready?"

"The White House is ready, sir. Just move in."

Despite what Hannibal had said in New York, Kay half-whispered, "You dare not. It is sacrilege."

"Nonsense," said Hannibal. "I'm the boss of this country. This is where I belong."

Kay could find no more to say.

The Americans had fled without burying their dead; and the bombs and the shelling had taken its toll. Kay followed with the entourage into the great building.

"So many dead, even here," she spoke unconsciously aloud.

"I'm sorry about them," said Hannibal. "But looking at it unsentimentally, Kay, no more are dead here or elsewhere because of this war than die hidden from your sight in hard times."

"Sophistry," said Kay. "You can't deny there are dead because of you."

"Hush," said Hannibal. "My argument with posterity is my own."

Steel Fists guards presented arms. There were more inside. Kay's lips curled. Already Hannibal feared assassination. But it wouldn't be assassination. Retribution.

Already Hannibal's scores of secretaries and officers were busy, and the large pleasant rooms where once the tourists were permitted to roam, were now filled with desks and scurrying figures. Hannibal, however, went upstairs and into the room that had been Lincoln's, where Lincoln had signed the Emancipation Proclamation.

This room was his private office and beyond were the rooms where he would sleep. Kay wondered if he would have the temerity to keep her here. Away from here, she might escape. Rejoin Spike. Ah, but was Spike alive? Her heart missed a beat. She saw Hannibal take out some papers and an attendant brought a microphone.

"A proclamation to your new subjects?" she said coldly.

"Not subjects," Hannibal took her scorn goodhumoredly, "Americans. Americans of the New Era."

18

YOUR SENESCHAL SPEAKS

SPEED WITH JOHN HANNIBAL was paramount; he had reached his objective and therefore must broadcast at once; so Kay had to sit there and listen. Listen as she knew millions of Americans were listening because Hannibal's Steel Fists had seized a million cheap radios and distributed them free among the unemployed. She saw him, who could be so hard and ruthless, adopt his engaging persuasive radio manner. She listened.

"Americans all! This is John Hannibal speaking to you from the White House in Washington. Sitting in the chair that Lincoln occupied, I speak to you. As leader, as Seneschal of America, I am going to tell you the truth.

"The rebellious American military leaders and their misguided soldiers have met with complete defeat. Now, this moment, they retreat in disorder into the Alleghenies, pursued by our allies of Germany and Italy.

"Henderson, the once-elected tool of the Communists and the rich, has fled the country. With your help the rebellious American armed forces are without munitions and supplies. I am in the White House and I now announce to you and the world the New Era government which will lead this country to peace, security, contentment. Presently, when voting machinery is arranged, you will be given the opportunity of approving or disapproving the plans of the New Era. So that you will know what these plans are, I outline now the new decrees to be promulgated.

"First: The national debt of sixty billion dollars is abolished, canceled, repudiated. Holders of such bonds who can prove they are workers, producers, will be paid in New Era dollars the face value of the bonds. The rich will get nothing.

"The railroads from this day forward are owned by the government. Workers and producers who own railroad bonds will be paid in cash. Freight rates and passenger tariffs are hereby reduced fifty percent.

"All corporations with a capitalization of two million dollars or more are hereby declared to be a public interest and shall be subject to strict government control.

"I will at once abolish the expensive and stupid state governments, as well as archaic county governments. State government debts shall be abolished, and only bond holders such as farmers and workers shall be paid the face value.

"All transportation and means of communication are hereby declared the property of the New Era.

"All banks are herewith branches of the New Era Treasury and will issue no credit or paper money without my approval.

"Relief will be administered pending revival of business when jobs will be found for all capable and willing to work.

"The public utilities of light, gas and electric transportation are also commandeered and owned by my government. The electric industry of this nation will be operated to give to every one the boon of electric power, and not operated in the interest of profit alone. Every farmhouse in this nation will have electric light to read by; electric power to do the chores, the washing, the back-breaking drudgery that has been forced upon you because for years the electric industry said, 'There's no money in stringing wires to a single or even a few farmhouses.'"

HANNIBAL PAUSED AND then he continued: "This is not only a totalitarian state, it is a state which is governed in the interests of all. In past years efforts have been made from time to time to stop the rich from getting richer and the poor from getting poorer. These measures have all failed because wealth is power, and power in the hands of an economic autarchy spells defeat for a government.

"There is only one thing that the dollar nobility understand—and that is force. I propose to exercise that force. I shall be not only your leader, but I shall be their leader. The law is that each shall work for his bread, and the rich—who will now no longer be rich—will work or they will die. There is no middle course.

"For you, the people who have created this wealth, what does the New Era bring you? Not wealth, because wealth is not an ultimate end. The New Era brings you something far greater. Economic security. Fewer working hours—the thirty-hour week will, with staggering national and state debts abolished—furnish all the wealth this country needs to consume. With fewer working hours, there will be more playing hours. And places and methods of playing will be arranged that the health of this country shall grow greater.

"Every man, every woman, will know that at the age of sixty he or she will have to work no more. A government old age pension sufficient to keep him or her in the standard of living they have known all their lives, will be awarded. No man shall want from his birth to his death if he work and create wealth in his vigor to take care of him when he is old.

"Instead of working for rich exploiters, he shall work for the state. Instead of the state existing for you, you shall exist for the state. There will be freedom to work and play; but not the license of exploitation and misery.

"That is my program. It has already started. That you will approve it I have no doubt. So I, John Hannibal, Seneschal of the New Era government, do hereby proclaim myself leader of the American people. And those who oppose the New Era are branded enemies of the state, traitors who deserve the sentence of death."

With a start Kay realized that the soft, persuasive voice had ceased. And as it stopped the convincing quality was gone. She saw the new policies as bait to bring fish to hook. She stared at Hannibal, revolted.

"You don't believe that stupid nonsense," she cried. "You're tricking them into giving you power. You're taking their rights and giving them nonsense."

"I'll see that they are fed, housed and amused," Hannibal said brutally. "What else do they require?"

Kay leaped to her feet. "You can't do it—it's slavery. Every man to live only for the state—to be the state's peon—they won't stand for it."

"But they will," said Hannibal.

"God help them," whispered Kay, shrinking to the door. Hannibal didn't try to stop her. He was smiling in a twisted fashion.

Kay at length said, "If I'm not a prisoner, I'd like to take a walk."

"You're not a prisoner," said Hannibal. "Take a walk by all means. And, remember, my dear, I've won. There is no turning back. So think of what you could do, what you could be as wife of the Seneschal."

He would have gone on—she saw it in his eyes—but now she could endure no more. She turned and fled to the freshness of the November dusk. And suddenly she knew she could not go back. She had stood all she could passively. Hannibal must be fought. There must be thousands, millions of Americans who would resist if organized, directed. Spike! How she wanted him now.

But he must be dead. She had heard no word. Hannibal had refused information. But there was David Farnham. In Juarez, calling on people to resent this madness. She would go to him. She turned blindly toward Pennsylvania Avenue. She did not know how she would flee, but flee she must. If she went back to Hannibal she would do one of two things—marry him to influence his decisions, or kill him to stop the madness.

19

THE STREETS ARE CRIMSON

ALREADY THE INTOLERABLE hush of frightened men lay over Washington; the alert, tense waiting—for what, no one knew. In the little house on P Street in Georgetown where Spike Brenn sat opposite Hawker, you could feel the waiting. Even their voices were lowered. Spike was nervous.

Yet even this vanished when he glanced at Hawker's white, grief-stricken face. Hawker had told him—centuries ago it seemed, although it was only moments—that his mother had been thrust off a curb by Steel Fists and her skull fractured. She had died, ignored and unattended, and Hawker had but recently come from the morgue where arrangements were being made to cremate her body along with the bodies of the dead left behind in the hasty exodus.

Looking at Hawker now, Spike was trying to recall the eager-eyed youth who had come to him shyly in New York and proffered him the honorary presidency of the "Hams of America," the amateur radio short wave broadcasting association.

"They barely let me go in to see her," Hawker was saying. "They said there was only room for the living now. They hustled me around as if I were a bum."

Spike said, "I know, kid, but we've got to think about the country now. We've got to think about how to stop this before it's too late."

"I'd stop it," said Hawker, "by getting a gun and shooting the swine—"

"And get yourself shot and do no good." Spike eyed the slim, dark-eyed boy, and sighed. "Lord, I wish I had your build. I'm so big I can't go anywhere without being recognized. So I'm passing the buck to you."

Hawker nodded, his thoughts falling back to Spike's original request. "You get the information to me," he said, "and I'll get it out somehow. We'll have to distribute it by messenger and those who have got electricity can re-broadcast."

"Yes," Spike agreed, "and those who re-broadcast will be in danger. Hannibal's men will have listeners on the wave lengths and will trace down the broadcasters by radio compass."

"Of course, one of us will make the broadcast and move," said Hawker. "None of us are working now, in this district, anyway. The fellows will be glad to do it." He suddenly stood up, swearing furiously.

"Who the hell does this Hannibal think he is?" he cried. "What right does he have to say I've got to work all my life at what *he* says I shall do?"

"That's what we've got to preach, boy," Spike said. "Hannibal will take our lives to do with as he pleases. They're not our lives to live any more if we let him get away with it."

Hawker paced up and down. "He's taken opportunity out of life. Suppose I do wind up, starved, finished, hopeless. At lease I've had my chance and if I didn't have enough on the ball to climb higher, it's no one's fault but my own."

Spike listened as the tirade went on, closing his eyes, visualizing hundreds and thousands of such ambitious youths. They would be the backbone of resistance to Hannibal. Other youths, fooled by Hannibal, would be the opposition. But the fight could be won.

He rose and his movement stopped Hawker. Spike held out his hand. "It seems like running away, me going to Juarez," he said. "But I guess my life's valuable enough to keep it going for a while until we can get organized. But I'll be back through here—and when I do it'll be for action."

Hawker said simply, "I'm your man."

At the door Spike said, "If you hear of Kay Carstairs, let me know. If she's in trouble"—he hesitated—"do what you can without betraying yourself. And don't take too many chances. You're valuable now."

HE WENT OUT to the street and caught a Wisconsin Avenue car and later transferred to a trolley that took him past the National Press Club Building. Blank and dark now. Spike smiled grimly, and he thought of his own offices up there, maybe never again to be occupied by himself.

Crowds milled around in that aimless manner of people with no place to go, no responsibility to attend to. Occasionally there were cries of, "Long Live the Seneschal! Hail, Seneschal!"

Everywhere were Steel Fists. They had swarmed into the city, and there were so many that the housing problem was acute, and some of them marched endlessly for want of a place to sleep. Spike got off, slouching his shoulders, half-crouching to keep his height from being so noticeable.

A man suddenly rushed out from a restaurant. He was waving a handful of money and he was cursing in a loud voice.

"What the hell is this?" he roared. "I offer him money and I can't get anything to eat."

People stopped to stare at him curiously. He went on, gesticulating to his vest. "I ain't eaten in two days and what does that sap in there say? He can't take my money because he don't know whether it's any good. He had the nerve to say that the farmers won't sell produce for this money. Good old Uncle Sam's money."

A mumble, inarticulate, unconvincing, went up from the hearers.

"Where's this New Era?" shouted the man, boiling mad. "I want food. I got kids home that want food. If Hannibal can't feed us, then what is this New Era—another gyp?"

Then suddenly the crowd broke, and through it came a pudgy Steel Fist corporal followed by six men. He had a round face with a small pursed mouth, and he walked mincingly. He stopped in front of the man who had come out of the restaurant.

"Cursing the Seneschal, eh?" he said shrilly. Awkwardly he swung his gun and struck the man in the face. "A traitor." Then, his voice rising to a scream: "All right, give it to him, men."

Standing there, his arms taut against his sides, Spike saw the six Steel Fists beat the man to the sidewalk and kick him until he lay silent, his blood spreading on the pavement. Once Spike glanced at the corporal: he was staring at the crumpled body, his face flushed, his lips parted. Spike turned away in disgust.

"Take him away," the corporal said at last, breathlessly. Red-faced, he looked around at the crowd on the sidewalk. "Anybody else think he's getting a raw deal? Anybody else want to talk against the Seneschal?"

There was silence.

Panting a little, the corporal cried: "You'd better be quiet." He made a fluttering gesture. "Now all with me; cry, Hail Seneschal!"

The crowd howled dutifully and the corporal with a nod turned away.

He followed his men who were dragging the senseless body of the beaten man to a patrol car. The crowd stood apathetically and watched. Spike studied them. They were like strikers he had seen who stood sullen in face of police force, not daring to resist.

"If the Steel Fists were removed, if Hannibal were removed—killed—the movement would fall apart," he told himself. He dismissed the peril of the invading force of

Italians and Germans. Without the Steel Fists they would have to withdraw. No, Hannibal and his key men were the crux of the situation.

He smiled grimly to himself as he walked south. He who had cried out in scorn at the assassins abroad who had ended tyranny with a knife, a bomb or a gun. And here he was, Spike Brenn, thinking of the same means. Not only thinking of them but wondering how Hannibal could be reached through the swarm of guards that surrounded him.

He passed an alley. A corner drugstore threw the light on his face. He tried to shrink a little under his hat.

And then the words, "Spike! Spike Brenn!"

He whirled and saw the shadow of her in the alley's darkness. He ran to her and silently took her in his arms and held her with a fierce strength that must have hurt her. But she did not cry out; silently she clung to him.

"Kay," he muttered. "Kay, how did you get here?"

She told him of the days with Hannibal, of the final supreme mockery of the broadcast from the Lincoln Study.

"I had to leave," she concluded almost breathlessly. "I've got to do something, Spike. Do something to stop all of this."

"Liberators," he murmured.

"What did you say? Liberators? What do you mean?"

"We're going to Farnham and Henderson and all the rest," Spike said. "We're going to be emigres—fugitives from our own land. We're going down there and work to overthrow a despot and his tin soldiers."

"We can try," she nodded, and took his hand. "We can keep fighting."

"And we'll win," said Spike in a queer tone. "Deep in

people, underlying hunger, thirst and cold, underlying greed, ambition and desire for luxuries is a spiritual hunger for freedom that will not endure regimentation. Hannibal's only hope lies in a new generation of children raised in his mad philosophy. We who believe in democracy will crush him before that time comes."

She turned to look at him, her eyes shining. "Spike, I—I never heard your voice like that."

"We who have enjoyed spiritual freedom will not be starved," he said gently. "Other men before Hannibal have tried to kill that desire for freedom—and they have failed."

He led her down the street to where the car was parked that would start them on the long journey to a foreign land.

20

FIRE AGAINST FIRE

THE SNOW FELL in big soggy flakes that melted almost
as soon as they struck the ground. But against the glaring
outside lights (Dorsey had had floodlights trained on the
White House to prevent a surprise rush) the flakes looked
lovely, and Hannibal swung his chair to stare broodingly
at them. It was midnight of this February day, yet he had
not finished his work, and was dreadfully tired. His headache was an agony like heavy blows on his skull. He would,
however, quit for the night now, and as was his custom he
reviewed the day.

His government, the New Era government, had been
recognized by Italy, Germany, Japan and all the South
American nations. That is, by Venezuela and Bolivia—the
rest had been annexed by Italy and Germany for exploitation.

He was dickering with Japan for a peace based on the
surrender of the Philippines, Midway, Wake and Guam
Islands. He would accept that.

He had written a note to General von Blutcher suggesting that since food was short, it might perhaps be better
for the expeditionary force to withdraw. No use having
the Italo-German army spend a winter here when he

had already opened peace negotiations with Volpi and Von Eitel on the basis of the abolition of the Monroe Doctrine and American recognition of their South American spheres of influence.

This seemed a lot accomplished but there remained yet so much to be done.

The question of money. Incredible that despite the severe punishments and even death inflicted by Dorsey's storm troops, the damned farmers refused to accept dollar bills that were the same in every particular as the old money except that they bore pictures of industry and agriculture instead of the heads of dead presidents, and bore the imprint of the New Era government.

He made a note to consult Hervey, his Secretary of Finance, as to how confidence could be restored in the money. This job of seizing grain and food by force and distributing it to the endless bread lines would have to stop.

He would, too, have to see Richards, Secretary of Industry. Manufacturing must be revived by spring. Yes, get going even if he had to offer the former executives better inducement than prison and lashes and castor oil. Funny, he told himself, that he had not figured on an utter paralysis of industry. He had not thought that executives were so important. But they were; what good did it do to have workers on an assembly line when there were no raw materials, no coordinated effort to have all the parts in plentiful supply and accurately made?

There were mumblings, too, all over the country. People used to eating well and bountifully were saying they starved because they only had bread and coffee and meat once a week. Hell, that would keep life together, and they had to

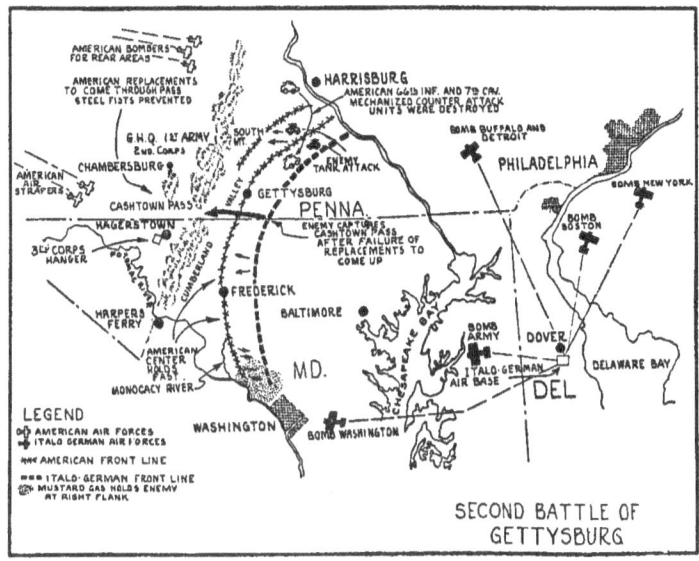

AMERICAN BOMBERS
FOR REAR AREAS

AMERICAN REPLACEMENTS
TO COME THROUGH PASS
STEEL FISTS PREVENTED

• HARRISBURG
AMERICAN 66th INF. AND 7th CAV.
MECHANIZED COUNTER ATTACK
UNITS WERE DESTROYED

G.H.Q. 1st ARMY   SOUTH MT.
2nd CORPS

BOMB BUFFALO AND
DETROIT

AMERICAN
AIR
STRAFERS

CHAMBERSBURG

ENEMY
TANK ATTACK

PHILADELPHIA

CASHTOWN PASS   GETTYSBURG

PENNA.

BOMB NEW YORK

HAGERSTOWN

ENEMY CAPTURES
CASHTOWN PASS
AFTER FAILURE OF
REPLACEMENTS TO
COME UP

BOMB
BOSTON

3rd CORPS
HANGER

FREDERICK

HARPERS
FERRY

BALTIMORE

BOMB
ARMY   DOVER

AMERICAN
CENTER
PASS
FAST

MD.

ITALO-GERMAN
AIR BASE

DELAWARE BAY

MONOCACY RIVER

DEL.

LEGEND

AMERICAN AIR FORCES
ITALO GERMAN AIR FORCES

WASHINGTON

BOMB WASHINGTON

AMERICAN FRONT LINE
ITALO-GERMAN FRONT LINE
MUSTARD GAS HOLDS ENEMY
AT RIGHT FLANK

SECOND BATTLE OF
GETTYSBURG

expect some discomforts when you shift from one form of government to another.

He saw on the desk a memorandum from Dorsey, "Must confer about action to be taken against Liberators."

Liberators! He stared at the snow, falling thickly, silently, bringing hush to the night and to the city. Scarcely more than two months in office and already conspirators against him had banded themselves together as the Liberators. A gust of fury swept him. He could attend to *them* tonight. He pressed a buzzer.

INTO THE ROOM came Dorsey, a little fatter, a little more shark-jawed, and exuding the sense of power that came to him as Secretary of War, Marshal of the Steel Fists, Chief of Transportation and Communications. A big man, Dorsey, but big enough for his job.

"Bad night, Seneschal," he said.

"Is it?" Hannibal swung in his chair and lit a cigar. "All

right, Dorsey, what authority do you want to wipe out these Liberators?"

"Liquidate them, you mean," Dorsey's mouth lifted maliciously. "Very simple, Chief. A decree authorizing the Steel Fists to seize all the leaders in every city of five thousand or more inhabitants. One out of every ten to be shot, and a warning that one out of every nine will be shot next, and so until they are all dead—unless the Liberators immediately stop their propaganda."

Before Hannibal could comment he went on, "We'll offer prison sentences to some of the ten if their friends or relatives will step forward with information about the Liberators."

Hannibal's anger faded. Killing again. He sat silent for a space. Then: "There are seventy thousand cities and hamlets. Would you kill that many? Seventy thousand?"

"Or ten times or a hundred times seventy thousand," said Dorsey savagely. "We've got to wipe out the old to make way for the new. In all revolutions the way to get rid of an old idea is to kill the man who holds it."

"But is it politic?" asked Hannibal. "We've got discontent because of concentration camps and forced labor. Aren't you going to make it worse? The idea is to conciliate—build friends and strength."

Dorsey, already arrogant in his power, exploded angrily. "The trouble with you, Seneschal," he snapped, "is that you're a damned idealist. Be real, look at things straight. You're trying to change men's thinking habits—habits established for hundreds of years. You're bound to have opposition from the stubborn."

He paused. "Wipe out the old. Our strength lies in the youth, anyway."

Hannibal shook his head. "Not by wholesale slaughter."

"Your hatred of bloodshed again," Dorsey's sneer was ill-concealed. "You can't have an omelette without breaking eggs. And you'll let a counter-revolt form to endanger us all because you hate to use the rifles. It's wrong, I tell you. You've got to be ruthless."

He leaned forward and took out some sheets of paper. "Now, I've got a membership list of these 'Hams of America.' Also of the Amateur Aviators—and those two organizations are behind the Liberators. Besides seizing the leading ten inhabitants of every town, I say we should seize every kin of these members who has not yet been arrested and executed."

"To what end?" Hannibal asked.

"Hold them as hostages. Announce that the next assassination of a Steel Fist leader by the Liberators will be followed by execution of the kin."

Hannibal considered this. You had to strike at fire with fire; and certainly these subtle assassinations in his eight key areas, destruction of valuable Steel Fist leaders, would have to stop.

"I'll sign this decree," he said, "but the arrest of the leading ten men in each hamlet—I won't do that. Too many innocent people will be killed, and too many enemies made."

"You're weakening," snapped Dorsey.

"Is that all you think of—butchery?" cried Hannibal. "Do you realize that scarcely a factory wheel turns in this country? That seventy percent of the people are standing in breadlines? We've got to get industry turning, and you can't do it without support from the people."

"The more who are liquidated, the fewer mouths there are to feed," said Dorsey. "And you've got to consolidate your hold—train them through fear that you are the chief. That this is the way things are and they have to take it."

Hannibal stood up. "The hostage decree I'll sign. The other, no."

Dorsey shrugged ill-humoredly. "Very well. If you must be kitten-hearted about it, I'll do the best I can. But I wish you'd raise the ante on Brenn and Farnham's head to a hundred thousand dollars gold reward, dead or alive."

Hannibal turned swiftly from the window. "You've got an idea about them?"

"I'm going to get rid of them," said Dorsey. "They're the backbone of the Liberators. Farnham has also your genius for organization, and that Brenn is not only a propaganda agent, but he slips in and out of this country leading some of these raids on our key centers."

Dorsey shook his head. "How he does it is beyond me. He's so big and so unusual-looking that you'd think he'd be spotted instantly."

Hannibal said soberly, "He has many friends who hide him."

"They won't hide him from me long."

Hannibal nodded. "Very well. A hundred thousand dollars gold, dead or alive. Have it put on the radio."

Dorsey picked up his papers and went to the door. Here Hannibal stopped him.

"And by the way, send word to von Blutcher that I'd like to see him."

"Why?" Dorsey turned alertly.

"With food as scarce as it is and the problem of distribution terrific, I see no reason to feed an occupying army, especially as peace is about to be concluded."

"I'll send for him," Dorsey agreed and withdrew.

HE LEFT HIS papers in his own office and glanced at his strap watch. One o'clock. Von Blutcher was a great one for girls and parties. He would still be up. Dorsey put on his quilted silver coat and his silver overseas cap. At the White House door was a limousine with a chauffeur sleeping in the front seat. Dorsey woke him.

"General von Blutcher's," he said.

He leaned back as the car started and closed his eyes. The plan which had been in the back of his head for weeks leaped to the front, and he examined it with care. He nodded and thought, "Now is as good a time as any."

Von Blutcher had a large marble house on Dupont Circle. Dorsey had been right, the general was up; the house blazed with lights and the sounds of music well-played drifted out on the silent snowy night. The general himself, a glass of champagne in one hand, was talking with a tall, voluptuous blonde.

Dorsey made his acknowledgments, went around the circle of officers and even indulged in a rare glass of champagne. But finally he got von Blutcher's ear and asked for a few moments alone. Von Blutcher sensed something important in the air, and invited him into his private study.

"What is it?" Von Blutcher asked, gesturing to a chair.

"Hannibal wants to see you about having the expeditionary force sent home," Dorsey told him.

Von Blutcher frowned into his champagne. He was

having a splendid time here; and was virtual master within his own sphere. At home—well, there was Von Eitel. Von Eitel who didn't like to share the glory with others. He shrugged.

"Is it safe? After all, winter has put an end to campaigning. But in the spring is there not fear of a revived American army making another attempt?"

Dorsey smiled inwardly. Most of the army, faced with a *fait accompli,* had joined the Steel Fists, now the official standing arm of the New Era. Those officers, many of them, who could not foreswear their oath of allegiance to the republic, had fled either to Mexico or Canada. Under present conditions there was no hope of a new military effort by the old regime. Dorsey knew that von Blutcher knew this.

Yet Dorsey replied, "It is a possibility. But the peril, in my opinion, is greater than that."

"What do you mean?" von Blutcher put down his wine glass and began to peer alertly at Dorsey.

"Counter-revolt!"

"Counter-revolt! Nonsense! You hold the whip-hand. Where—"

"General," cut in Dorsey, giving the German a bold stare, "you have, naturally, heard the statement that there is a man for every event."

"Ah!" murmured von Blutcher, "I have, indeed."

"Hannibal's organizing and military genius made this revolution possible. I am the first to admit it. But after the initial overthrow comes consolidation, entrenchment. In my opinion it takes an entirely different sort of man to accomplish those objectives."

"You're very interesting. Go on."

"My meaning is this Hannibal hates blood. He was badly wounded in the World War, you know. He hates to shed blood. He is trying to change people's thoughts and manner of living without liquidating the unchangeables."

Dorsey paused. Then: "You have heard of the Liberators?"

"Something," nodded von Blutcher. His eyes were shining. He sat immobile, listening.

"There is a counter-revolt growing. So far it has made no great headway. Forays and propaganda. A few murders of our key leaders in the eight areas into which we have divided the country. But unless it is squashed, and terribly, finally, ruthlessly liquidated, it may grow. I have advised that course. Hannibal refuses."

"And your alternative?"

"Let us talk realistically, General. Germany and Italy have aided Hannibal for one reason and one reason only. That is to have a free hand for the development of South America. South America has more resources, more fine white man's climate than any continent now possible for you and the Italians to exploit."

"I know that. Don't go over ground already seen. Get on with it, man."

"Patience, General. Here is my point. If the counter-revolt succeeds, and the United States returns to the old regime, then its first move will be to re-establish the Monroe Doctrine."

Dorsey smiled. "With a powerful United States—and leaders opposed to Italy and Germany in South America—you would have to abandon South American conquest. You could not support expeditionary forces in South America with an American fleet to cut your transport line."

"Oh," murmured von Blutcher. "Quite so."

"Precisely. Now, if Hannibal goes on as he is going, trying to make friends with the old regime, he will fail as Bela Kun failed in Hungary. As Lenin told Bela Kun he would fail unless he liquidated the old regime, permanently. Hannibal is no longer the man for the task ahead. He is an idealist, and a realist is needed."

"Quite true, as you put it," assented von Blutcher. "And, I take it, you are suggesting yourself for the task."

"I am not afraid to purge this country until the possibility of the old regime coming back is overcome," growled Dorsey. "I am organizing the New Era Youth Movement. I am placing all my faith in the new generation that will have brief memories of the old. And I am placing my faith in the permanent liquidation of the old regime."

"I see," said von Blutcher, "you want a palace revolution, in other words. You want to turn out Hannibal—or liquidate him—and put yourself in. Have you got the following?"

"The Steel Fists are faithful to me," said Dorsey, though he could not be positive of this. "The Shock Troops are my creation. The Youth Movement is mine. Hannibal in his preoccupation with organizing industry and banking, has left all that to me. He is out of touch. In case of a 'er—change, the trained men would rally to me. Particularly if the change was cleverly made."

"How do you mean, cleverly made?"

"Suppose," said Dorsey, leaning forward, "Hannibal were to die and his death be charged to the Liberators?"

"Ah," said von Blutcher, "I begin to see. The Steel Fists would be in the mood for a purge to avenge their martyred leader. The mantle of leader would fall naturally to you, and there would be no question of loyalty to you."

"There, General, you have it in a nutshell."

21

THE VICEROYS

GENERAL VON BLUTCHER picked up his champagne glass and drank the few drops in the bottom. The pleasant glow he had had from the wine was gone now; he was a cold, cleverly calculating man. He knew Dorsey, knew him for an ex-American officer cashiered for speculating funds entrusted to him. He knew how far Dorsey could be trusted—which was only as far as Dorsey's self-interest led him to cooperate.

"I presume," said von Blutcher, "that if you were raised to Seneschal, there would be no question about interfering with Germany's and Italy's manifest destiny in South America."

"Of course not," replied Dorsey instantly. "Look at the problem realistically. The New Era, even with proper purges and good organization, will need years to settle and consolidate its power. I have made up my mind to make war against Mexico. Not a difficult campaign perhaps, but after Mexico is conquered it will take more time to digest Mexico, organize it so that its resources properly come to us."

He shrugged. "After Mexico is conquered, I'm going to take the North American continent to the Panama Canal.

That also requires organization and time. In short, General, the New Era program will require ten years minimum to settle itself. In that time you should have done equal work in South America."

This was true; this was sound and von Blutcher knew it. He toyed absently with the champagne glass. "If this *coup d'etat* is to come about, just when did you have an idea of accomplishing your end?"

"As soon as possible."

"I must consult my government," shrugged von Blutcher. "So must Gravi."

"Granted, but that does not take forever, General. Listen! Hannibal has set March 4th as the date of the plebiscite on his New Era program. He will be doing a great deal of campaigning until then. The result is foregone, but he thinks of England and France and world opinion.

"He will be moving around, then; speeches in New York and Chicago and San Francisco. He intends to make a lot of radio addresses. Some time during that period when he is away he can be removed. I shall be at the White House on my other duties. I can make the radio announcement, declare my assumption of power as Seneschal."

Dorsey shrugged. "You will have to preserve order, to help me get rid of those too faithful to Hannibal—or too ambitious for themselves. So we must act within the next fortnight."

"Yes," said von Blutcher and again, "Yes, of course. The timing is fortunate."

He rose from his chair. "I shall communicate with my government at once. Within a few days you shall have the answer. I may say, for my part, that I shall recommend the step."

Dorsey's face gleamed with the sudden savage joy within him.

"Thank you, General. I shall lay my plans accordingly."

Von Blutcher showed him to the door, but did not rejoin the gay party. Instead he sent an orderly for Della Gravi, his co-commander of the Italo-German Expeditionary Force.

Della Gravi came reluctantly, a little high and his face covered with lipstick. But he wiped off the smirk and the red rouge when von Blutcher told him what was in the air. His little dark eyes gleamed.

"It is what I was telling you the other day," he cried excitedly. "Here is not only South America but North America to be had for the taking. Did I not tell you that seven hundred and fifty thousand more men and equipment would let us keep the United States to ourselves?"

"You did," nodded von Blutcher dryly. "And I agreed. But I said none of us should bite off more than we could digest. I had Hannibal in mind, of course, because Hannibal is a patriot, and he would resist us. But Dorsey's suggestion puts a different complexion on matters."

"It does, indeed," assented Gravi. "And we should by all means let him have his palace revolution. We can handle him. And we can't handle Hannibal. Let Dorsey keep the apparent power and he is swine enough to let us do as we will."

Von Blutcher said thoughtfully, "We have sixty days in which to move troops. We could seize the munitions plants and use them to our own ends. We can live off the country, thus cutting our communications problem to the minimum. We could conquer the United States and hold it—with Dorsey's aid."

He sent for a bottle of champagne. "As for me, Gravi, I am cabling Von Eitel tonight." He stared at the wine that the orderly poured. He held it up and smiled complacently. "Marshal von Blutcher," he murmured, "that would be a nice title, Gravi. Marshal von Blutcher, viceroy of North America."

"Of part of North America," corrected Gravi, sipping at his wine. "I, too, should like to be Marshal and, say, viceroy of Eastern America."

Von Blutcher foresaw trouble here, but there was no use rousing it until the proper time came. When it did he had an idea a brief brush with the Italians would show them they were no match as fighters for the Germans.

"As you like," he murmured, and clinked glasses.

DORSEY WAS IN his own quarters, the light burning, calculating, figuring along a list of names that included all to whom Hannibal had delegated part of his enormous power.

Not a hundred yards away John Hannibal sat in his son Stephen's room. A single night light burned and cast a soft gentle glow upon the quietly sleeping boy. Hannibal could not sleep. His head was still throbbing. Looking at Stephen, he reproached himself for neglecting the boy. Once they had been together constantly; now he rarely had a moment from endless conferences and problems. This reproach set him thinking of Kay. Why couldn't she see things his way?

Why couldn't she perceive that all was for the best; that instead of the country living in a welter of idealistic patter lipped by stupid politicians, the country should live realistically and revive under a single dominant control? A corporative control; like a business, one head, one director.

He looked at the flushed face of the sleeping boy. A sense of loneliness swept him; some day the boy would be Seneschal, trained for the task as other youths would be trained to his aides. But meanwhile, Hannibal knew he was alone. He could talk to Dorsey but he couldn't trust him, any more than he could trust the others who paid lip service to the New Era but served themselves and their greed for power.

And in this endless task of rebuilding from the bottom, Hannibal wanted someone to trust, someone to whom he could unburden his thoughts and problems. Kay! More and more he wanted her. He had been a fool to let her go. And somehow, in some way, he must have her back.

He bent and brushed the boy's yellow hair with his lips and stole back to his own room to spend another sleepless night.

AT THE JUAREZ airport Big Spike Brenn walked out to the low-wing transport plane. Ahead of him streamed seventeen men, picked men, every one of them. They carried automatic rifles, pistols, while on the plane other men loaded heavy belts of cartridges for the light Browning, and musette bags full of clips for the automatic rifles.

David Farnham, now the heart and soul of the Liberator resistance, strode beside Spike. "I'd as soon you didn't go tonight, Spike," he said, plainly put out.

"I have to go," responded Spike. "The man is worse than a murderer, he's such a swinish brute that to let him go on would lose us all we've gained."

"Oh, I agree with you there. But can't Duval or Harmon attend to him? After all, you're needed here for propaganda, not running off on raids."

Spike laughed boomingly, and his pace quickened. It was on his tongue to tell Farnham that he loved these raids; the sudden savage hand-to-hand attack, the whine of retaliatory bullets, the pursuit and the final escape. These adventurous interludes came like a breath of fresh air after the constant, endless grind of running propaganda machinery, getting out the newspaper, the *Liberator,* hooking up the "Hams" by radio to spread the truth throughout the country, to tell people hopelessly facing tyranny and oppression that liberty fought on.

But Spike knew Farnham would not listen to such childish explanations as a love of danger; Farnham was like a machine, drove himself as one, and expected others to do the same. So Spike pretended anger.

"Listen," he snapped. "The man's a swine, and he's butchered right and left. If he's not taken care of, what good is our propaganda or organization when people will be afraid of joining us for fear of this animal?"

He paused at the plane door. "Attending to this chap is as necessary as anything else, even more so. Because it will serve as a lesson to other Steel Fist administrators, and will show our friends that they cannot be slaughtered without us striking back."

Farnham could understand that argument. Above all else it was vital to maintain the friends and supporters of the Liberators in the United States and increase their number. Spike's raids would do that.

"Still," said Farnham, "you don't have to go. Duval could lead just as well."

"There must be no chance of failure," said Spike. "So I go."

Farnham acquiesced without good grace. Kay came up, fingers still grimy from reading and correcting proofs of the woman's page in the *Liberator*. She heard part of the argument and said, "Dave, there's no question but what Spike must go. He has the men's confidence."

Spike threw her a grin. Major Pablo Martinez, commandant of the Mexican airport, came up, saluting, and bowing to Kay. "You make new raid, eh, *Señor* Spike?"

"Yes, Pablo," said Spike. "Have your men checked the border?"

"*Si, Señor,*" grinned Pablo. "You will have to detour south and west and cross well above here. My two *pilotos* are pulling the Steel Fist air guards well to the east."

Spike shook hands warmly. Pablo said, "*Señor* Spike, theese Hannibal he go too far. Today he write President Diaz that El Presidente surrender all of you, my good friends, or Mexico, she pay with war."

"What will Diaz say?" Farnham asked.

"He will say, *Señor* Hannibal, Dictator, you go to 'ell, eh? *Si*, that is what he say. I know Diaz depends on you to save us from invasion. Surrendering you will only shortly cut El Presidente's throat," Pablo made a sound with his tongue.

The pilot called out of the transport window. "Okay, Spike, when you are."

"Coming." Spike bent and kissed Kay and shook Farnham's hand. "Back by four," he grinned.

Down the field a small cabin job filled with copies of the

Liberator and world newspapers such as the London *Times* and the Paris *Le Soir* took off after a short run and headed into the detour for the long run to Indianapolis and back by dawn. Later, as Spike knew, other fast planes would fly to other key centers to leave propaganda and instructions to keep alive the spark of revolt.

Pablo came back again to give the all clear signal. Spike hopped into the transport and closed and locked the door. He waved through the window at Kay and Farnham. The pilot gave the three engines the gun and the big transport, loaded with armed men, taxied down the field, turned into the wind and roared high into the night.

22

THE LIBERATORS

IN THE CENTER of Phoenix, Arizona, stands the Verde Hotel, a small quiet hostelry devoted to transients, chiefly housing executives of the copper and gold mines located in the Superstition range to the eastward.

On this night, from the opened windows of the second story, came a series of harsh, horrible screams, interspersed at times by a howl of pain. Underneath, like an accompaniment, was the weeping of two children. Downstairs in the lobby men stood rigid, fists clenched, eyes pale and faces white. But they did not cry out in protest against what was happening, nor make any move to interfere. The lobby was filled with Steel Fist Shock Troops, and to make a move was death and they knew it.

Upstairs, leaning against the jamb of the opened door, Stash Calder, Colonel of the NESP (called the Wasps, but actually the initials of the New Era Secret Police) grinned as one of his men laid on with a mule whip across the naked back of a spare, bald man about whose face nothing could be told because of its contortion of pain.

Stash Calder held in his hand a throw-around.

RESIST! ALL AMERICANS RESIST HANNIBAL

AND HIS MURDERERS!

Hannibal and his cut-throats intend to forge on your wrists the chains of Fascism. They are trying to kill forever the traditional liberty of America, the liberty that has made you free men. Your friends are being murdered; your country's wealth is being destroyed; you are being made slaves who will labor to support the dregs of human kind in their power and arrogance.

These swine have betrayed the country to a foreign invader. Your brothers have been shot. Unless you join with us to destroy this menace, your sons will live in slavery.

RESIST! JOIN THE LIBERATORS AND
PROTECT THE LIBERTIES OUR ANCESTORS
FOUGHT AND DIED TO GIVE US.

The man on the floor fainted at the cruel sweep of the whip-lash. Calder said, "Throw some water on him, Jerry." One of the Steel Fists went to the bathroom and came back with some water. The woman who crouched, half-fainting, between two other Steel Fists guards, cried, "Dear God, don't beat him any more. You'll kill him."

"And so what?" snarled Stash Calder. "He had these dangerous sentiments on him, didn't he? He is a traitor to the New Era. And he'll tell me where he got this paper or I'll cut his skin off inch by inch." She struggled but cruel wrenches at her wrists flung her back in pain. The two children, a boy and a girl of eleven, cowered and wept the more. Stash threw them a harsh glance.

"Cut out that bawling. There's enough noise in here without yours."

He looked down at the man whom they were trying

to revive. "Harvey Beckwith," he mused, "in the mines at Miami he didn't think anything of murdering us poor lugs off. Sending us down in the earth with lousy equipment to mine copper to make *him* rich."

His own mind went back to the time he had been caught trying to hi-grade a streak of gold ore that had been cut by the shaft. Beckwith had cursed him, discharged him, and had him arrested and sent to prison for two years. Well, it was his turn now.

The beaten man showed signs of reviving. "Are you going to tell who gave you this message?" Calder asked.

Beckwith was too far gone to speak. But his eyes flared in defiance.

"Yeah?" Calder yelled savagely. "Lay it on and don't spare the horses."

The beating began, but mercifully could not last long because Beckwith shuddered a little at the end of the fifth lash and collapsed.

"Pour on the water," Calder said.

Jerry straightened up, his face queerly pale. "No use, boss, this guy croaked on us."

Calder didn't show any emotion. "Dammit, I'd like to find out who's spreading this propaganda. Well, somebody else will get caught—they always do. Take the stiff down to jail. We'll plant him out back in the quicklime."

THE WOMAN TRIED to fly at him with ten outstretched clawing fingers. He struck her in the face and turned and walked down to his car. No one spoke to him; all drew aside to make room for him to pass. He smiled; they hated him, but they feared him, too.

He stopped downtown to see the New Era High

Commissioner, one Leffingwell, who had been sent from Chicago.

Stash said, "I traced the propaganda to Beckwith and just put the lash to him. But he up and croaked on me."

Leffingwell was a big, fat man with a putty face. He turned a little bleak.

"That's the fourth man you've beaten to death, Stash," he said. "They ain't going to like that in Washington."

"They hell they ain't—Dorsey is. He wants these Liberators smashed, and you ain't gonna do it with kid gloves."

"We'll have to explain Beckwith's death. After all, he was a mine owner."

"That's easy. We were going to put him under protective arrest and he tried to escape and was accidentally shot," grinned Calder.

Leffingwell didn't say anything and Calder got on to the business that had brought him.

"You got ten thousand bucks from old man Consadine for letting him get away to Mexico. Where's my half?"

"Now, Stash, you—"

"Cut the gab. I want my cut."

Leffingwell got angry. "When you grabbed those diamonds from Mrs. Arnold you didn't count me in."

"Because you held out on me when we bumped old Cosgrave. Come on, dish out the dough, less'n you want me to do bad by you in Washington."

Leffingwell flinched. Stash stood well with the Steel Fists while he, Leffingwell, was just a disbarred lawyer. He reached into his desk and counted out part of the pile of bills he had.

"Is your greed endless, Stash?" he asked. "You must

have made a hundred and fifty thousand in the last three months."

"And I'm gonna make twice as much as that before spring." Stash laughed as he counted the bills. "Listen, guy, when you're on top you cash in. The big guys did it in the old times, and I do it in the New Era. I'm gonna have a million before I'm through."

He pocketed the money, said a surly goodbye, and went down to his car. He was driven to the hotel whose mezzanine floor was his new headquarters.

Night had fallen and the dust of Arizona's desert lay like a pale gauze veil under the moon. He thrust his assistant, Slugger Scott, out of his swivel chair. Scott grunted.

Stash said, "What'd you do with Mrs. Beckwith?"

"Took her home. Say, Stash, she's almost nuts."

"What of it? She had it coming. Last summer she wouldn't have spit on us." Stash lit a fat black cigar and inhaled deeply. "Time she knew Hannibal's turned this country back to us."

"Yeah," said Scott. "Listen, this telegram came while you was away. I kept the boys hanging around."

Stash picked up the telegram. It was from Geary, the High Commissioner at Los Angeles. Marked urgent.

RADIO COMPASS HAS LOCATED ILLEGAL
SHORT WAVE RADIO IN TEMPE BELIEVED TO BE
LOCATED IN HIGH SCHOOL BUILDING RAID AT
ONCE AS STILL OPERATING SENDING PERVER-
SIVE PROPAGANDA

Stash smacked the desk with his fist. "That new teacher,

Callan," he exclaimed. "I thought he's been yelling too loud for Hannibal." He jumped up and reached for his cartridge belt and holster. "Get the boys, Slugger. I'll show that guy. I'll make a real lesson of him."

SLUGGER WENT OUT and Stash buckled on his belt, muttering to himself the while. He paused to take a handful of cigars and thrust them into his pocket.

"Stash," called Slugger.

"Colonel to you," growled Stash out the door. "We gotta have discipline? You read the order from Hannibal."

Scott's laugh sounded harshly from outside. "Sure, I read it. No lootin'. No murder, and everybody to have a square deal and honest trial. But if you've overlooked a watch since this here revolt started, I'd have got it and I ain't got even one. You—"

He stopped speaking. Stash said, "Damn you, if you think you can talk to me like that—"

There was a lot of noise from down the hall. Stash took out his cigar and spat.

"Them guys of mine is drunk again," he muttered. "I'm gonna—" He became silent as boot heels thudded in the hall. He caught the gleam of guns and uniforms.

"Stay there," he called. "I'm coming. And you guys gotta quit drinking on the job or—"

He ceased to speak. These men came on and he didn't know them.

"Say, what's the idea?" he shouted angrily.

The leader, a huge man of six feet five, said, "We've come for you, Calder."

Stash went for his gun. But his hand fell away when he looked into the muzzles of three automatic pistols.

"I don't savvy," he said, falling back into his office.

"You will," said the huge man.

"Say," said Stash, seeing the Steel Fist uniforms. "If you guys are tryin' to cut in on my—"

He stopped, a sudden fear gripping him. From behind the four men suddenly stepped a tall, gaunt woman.

"Mrs. Beckwith!" he gasped.

She ignored him. She said to Spike, "He killed my husband. Tom wouldn't betray—betray—" her voice cracked. A taut, terrible silence came to the room.

Spike said to her gently, "I know, Mrs. Beckwith. Your husband was a patriot." He turned to Stash Calder.

"We're the Liberators, and we came here to try you on another charge of murder. But it seems fitting that you should answer for the killing of Beckwith."

Calder swallowed hard and the crackling sound was audible.

"I want—you can't—I'm the police—" he stuttered. He took a deep breath. He screamed, "Sam! Slugger! Harry!"

Spike said, "Your men can't help you, Calder. You're charged with the murder of John Beckwith! How do you plead?"

"I want a lawyer. A New Era lawyer," croaked Calder. "I want a real trial."

"You're getting one. How do you plead?"

Calder's nerve broke. He screamed. "Beckwith was an enemy of the State. He was a traitor to the New Era."

"You had him beaten to death?"

"My orders are to—yes, I executed him. Executed him like I had a right to do."

In the sharp silence he knew he had said the wrong thing.

Spike said, "I guess that's all. Get the rope."

Stash suddenly understood; they were going to hang him. He was not one to die without making an effort. Regardless, he jerked the gun and leaped to one side, trying to shoot in the same movement.

Spike's gun tracked him, and two thuds of explosion roared in the room. The reek of cordite made a fog inside. Stash fell, his shoulder smashed by the heavy .45 slug. Spike's men dragged him out. They worked fast under the cover of their comrades' guns…

When the red sun came out of the desert at dawn, the early risers in Phoenix saw a body dangling from a lamp-post by a string around the broken neck. The placard read, *Executed for murder by the American Liberators.*

23

TWO MEN MUST DIE

THERE WERE RAIDS into Louisiana. A quick descent on Atlanta, Georgia; and a miracle of a raid on Kansas City where the dawn found not only the High Commissioner of the Upper Mississippi Valley District, but also his two aides and the Steel Fist Secret Police chief, swinging from the lampposts. As Spike could tell from the Steel Fist newspapers, news of these retributive acts was strictly suppressed, but the *Liberator* paper smuggled out three times a week by airplane saw to it that the people knew.

And as reports to Farnham showed, the deaths of the most vicious of the Steel Fists had a definite effect on the morale of those who were still secretly resisting. More adherents joined.

Set-backs were suffered when this happened because Dorsey's Secret Police sent out a myriad of spies and, despite all precautions, some of these were taken into the Liberators. Where they were taken in, wholesale slaughter followed.

In Indianapolis, on Monument Circle in front of the old English Hotel, eighty-five Hoosier members of the Liberators were sprayed with machine-gun fire until the gutter ran with blood. But within forty-eight hours Farnham held a short wave message out to Spike to read, a message from a railroad roundhouse foreman.

LIBERATOR UNIT HERE REORGANIZED
STOP KEEP THE HELP COMING

Farnham's eyes were bright. "America is stirring, Spike. We're beginning to win."

Spike, irritable after two sleepless nights, and discouraged because when he had arrived at Cleveland he found all the Liberator leaders murdered, was not so sure.

"The people are aroused, a lot of them," he admitted, "but what good does it do? Hannibal has made the Steel Fists the regular army, and raised them to a million and a half men. Fully equipped. What good does it do for the people to arouse themselves when they're unarmed at the mercy of a million and a half gangsters, armed to the teeth?"

"It took time for this condition to come about. It will take time for us to drill and arm the Liberators."

"You haven't that much time," said Spike. "Look, I go around the country executing a few rats. Where I should hit is at the White House. Destroy Hannibal and Dorsey and you've wrecked the thing at the top."

"Don't hurry matters," said Farnham, and went back to the consideration of his finance reports. Money from liberals throughout the world was pouring in, but not enough for what he wanted to use it for. It took more than a few millions to win back a continent.

But that Spike's daring raids (to which he now devoted himself almost entirely) were having their effect, was evidenced a week later. Spike and Farnham, together

with five other regional directors of the Liberators, were
together considering a smuggled-in report from Admiral
Evelyn, of the Pacific fleet.

It was the queerest situation an admiral ever found
himself in and Evelyn was expressing his dilemma well.

Japan has recognized Hannibal's New Era government as
the de jure government of the United States and is working
out terms of peace with Hannibal's representatives. What am
I to do? You have President Henderson with you, but does
he or does he not represent the will of the majority of the
American people?

Even if I was fully equipped to offer battle to the Japanese fleet (which I am not, as my requisitions for supplies go
unexecuted on the mainland) should I do so? After all, I am
the admiral of the American Fleet. The fleet of the people. If,
as I am told, the people are for Hannibal, then the fleet also
should be under Hannibal's authority. I do not believe they
are for Hannibal. But what can I do?

At the moment I hold Hawaii. I cannot attack the Japanese; and in a few more weeks, due to lack of supplies for
re-fit, I may not even be able to defend against the full Japanese fleet. Intelligence tells me that the Japanese intend to
seize this moment for a swift blow to destroy my fleet, seize
Hawaii and annex it.

The reason the Japanese can do this is because my fleet is
weakened by lack of help from home. So here is my problem:
I can recognize Hannibal as the vested American government, tell him of the treachery Japan is planning. With
supplies now forwarded from the mainland, I can meet the
Jap fleet on equal terms. And prevent the destruction of

American seapower which would cripple us for fifty years to come. In fact, if I make my peace with Hannibal and the Japs find it out, they will not try such a back-handed blow because they would know the battle answer beforehand.

So you must tell me what your chances are of quickly regaining control of the nation. I must think first of all of the people and of my country. If you have a chance of victory within a few weeks, I shall hang on. If you have not, then I must, on my conscience as an American, recognize Hannibal as the *de facto* government and prepare to defend our seapower and our shores.

THERE WAS A moment's silence after Farnham finished reading Evelyn's letter. It was a terrible blow and all of them knew it. Part of Farnham's scheme for spring had been to have the Pacific fleet steam secretly to the California coast, and with the aid of the guns and fifty thousand sailors, seize a toe-hold of he country, perhaps Oregon, Washington, California and Arizona, as a base from which to start re-conquering the rest of the nation. With Evelyn in his present predicament, this was impossible.

With the fleet lost, then years were added to the task of winning back the nation. Henderson, a hollow-eyed old man, crushed by age and sorrow, looked helplessly toward Farnham.

"Couldn't Evelyn steam forced draft at once?" he asked. "Couldn't he seize the Pacific coast now? Half our trouble in getting foreign aid is that we're exiles from our own country."

Farnham made his decision instantly. "No! Impossible! You could not keep Evelyn's fleet movements hidden from the Japs. They would seize the chance and fall upon undefended Hawaii and capture it. Evelyn would then be forced to base on San Pedro. He would be caught between the Japs and the Steel Fists and lose his fleet."

"But we can't let him go over to Hannibal," cried Vice President Barnes. "All Hannibal wants is the fleet to start a war against Mexico to distract the people's minds. He may start the war anyway, but with a fleet to blockade the coast and start a force inland from Vera Cruz, as well as an attack along the border—he'd be bound to win."

Spike said dogmatically, "I've been telling you all along we're striking at the wrong men. Hannibal is the one we should strike at—Hannibal and Dorsey. Crush them from the top."

No one ever had a chance to answer that point. The walls of the ash-gray, sun-bleached house that was headquarters, were paper-thin. And now, from the direction of the International Bridge, came a few scattered rifle shots. Then a sizeable volley. Then the roar and reverberation of sustained small arms fire. Rifles, machine guns and the sharp bark of one-pounder cannon.

Every one leaped to his feet. A few seconds later Colonel Pablo Martinez rushed in.

"Run, *señors*," he yelled, "for your lives. The Steel Fists— they come—an army of them. They kill my people; they seize the bridge. They will kill you."

Spike's hand streaked from his pocket and a shrill blast of a whistle bit through the night.

"Rally your men, Pablo," he cried. "O'Hara can hold this house until you get the main force up." He turned to Farnham. "The rest of you—into the shelters."

He turned and raced from the room, his whistle blasting again. O'Hara had heard the shrill of warning, and his finger was pressed on the button of an old air raid alarm siren whose moan rose to a shriek in the night.

Juarez was full of American army officers and even soldiers who had refused to bow to the New Era government. These had been formed into companies and drilled by O'Hara and others for just such a contingency as this. Bomb-proof shelters had been constructed against the possibility of the Steel Fists trying to destroy them by an air raid. Toward these shelters now every one rallied. As Spike knew, everything now depended on the size of the raiding Steel Fist party. If there were thousands, then it was all up.

Due to conditions across the border, President Diaz had stationed a division of Mexican troops around Juarez. But it would take time to rally them, particularly at night. Spike was grateful for O'Hara now, and for the smart, intelligent discipline that had always prevailed in the regular American army.

WITHOUT CONFUSION, WITHOUT the loss of a precious minute, the tiny army of five hundred men slid into its place, each man to his task. There were anti-tank guns for the big lumbering Steel Fist tanks coming down the street; automatic rifles for a sizeable volume of fire on the combat patrols following and Browning machine guns that tore widening gaps—Americans against Americans.

The Steel Fists had evidently depended upon surprise and night attack. And since surprise had failed, the night attack was fatal. They had on their clothing huge white steel fists to identify them to each other. And these, now, under O'Hara's searchlights, made them splendid targets.

Four of the tanks that were literally tearing down Juarez house by house as they came along, were stopped by anti tank guns. Two others, with roaring three-inch guns in their turrets, were charging in, and these alone promised to turn the tide in favor of the Steel Fists.

Spike leaped from his embrasure. "Okay, tank killers out!"

He had little to do with the subsequent operation except to cover it with his gun and be there.

Out leaped three regular army soldiers who, taking advantage of every bit of cover, raced toward the slow moving tank. They carried things. They got under the flank of the tank which could not shoot at them, itself, and whose size protected them from the fire of the Steel Fists pressing behind.

One man jerked out a bottle. Through one of the air slits in the steel he poured the gasoline. Touched it off with a match.

The fumes had filled the inside of the rumbling tank. These ignited and with a furious roar almost like an explosion, the inside of the tank became a raging inferno.

Spike grabbed out a hand grenade from his pocket, jerked the pin and drew back his arm. Driven frantic by the raging fire within, the tank crew opened the top steel hatch and tried to come tumbling out. Spike's grenade, timed to the second, hit the hatch and roared. The two soldiers who had accompanied the gasoline artist also threw their grenades. The tank crew died to a man, and the tank burned for a half-hour or so, offering excellent illumination to the defenders.

But with the failure of the tanks upon which they had evidently counted to tear through, the Steel Fists began to retreat before the accurate fire of trained soldiers. They were taken in flank by a hurry-up battalion of Mexican regulars, and their retreat became a rout.

Within an hour after the first shot, the raiders were back over the bridge, minus some hundred and ten of their number.

Farnham summed it up. "Hannibal's getting hurt by our raids and propaganda," he cried. "They even dared invade Mexican territory to try to kill us. We're winning, I tell you!"

TWO WEEKS AFTER the abortive raid to seize the Liberator's headquarters, Spike and Farnham learned vital news that changed the whole aspect of affairs. Prior to its arrival, Spike was talking to Farnham and Spike was in one of his stubborn moods. Because of his forays with the raiding parties, because of his constant recruiting among the "Hams" who relayed the short wave news, he felt himself to be better in touch with what was happening among the people of America than Farnham. And he was frankly impatient with what he considered Farnham's Fabian tactics of delay.

"Hannibal's building up a terrific propaganda," he said; "he's literally buying the people by all kinds of devices; bread and circuses for the people on relief; electrification of farmhouses at no cost and small electric charge afterwards; and a promise of a special processing tax to raise the farmer's income. And between the farmers and the workers he's got enough votes to carry his plebiscite overwhelmingly. And once he wins that, we're lost."

"We'll be badly checked," admitted Farnham. His dark sleek head was covered with gray; and he had aged twenty years, it seemed.

"More than checked," argued Spike. "If Hannibal can show the world a vote of confidence in him, then he gets recognition from all nations. You and I and the others then are conspirators, outlaws, and he can take even more drastic attempts to quell us than he has. We won't even be safe in Mexico or Canada, for he can say to those governments that giving us sanctuary is an unfriendly act, and to save trouble they'd either kick us out or surrender us to Hannibal's agents."

"All right, all right," snapped Farnham impatiently. "It takes time to organize a counter-revolt, overcome mass inertia. What have you to suggest in place of what I'm doing?"

Meanwhile, Henderson and the other leaders of the Liberators had drifted in; they all looked expectantly at Spike.

Spike was ready. "Capture or kill Hannibal," he said. "Strike at the main spring. Get rid of Dorsey and Hannibal, and even if the movement does not fall apart, there will be squabbles among the other Steel Fists for power; dissension and thus weakness."

No one in the room spoke or seemed to breathe.

He paused, then went on: "Finally, if we do that we postpone this plebiscite and give you, Farnham, the time you want. And we must delay the plebiscite or consider ourselves lost."

There was a murmur of approval to this. Farnham leaned back, clicking a pencil against his white teeth.

"I am not squeamish," he said, "and in a matter like this, Hannibal's death is to be welcomed. Killing him and Dorsey is easy to propose, but can it be done? If you try and fail, all measures Hannibal takes thereafter—and they will be terrible—will meet with foreign approval and cut down the money gifts we get to finance our efforts."

"Yes," said Henderson. "I understand a whole battalion of Steel Fists surround the White House. Lights have been installed so even a mouse can't move unseen. No one can get in to Hannibal who is not checked for firearms. He wears a bullet-proof vest at public appearances. And in speeches no one is allowed within rifle distance without being closely watched—even searched."

"It would take time and planning," said another.

"We're making headway," spoke still a third, an ex-senator from Minnesota. "The northern Mid-West states are nearly ready to revolt. We might ruin all we have done by trying and failing at assassination."

Spike did not quail at the word. He simply reiterated, "Hannibal and Dorsey must be gotten rid of. I'll take time to plan it; go to Washington myself. The rest of the work can be carried on. All I say is that it must be done, and I'll make certain there is no failure."

"And the boy," said an ex-congressman from New York, "Hannibal's son. We have it on good authority Hannibal is grooming the boy for his own job as dictator when the day comes."

"I don't make war on children," said Spike. "If Hannibal falls, the whole house falls. I—"

THEN IT WAS that the messenger from Virginia Beach entered. An ex-army officer, retired, called to duty and now forced to flee, he immediately sought Farnham's ear alone. After he had whispered for five minutes, Spike saw Farnham's face become suddenly pale and tense.

Farnham turned. "This is for all of us to know. Gentlemen, this is Colonel Bagby from Virginia Beach—just east of Norfolk. He brings news we must consider at once."

The introduction was acknowledged. Then Farnham said, "Colonel Bagby informs me that for the past four days troop transports from Italy and Germany have been landing troops at night along the Chesapeake. Already, he says, about twenty thousand additional troops, fully equipped to fight, have been brought ashore. The rumor is that many more are coming.

"The Italians were openly boasting that more than three hundred thousand were slated to come. They spoke as if they expect to conquer the country."

Spike said, "And as many Germans?"

"Yes," nodded Bagby, an old, tough-faced man with three campaign ribbons in his buttonhole. "At least three hundred thousand Germans. And lots of German supply ships with mechanized stuff, armored cars, tanks, and motorcycles for long-range reconnaissance work."

"What can it mean?" cried President Henderson.

"Yes, what?" asked the ex-senator from Minnesota. "Hannibal's last radio address said specifically that, confident that the plebiscite would favor him, he was asking Italy and Germany immediately to withdraw their troops. Is Hannibal afraid of our counter-movement?"

Spike quickly shook his head. "No. He's got sufficient

Steel Fists to police the country; and—" he turned to Farnham quickly. "Is there any rumor that England might intervene in our behalf?"

"No. England is too harassed maintaining herself, and besides, her re-armament program is still far from complete. It is not that, I am positive."

"Then what?" asked President Henderson. "With a quarter of a million Italians and Germans already here, the addition of six hundred thousand more—why, that's three field armies."

Spike pounded his right fist lightly into the palm of his other hand. "Whatever Hannibal's intentions, I tell you this: if the coalition forces get eight hundred thousand men into this country, we're done for—at least in the lifetime of every man in this room."

"Possibly," said Farnham, "but what do you mean?"

Spike smiled. "I mean there is no time for delay. Look at it this way: suppose we get rid of Hannibal and Dorsey and throw confusion among the Steel Fists. Suppose we can seize and hold some communications and get word to the American people that a conquering force which will reduce them to slavery to a foreign power is about to take over.

"Why," he shrugged, "we can get the explosive reaction that will arouse almost unanimous revolt. With internal Steel Fist dissension and no leader, the Steel Fists can be overthrown. That done, we can risk Japan's seizure of Hawaii, recall Evelyn and his fleet. Re-fitted, the fleet can cut the Atlantic communications line of the Italian and German invading forces. We oust them. As for Hawaii and what happens to it—why, we can wait until the country has recuperated before deciding that issue. And, anyway, for my part I'll swap Hawaii for my own country any day."

A MURMUR OF approval went up at this. Farnham, who had discussed the same strategy based on a longer campaign, said, "But everything hangs on getting rid of Hannibal and Dorsey. How do you propose to do that?"

Spike fumbled for his pipe and began to fill it.

"Gentlemen," he said quietly, "I'm a reporter, and not an emotional person; not a sentimentalist, nor one given to melodramatic ways of thinking. But after all, I *do* love my country, as do we all, though we may not get maudlin about it. I am stirred by the thought of what may lay ahead for her and for her people if this vital moment is not seized. So..." his voice died away.

No one spoke. Kay had come into the room and Spike paused to look at her. His face still held a gentle, a sort of ecstatic expression. He even smiled at her.

"So," he continued in a low voice, "I'm going to Washington. I'll take a few people with me. Volunteers because none of us, I expect, will come back. But we shall rid the country of Hannibal and Dorsey. How, I cannot say, but we will do it. I swear to it."

He did not raise his voice, but there was no need to. They knew he would do this—offer his own life for the life of Hannibal. Kay knew it and she paled as she kept coming forward. But she did not speak. No one else broke the sharp silence.

Farnham, who was watching her and saw her reaction, looked a little bleak. But when he turned to Spike his face had the same serene patience it always had.

"I can't say you're wrong," he said, "because you're not.

You're right. If we are going to reclaim the nation, we've got to do it before Italy and Germany get some overwhelming numbers landed. They'll take weeks, even two months, to ferry over such an army. But we've got to get rid of Hannibal and Dorsey at once. If you want to do it this way, Spike, I cannot, will not, stop you. I can only say we will go on as we have been going and pray that you are successful."

The group dispersed a few moments later. Kay stood beside Spike. "You risk failure, no matter how clever you are. I could go to Hannibal and make certain of the ultimate end."

"When you saw him face to face," Spike said bluntly, "you wouldn't dare. He's too strong for you."

She knew this was true. She had thought often of what would occur if she was armed and face to face with Hannibal. The man held some sway over her that took will power to break. But thinking of the peril Spike would run, she said, "I could do it. I would."

"No," said Spike. "But you can help. You know his people; the ones we can or cannot work through. So you can go to Washington with me if you wish."

Farnham gave Spike a quick sharp look. "Would you make her run such a risk? This would mean her death."

"Yes," said Spike. "And why not. This is no time to be thinking of my life, or yours, or hers, precious as it is to me." He stopped speaking for a second, and his face took on a dreamy, abstracted look.

"When I was a kid," he said almost to himself, "I used to read stories about men like Nathan Hale, and other chaps who put principles before life. They seemed real enough then; and I thrilled to them. Later, as I grew older and saw and met people, I figured they were romances made up by historians with nationalistic ideas. Maybe my later idea was right but now, looking back, I can see that in our time people had only to think of themselves. They never had to weigh life against principles. Because of what a few brave, stubborn men did in 1776 and 1812 and 1860, our generation, until now, has had it easy. They could listen and laugh at politicians prating about a country born in the blood of sacrifice. But it was—this country—born just like that."

He shrugged, squared his shoulders. "And the time is here for us to think about those principles again—the principles of freedom and opportunity for all, and free press and free movement and government of laws and not of men. And if we have to die for those principles, then it's because the wheel of time brought this task to us and not those of the next nor the last generation."

He suddenly laughed self-consciously. "Damned if I don't sound like a guy running for alderman in the fourth ward."

But Kay and Farnham did not laugh. Kay's eyes were brilliant as she studied Spike's face.

After a moment Farnham said: "When do you leave, Spike?"

"As soon as I can get the volunteers and a plane."

Farnham held out his hand. "I say no more," he declared quietly. "You're right, of course, and Kay must go and so must you. Good luck—and—well, good luck."

24

BULL-WHIP RULE

WASHINGTON WAS EASY to get into from the Maryland farm country where Spike's pilot landed the plane. The highways swarmed with trucks and motor cars, all bearing the Steel Fist device on the side to proclaim them government property. The railroads ran ninety and a hundred car trains, loaded with material. When Kay and Spike registered in at a small side-street hotel, the Harbord, they found out why. Washington's population had trebled, even quadrupled. All was feverish activity.

Old buildings along Pennsylvania Avenue and to the east of the Capitol were being torn down, and already foundations were being poured for vast new structures. Probably the greatest building program Washington had ever known was under way. In one of his many speeches Hannibal had said, "I will make Washington the most beautiful capital in the world."

Apparently he was doing just that, for workmen were razing every old structure that had stood since before the turn of the century and others were re-building whole sections of government buildings injured by bombing. Spike saw much else besides; the city swarmed with Steel Fists in uniform, carrying either rifles or sidearms.

These were fraternizing heartily with the Germans in the coal-scuttle helmets and *feldgrau* uniforms; and with Italians in dish-shaped helmets and green uniforms. There were many of these last; more, Spike thought, than were necessary.

Kay pointed out something else. Over the White House floated a most peculiar arrangement; it looked like a fish net suspended by huge floats. The net made a huge circle at about four thousand feet altitude. Spike knew what it was; the floats were small captive balloons and strung between them was a net of steel wires. Airplanes flying at night, particularly, and trying to come down, would drive their propellers into the steel mesh and thus be destroyed.

"Hannibal's taking no chances on being bombed out," Spike muttered.

He saw also, a flight of six planes circling high above the net. At the end of two hours another flight came up and those which had been on air guard descended to Anacostia Field.

"That prevents any attack from the air," Kay said.

"It does," admitted Spike grimly, "unless you had a dozen men willing to smash up to wreck the defenses and make an opening for others to come through."

On billboards they saw huge posters that read:

VOTE AYE ON SENESCHAL HANNIBAL'S
PROGRAM. INSURE THE FUTURE OF YOUR-
SELF AND OF THE NATION.

Where workmen were clustered, an outside radio blared

*Spike stood
silently before
John Hannibal*

somebody's speech extolling the merits of the totalitarian state.

Spike and Kay strolled up Executive Avenue, Spike slumping and shambling to hide his height. Across from the White House Steel Fists were encamped in hastily erected huts; and a tight patrol of them guarded not only the street but the lawn itself. As Kay and Spike approached closer to get a better estimate of the number, a Steel Fist corporal with four men came jouncing down upon them.

"Well," he said, "where do you think you're going?"

Kay took up the burden. "We're—we're on our honeymoon"—she blushed prettily—"and we thought if we walked down here we might get to see our Seneschal— see Mr. Hannibal."

The corporal laughed. "Fat chance! Nobody's allowed down here but us who're running the government. You'll have to go back." But he said it kindly and gave her an appreciative look and a grin.

While Kay and Spike were strolling back, a sixteen-cylindered car whirled past. A tiny forked pennon bearing a steel fist and a gold star floated from the radiator. Spike caught a glimpse of Dorsey, his shark-mouth tightly clamped. The Steel Fists snapped to attention and presented arms as the car turned in at the White House driveway.

"It's impossible," murmured Kay. "I don't see how you can possibly get to him."

"Nothing is impossible," replied Spike, "but it is tough."

THEY WENT OUT to Georgetown at dusk and sought out Hawker on P Street. His face showed the strain of the last few months; and his expression had the cautious air of one who carries his life in his two hands, expecting momentarily to trip and drop it. But he instantly agreed that his house be a rendezvous for the plan.

"More and more Hannibal is having his way," he said. "People are eating, and listening to his promises of the future. That and mass inertia are making them swing toward him."

"You think he'll win the plebiscite then?" Kay asked.

"Using Hitler's methods," smiled Hawker, "he ought to get eighty percent—and the other twenty will be liquidated or placed in concentration camps."

Driving into Virginia to pick out an isolated landing spot for his volunteers, Spike got a look at what happened to those men sent to concentration camps. Hawker had a friend, a member of the Liberators, who worked for the New Era government. He was a road engineer in charge of the widening of the highway between Norfolk and Petersburg. An eight-lane road it was and Spike, seeing the concentration of German and Italian troops along its length, gasped. A mechanized army, he knew, could speed

from the camp with amazing swiftness to Washington
along that road.

And along that road Spike saw men under the Steel Fist
bull-whips. Men whose aged bodies and fine faces told
they were not road laborers, but men who had once known
authority, money and cleanliness. They were filthy now;
half naked in their rags, and doing the work of mules with
a Steel Fist private over them. Carrying logs, for instance,
or loading wheelbarrows with rubble and pushing them
to a dump heap. Let a man falter and the bull-whip hissed
and a red lash of pain lay over the man's back. Spike saw
them fall, be whipped until they howled, and drag themselves upright in agony to try once more.

Hannibal could say he executed none of the old regime;
he didn't have to; he worked them like this with poor food
and thin clothing, with a bull-whip to lacerate their backs
until they died of exhaustion or strung themselves up by
their rags.

At another time Kay came back one evening, trembling,
and threw herself in Spike's arms and sobbed.

"I danced with him at my first cotillion," she panted.

Spike shook her gently. "Who?"

"Young Bob Ahern." She clung tighter. "I saw him working on one of the concrete mixers by the Union Station.
He was being beaten—horribly." She shuddered, and Spike
had to keep her from falling. "He broke away from them.
He—oh, Spike—he threw himself into the mixer."

Spike got out a bottle of Scotch and poured her a stiff
drink and one for himself.

Deliberately he said, "I heard from O'Hara today. The

transport planes are going to be available. Enough to carry three hundred of our men."

She didn't appear to listen, so he shifted and told her of a half-wit in tattered remnants of a Steel Fist uniform whom he had seen. "And he was singing this, darling: 'Oh, Hannibal's the Seneschal and chief of all the land. He'll make us great, he'll make us rich, we'll never go back to digging a ditch; ain't it gonna be grand?'"

After a while he got her quieted and told her that O'Hara had forty pilots to volunteer to break through the screen of balloonettes.

"It'll only be a diversion," he went on; "they can bail out when their planes hit, and if we win on the ground, they'll be saved."

"Killing," she said, "murder. The way I feel now I could go to Hannibal and—and be a Messalina or a Madame de Maintenon—"

"But you won't."

She didn't reply, but for the rest of the evening when the Liberators, one by one, drifted in to report and to receive new instructions, she was quiet and watchful. Spike, busy with his plans for the raid, did not notice until some time later that she had quietly slipped out.

KAY HAD ACTUALLY gone out because she wanted to think, and think straight. Under the spell of Hannibal she had thought in terms of abstract philosophy; the greater good for the greater number; a change that would bring security and happiness to all.

Listening to Spike, she also thought in terms of principles; freedom of opportunity, justice to all and free concourse of men to guide their own destinies.

But the death of Bob Ahern, the son of the president of American Foods, had changed all that. She had known him as a decent, hardworking lad who, graduated from Yale, was about to start at the bottom in his father's corporation and prepare himself to manage it one day. She knew him to be kind, courteous, an average young American, fortunate to be born of wealthy parents.

And now he was dead; driven to the most horrible form of self-destruction by a merciless tyranny that the human spirit could not endure.

That was the reality of it. Youth dying while two factions played at their game of principles and philosophical dicta.

She walked toward the Mayflower Hotel, scarcely seeing where her feet took her. She wanted to find the answer—to satisfy herself. How many other young men who, in the ordinary course of events, would become leaders and executives, were being driven to suicide or death? How many more would be destroyed? Many, she knew, thousands.

And suddenly she had the answer. Men like Hannibal and Spike could dream their dreams, work out their theories, adhere to their principles. But when the time came for action, Hannibal alone could not carry out his plans. He had to have help. He had to call on many men—thousands and thousands. And they were the fault. Hannibal himself resented and feared bloodshed except in dire emergency, but his pawns, his sub leaders were human, filled with the ordinary deficiencies of the human kind—greed, selfishness, a certain brutality among many, lust and ambition.

These weaknesses could not be ironed out in one blow; if they could, then the world would have been a Utopia two thousand years before. One man might have a vast vision but he could not impart it to weaker men who must help him.

So Hannibal was entirely wrong, and Spike was right. The answer must be what all thinking men had declared it to be; a long process of human evolution in which the number of men capable of understanding and putting into effect a great vision should increase.

Spike was also right when he said that to save many thousands of lives the life of one man did not matter. Life must follow its predestined course of slow and painful evolution and he who would hurry this, complicate the process, was an enemy of the world.

She took a big breath. She who had never killed anything was trying—

Her thoughts were brutally interrupted by a hand grasping her shoulder and whirling her. Her head had been sunk in thought, and her dark clothing was unobtrusive. But as the hand whirled her, her shoulders squared, her head flung up, and she turned a sudden furious gaze on the man.

But this was no amorous Steel Fist. She was looking into the shark-like face of George Dorsey.

He thrust his tongue against his teeth and whistled shrilly, keeping his tight grip the while.

Steel Fists came running. Dorsey said, "Arrest this woman. High treason against the State!"

Kay had no chance to protest, nor to struggle. Her arms were black and blue from their brutal grips; her body was swirled until she was breathless. She heard Dorsey call after the Steel Fists, "No record to be made of this arrest—and you know what to do with her."

She knew then she was lost. Hannibal would have

protected her, but Dorsey was going to make certain
Hannibal knew nothing of this.

25

WANTED FOR TREASON

SPIKE WORKED UNTIL midnight and when he at last straightened up from the papers and rubbed his tired eyes, he knew the plan was complete to the last detail. The plane attack would smash from the air, and the ground forces would disable the AA guns mounted on the White House lawns. This would draw off part of the force of defenders. And with three hundred trained soldiers, and the additional two hundred to be recruited around Washington, the rush would be made on the White House, and no one would retreat until Hannibal was dead.

The only fact left missing was the precise time on March 4th. Spike deliberately left this blank because he had to make certain that on that date Hannibal would be in the White House. The man was scheduled to make a radio address on that night; everything pointed to him being there. But in these days, changes were quick and surprising. So while the men would be moved from Juarez, while the planes would be gathered and gassed and made ready, the final flash would go out from Hawker on the short wave.

Hitherto, Hawker had not used his own set, because he was more valuable under cover. But he could do so this night because if there was success, it didn't matter, and if there was failure he would be dead anyway.

Spike had checked and re-checked. He knew O'Hara as a master of logistics and organization. So he straightened his cramped shoulders, looked around, and suddenly said, "Where did Kay go?"

Hawker said, "Why, she went out a while ago. I didn't notice."

Spike filled his pipe, lighted it and leaned back. "Well, it's done—we bet all the chips on one roll of the dice."

"All our chips," said Hawker. "We may lose. But there'll be other players, Mr. Brenn—"

"Spike to you, my boy."

"Well, Spike. There'll be other players after us. And somebody is going to win. This condition can't go on."

"No," said Spike, "it can't." He suddenly stopped, startled, shocked. "Out, you said. I mean Kay. Did you say she went out—outdoors?"

"Why, I don't know. You were talking about the automatic rifle equipment and cartridges and—"

Spike got up. His mind was suddenly clear on one point: Kay was violently upset over the death of this Ahern. She had said something about going to Hannibal. Could she have done so? He hastened to her room. It was empty. Her hat and coat were gone.

Spike swore, and hurried to his own room. Firearms for others than Steel Fists were forbidden by drastic punishment, but he had a .45 automatic pistol and he thrust it in his pocket now. Kay had gone out. Had she gone to Hannibal? He groaned and hastened out into the night.

Hawker called from the door, "Don't go out, you idiot, you'll be—"

Spike heard nothing else of what he said. He had to keep moving; he was so torn inside that without movement he would lose all control. He did not get very far. At the corner of Fourteenth and K, opposite the Ambassador Hotel, a Steel Fist guard suddenly thrust a rifle muzzle at him.

"Okay, buddy, where's your pass?"

"Pass?" Spike looked up, dazedly.

Other Steel Fists drifted across the road. They had been listening to the music in a night club.

"Yeah, pass," said the Steel Fist. "You know there's a curfew in this man's town. Nobody out after nine o'clock less'n he's got a pass."

Four against one. Spike said, "Aw, have a heart. I been seeing my girl. I forgot what time it was—you know how it is."

"Where do you live?"

Spike gave an address on Twelfth, South East. The guard grinned. "Kinda forgot what time it was, huh; it's midnight now. Well—"

A corporal said, "Where do you work?"

"On the new Education Building," Spike said.

The corporal nodded. Suddenly he struck Spike between the shoulder blades. "Straighten up. A guy like you oughta be in the—well, I'll be—"

Spike had automatically straightened and it added those last few inches that made him a huge man. Another Steel Fist said, "Why, you know, that placard in the barracks. Damned if he don't look—"

Spike knew it was all up. He went for his gun. He had it

out and he shot the corporal before any of them could act. He backed away, swiveling the heavy weapon on the other three. He might have made it, but there were other Steel Fists whom he didn't see. Behind him, a gun butt whistled through the air. The wood crashed against the side of his head. And he went down as if he had been pole-axed.

IN THE WOMEN'S section of the Washington jail, the big matron said, "Now, dearie, remember, you're a criminal and you can be shot for your crime. Better be a nice girl and tell Aunt Clara where this Spike Brenn is."

"I can't—I won't—I don't know," Kay panted.

She was naked to the waist in that dreadful cell, and the buxom matron who had a hard, dissolute face and a breath that smelled of gin, held a light whip—a dog-whip, the end of which had been dipped in resin and hardened so it would cut and flay.

"Now, don't be a damned fool," the matron who called herself Aunt Clara was losing patience. "I got orders to learn where this guy is. I get a reward if I do. So you'd better start talking, dearie, or I'll flay that hide right off 'n your back."

Kay tried to cover herself with her hands. She was frightened, in utter terror. Since she had been in this place she had seen other women beaten; she could, if she'd listen now, hear the moans of them. It seemed that in the New Era women not only did their share of the work but also could be beaten—by other women, of course.

"Come on, dearie, let's both get to bed. Where is this guy?"

"I don't know," reiterated Kay.

"Well, you dirty little bum, it's up to me—and me with

arthritis in my arm, too. But I'll get it out of you—yes, I will."

She struck once, savagely, with the lash that cut across Kay's smooth back and raised a red welt. Kay had never been hurt before in her life. The effect of the blow was both physical and mental. The shock, the amazement, the sudden anguish, aroused a fury that sent her springing like a tigress at the matron. She struck and then tried to kick.

The matron weighed two hundred pounds and she was a tough woman.

"So that's it. Well, bite on this." She drove her fist into Kay's face, sent her staggering back, and then struck again with the whip. Thrice, and again and again, the lash stung and raised welts on the soft skin.

Kay tried to hurl the chair. A blow across the face half-blinded her. She sank down.

Aunt Clara desisted. "I don't like to do this, dearie," she panted. "But I gotta know because it's my job. Tell me where this Spike Brenn is and I'll bring you some nice ointment. Your face is a mess, dearie."

Kay still refused to speak, but she was not beaten again then. Footsteps echoed in the hall and the matron, dropping her whip, hastened to unlock the cell door.

"Why, General," she said to George Dorsey. "I didn't expect you. The little tramp won't talk yet, and I was just using my persuader on her."

Dorsey looked at the half-naked girl. She was beautiful, he thought. Then as Kay lifted her face, he saw the welt whose swelling had practically blinded her.

"Damn you for an old biddy," he snarled at Aunt Clara.

"Why did you hit her face? If he—why can't you learn to hurt somebody without marking them up?"

"Well," said Aunt Clara sullenly, "she ran into it. I was swinging for her back."

They argued acrimoniously and Dorsey almost struck the old woman, but Kay didn't hear any of it. A roaring was in her ears. She was, she knew, about to faint.

A strange note in Dorsey's voice drove back the blackness. She became acutely aware of the horrible stench, of the groans, the dampness—of her nakedness. She snatched her torn blouse from the wet floor and held it over herself.

Dorsey was saying, "Listen, I know your friend Brenn is in Washington. We got word from our agents in Juarez. Now, you tell me where he is, and I'll get you out of here and give you a pass to go where you like."

Kay said nothing. Her smouldering eyes, shot with pain, fright and a murderous fury, did not even look at him. He repeated his question; coaxingly, then persuasively, finally threateningly. She did not reply at all.

"You see," said Aunt Clara, "she's a stubborn piece. I can't do nothin' with her, either."

Dorsey looked at the swollen face, so much beauty so suddenly bruised and battered. If Hannibal ever discovered she was arrested, saw her like this—and Dorsey's plan not ready for operation yet— A moment of cold fright invaded his heart. It was important to get Brenn—all kinds of rumors of a counter-revolt were coming in—but it was much more important at the moment that no wind of this reach Hannibal.

"I'll come back and talk to you later," he growled. "Clara,

put the wench in the black hole. And don't let anybody know who she is or why she's there."

He went out. Kay refused to move, but Clara picked her up bodily and carried her. The black hole was the solitary cell where recalcitrant prisoners were sometimes placed to meditate. It was below the cellar level even—just a square hole, six feet by three without lights and containing only a rotted canvas cot, a stool and a small wooden table.

"You ain't gonna like it in here, dearie," said Aunt Clara. "The rats just come right up and shake hands. Tell me about this Spike Brenn and I'll let you sleep in my quarters under real sheets."

As Kay staggered in under the beam of the matron's flashlight, she saw the iridescent eyes of a rat that scurried as she went to the cot and sank down.

She didn't say anything and Aunt Clara grunted, swore a good man's oath and went out, slamming the solid steel door. Kay was shut into utter blackness, with only the scurrying, whispering sounds of the rats to break the horrible silence.

26

OMNIPOTENT AND ALONE

THOSE WHO SINCERELY believe that a higher authority moves to control the destinies of man and nation might have had some confirmation this particular night in John Hannibal's Lincoln Study. He did something he was not supposed to do; he did something he had neither time nor inclination to do. He called for the list of those enemies of the New Era movement who were either under arrest or who had been executed. Many will say it was fate, predestination, for him to make such a remarkable request.

Actually the reason was much more simple and human. He had before him a clipping from the London *View*, the last remaining liberal newspaper in the world. Somehow the American correspondent of the *View* had managed to smuggle to Mexico and thence by wireless to his paper, a blunt, searching report of the New Era government.

This, in itself, was nothing unusual; other British journalists as well as Canadian reporters had sent out accounts openly criticizing the New Era government, politically, philosophically and economically. But the *View* journalist had included in his statement a sharp, terrible accusation.

One can say that the New Era government is a government

of murder. One can say it is causing its own destruction by destroying all the brains that made the United States a world power before the present cataclysm. I say destroying itself because more than two hundred thousand men and women have been executed, some with tawdry pre-decided trial, others without even this semblance of an excuse.

I can say without being disproved, that more than two-thirds of those executed—the brains, the creators, the producers of wealth, the real upper middle class—were murdered not by the higher authority of the New Era, but for personal revenge, jealousy, and the desire of underlings to rob the dead. Many of them died because they would not stand idly by and see the savings of a lifetime stolen by gangsters in Steel Fist uniforms.

Those dead are not persons of hereditary wealth. As in the case of England, hereditary wealth has produced no outstanding geniuses. Those killed were presidents and directors of great corporations; bankers, manufacturers, engineers, technical experts of all sorts; they were men who, by education and ambition, had started up the ladder of opportunity which the United States held out to its citizens as it has never been held out to the citizens of any other nation.

Hannibal's Fascism is destroying the very bulwark of American greatness. It was this democratic opportunity, these struggling ambitious men who by their industry and brilliance, placed America in the forefront of nations building the new civilization. With them dead and none others to take their places until the New Era Youth Movement can produce (if it can) new mechanical and technical geniuses, the truth must be faced that the United States as a world leader in civilization will slip far down the list of great nations. I might almost say it is doomed to be a second-grade power—and it is possible that its destiny of being a free nation, not troubled by the greed of other powers, is now lost. It may be overrun, split up into segments, become Balkanized, divided as Poland was divided, annexed and exploited by stronger nations who have not wasted their resources and power in a bloody shambles. All this because a one-man dictatorship in America is impossible; the nation is too big, too broad for one man to control. His agents fail him.

The full significance of this statement did not strike Hannibal at once. He was annoyed because he thought it mostly lies; the sort of propaganda that one nation puts out to save itself and its ruling class from a similar fate. The part about being Balkanized, partitioned as the subject of European powers, made him smile.

What grated most was the charge of murder. You could not call executions for the safety of the State murder. A government in power has the right to safeguard itself. In changing from the old order to the new, there were those who could not be re-oriented; and if they were active in their hostility, then they had to pay the price of death. But murder!

Nonsense. Yet the charge grated, particularly the part that accused his Steel Fist leaders of executing to gain wealth and revenge. So he sent for the lists. Not with any idea of perusing them; the endless names would have meant nothing anyway. But he wanted to glance through the important ones; and he wanted to check that figure of executions.

DORSEY WAS NOT in when he pressed the buzzer. Dorsey

was scarcely ever in now. Hannibal sighed and checked himself with a sharp inward curse. He thought of the radio speech he must make tonight; he thought of the speeches he must prepare for the morrow and the one for the morning of the election the day after. He thought of the treaties which must be signed; of the decrees regarding wheat and relief, and the compulsory acceptance of New Era dollars. He half-reached for the buzzer to countermand his order. But he did not. A secretary brought him the papers.

So presently his eyes ran down the list of names. Not all of them, of course; just the prominent ones. Dozens of them, aye, hundreds of them meant nothing to him; his eyes slid over them as if they were listed in a telephone directory. But occasionally a familiar arrangement of letters would halt his gaze and he would recognize the name of some political leader, some labor leader, some banker, some president of a great nation-wide corporation. He would shrug. Naturally these chaps had to see the light or take the consequences.

Then his gaze halted at this:

> Jason (Spike) Brenn. Charged with murder of Corporal John Corbin, U.S. Steel Fists; high treason, conspiracy against the State; plotting to disseminate false information regarding the New Era government. Alexandria concentration prison, awaiting trial. (Note: Privates Able and Martin and Conway claim reward of one hundred thousand dollars offered for the capture of this man dead or alive.)

Spike Brenn! The name conjured the vision of the huge, bushy-haired man whose vital personality he had known

from Damascus to Mukden. Again he pressed for Dorsey.
The Steel Fist marshal's secretary popped in.

"General Dorsey is not back yet, sir."

"Why was I not informed of the arrest of Spike Brenn?"
Hannibal demanded.

"Spike Brenn!" The secretary looked bewildered. "Just
a moment, sir." He popped back to Dorsey's office and
returned in two minutes. "Sir, the name has just appeared
among those arrested night before last. It was a routine
arrest, a man resisting Steel Fist discipline. It was not until
later that he was identified as the arch-traitor wanted. The
name was delayed coming in. General Dorsey hasn't seen
it yet, sir, I am certain."

Hannibal nodded. "Have Brenn brought to me here at
once."

"Very good, sir."

The secretary went out. Hannibal eyed the piled work
distastefully. He supposed he should utilize the interven-
ing minutes; his days never seemed long enough. There
were reports; the alarming increase of imports from the
Argentine of beef; the drop in the gold reserve; the still
partial paralysis of industry which had not responded to
repeated tinkering.

Instead, he began to think about Kay Carstairs. Spike
would know where she was. He'd like to talk about her,
climb down from this aloof pedestal where he stood alone.
The very vision his brain conjured of her aroused desire
within him. He rose from his desk restlessly to pace the
room.

He considered the possibilities—brutally because he

needed her so much. "She loves Spike. All right, let her make a trade. She can have his life if I can have her."

He knew he should be appalled by the thought. He who had tried above all things to remain impartial, cold, aloof, as unbending as the scales of pure justice. Yet the thought came back again. Why remain alone up here, surrounded by a vacuum of authority? He hated Dorsey too much to make a confidant of him; the others bowed down to him as someone not made of human clay; his son was someone to love and play with and shield.

His loneliness combined with the memory of Kay's beauty sharpened the pain in him. He turned thankfully when the door opened and two Steel Fist guards thrust Spike into the room.

SPIKE WAS HANDCUFFED and his ankles were held by leg irons which permitted him eight-inch steps. He was unshaven and his face was a mass of bruises as was that part of his body which the ragged shirt revealed. But in his eyes was the same bold look that Hannibal had seen there many times. He even smiled mirthlessly as Hannibal's eyes encountered his.

"I didn't want to see you, Hannibal," he said, "but they took me anyway and promised a bath. I didn't get the bath. I hope you can stand the smell."

"Sit down, Spike." Hannibal's blazing blue eyes did not relent.

Spike chose a stuffed chair with an antimacassar that his head instantly dirtied.

"It's softer than stone," he said.

"And don't," said Hannibal softly, "set yourself to spring and bash my head in with those handcuffs." He reached to his desk and revealed an automatic pistol under the papers. "I couldn't miss and, besides, you're temporarily valuable to me."

Spike relaxed; but he did not abandon hope of catching Hannibal off guard. His own life didn't matter if he could kill Hannibal.

The Seneschal said, "Why did you come back to Washington?"

"Why do you think?" Spike grinned defiantly.

Hannibal ignored the mockery. "I had hoped that perhaps, now that I am supported by the majority, that you had come to see my way of it."

Spike shook his head. But inwardly he was thinking that Hannibal was still obsessed; the man was still following a mad dream to disaster.

"You and I will never see the same thing," he said in a quieter tone.

Hannibal's nod was weary.

"No, I suppose not. You who had it easy, had money and fame and luxury under the old regime, would never want a change."

Hannibal fell silent, but the real reason for calling Spike here would not let him remain so.

"Where's Kay?"

Spike reared up sharply, his lips curling. "You should ask that—you who had her arrested! That's what I want to ask; what have you done with her?"

"I? I know nothing about her. Don't talk like a fool."

"You must have had her arrested. She went out the other night and she never came back."

Hannibal sucked in his breath with a quick sound, and

strode to the desk. He picked up the alphabetical list and his eyes ran down the names. Spike, watching him, thought that Hannibal was either telling the truth or was a superb actor.

"Her name's not here," growled Hannibal. He strode to Spike. "Don't lie to me, Brenn. You know what she means to me. Where is she?"

"I tell you she went out the other night and did not return. She must be arrested; otherwise I would have heard from her. I went to look for her; that's why I was picked up by your cut-throats."

Hannibal pressed a buzzer, and Dorsey's secretary popped in.

"Marshal Dorsey is not back yet," said the secretary.

"Do you know anything about the arrest of a woman named Kay Carstairs?"

The secretary thought a space. "No, Seneschal, no women that I know of have been arrested in the past forty-eight hours—not here in Washington."

Hannibal strode to him. "You're not lying?"

The secretary obviously was not. His eyes grew frightened. This was a soft job until you made an enemy.

"No, Mar—er—Seneschal, I swear it."

"Check the prisons now—particularly the women's ward in the city jail. Get me a list of every person in there—look at them yourself. Here"—he went to his desk—"here's a photograph of Miss Carstairs. If you find her, bring her to me instantly."

The secretary vanished. One of Hannibal's secretaries knocked and entered by another door. "You'll be on the air in an hour, Seneschal."

Hannibal waved him out brusquely. He turned to Spike. "Why did you bring her to Washington with you? Talk, Brenn, or I'll get it out of you."

HIS BLAZING BLUE eyes were maniacal in their intensity. Spike said, "Go call your murderers. You'll get nothing out of me. Except that we are both against you and your foreign hordes."

Surprisingly Hannibal relaxed. "So she can't see my viewpoint. You and she were conspiring here—representatives of Henderson and his gang, I suppose."

Spike said nothing.

In a calmer voice Hannibal said, "Now that the plebiscite will support me, can't you and she see that you're bucking an accomplished fact? The New Era government is here to stay."

"Perhaps," growled Spike, "but I see you're not certain enough of the result but that you're importing another half-million of your German and Italian allies. What are you going to do—kill all those who vote against you?"

At Spike's words Hannibal had stopped in a queer intent posture. Very slowly he pivoted until his glance was level with Spike's. He pressed his hands to his forehead—his headache tonight was a pounding agony because he had cut down his morphine injections.

"What did you say?" he asked in a low tone. "What was that about Germans and Italians?"

"Hah! That's a laugh. Me, an outsider, telling you about the landing of the German and Italian troops. As if you didn't know."

"But I don't know; and I don't believe it."

Spike stared at him. "By Heaven, I believe you're telling the truth."

"You must be lying. I have the promise of Von Eitel and Della Volpi that the expeditionary force will be moving out by June first. Instead of coming, the coalition forces are going. That was my pledge on the plebiscite."

Spike could not hide his astonishment. Here was a situation that demanded thought. Here was a new factor on which he had not counted at all. But if Hannibal had not imported more occupying forces, then who had? And why?

He glanced sharply at Hannibal and relaxed. "Listen, don't tell me that eighty thousand-odd foreign troops can land in this country, with more coming, and you not be informed. You're running this racket, aren't you?"

Hannibal did not appear to hear. He was staring intently at Spike. For a longish minute he held this position, his blazing eyes boring in.

"You're not lying. There have been troops landed. Tell me. Where? And how?"

"I smell another scheme in this," muttered Spike. "Somebody else has got ideas about the future besides you."

"Answer my question," shouted Hannibal furiously.

Spike made a quick decision. The thing he had hoped for had occurred; there might not be dissension in the Steel Fist ranks but there was scheming for power. It was best to tell Hannibal and, while he was aroused by the news, there was a chance of Hawker and O'Hara striking. They didn't need Spike; the plan was too well made for that.

"I'll tell you," he said, and reported all the facts that Intelligence had brought to Juarez. Hannibal listened intently, scarcely moving.

"The estimate is," concluded Spike, "that around eight hundred thousand troops will be landed in the next sixty days."

Hannibal stood quietly, his fingers interlocked. Spike said, "How does it happen that you, the Seneschal as you call yourself, don't know this?"

"Eh? What?" Hannibal gave a start. "Why don't I know?" His lips curled. "If you had ever sat in the vacuum of power, Brenn, you wouldn't ask that. I delegate my authority to this one and that one. They bring me news they think I should have and no more. This, apparently, was something I was not supposed to know."

He took to pacing the floor. Spike watched him for a while. Then he said casually, "Somebody has double-crossed you. Maybe your friends Von Eitel and Volpi have an idea they could *conquer* this country and partition it."

Hannibal nodded. "Undoubtedly. But they are not alone in that belief. As long as I am in power, Volpi and Von Eitel know such a thing is impossible. No, this is Dorsey's work."

"Dorsey?"

Hannibal nodded again. "Of course. He wants power. He can't beat me without outside help. He's made a deal with Germany and Italy. He—"

He broke off. The door opened and Dorsey's secretary entered. He was helping, almost supporting, a slim, ragged half-naked girl, covered only by a torn skirt and a black wool shawl.

SPIKE GROWLED IN his throat, leaped upward, and tripped over his chains.

"Kay," he cried. "My God, Kay!"

He fell to the floor, twisted and turned blazing eyes on Hannibal.

"What have you done to her, you dog?"

Hannibal was looking at Kay. The swelling had not left her face; she was nearly blinded by it and the sharp light after the endless hours in the utterly black hole underground. Where the shawl did not cover her torso completely there were more swollen welts.

"Hush, Brenn," he said and darted to her side. "Kay! Who has done this?"

She drew herself up with some of the hauteur of the Kay he knew. She flung back her head, trying to see him there.

"Your swine Dorsey," she said. "Dorsey!"

Hannibal turned to the frightened secretary. "Get out," he said.

The man stood, terrified. He stammered, "The woman didn't want to surrender her—she said this girl was a special—"

"Get out," thundered Hannibal.

He took Kay's arm as the secretary fled to the door. He led her to the far end of the room.

"There's a bath in there," he said gently. "There are some pajamas and a dressing gown. I'll send for my own physician."

She was silent, and her very silence cut him like a whip. He said, "Kay, Dorsey dies for this. I swear it—you must believe I knew nothing of it."

"Let go," said Kay steadily. "I can walk alone."

She did, and opened the door. For a space she stood there. Vaguely she could see Spike trying to crawl to her. She smiled, actually smiled.

"Steady, darling," she said. "I'm all right, really I am."

Spike sobbed in his throat. "Get these cuffs off me, Hannibal, damn you! Let me get at the swine. Let me—"

"Hush!" said Hannibal. "I didn't know. I—"

"But you see what happens in your damned insane scheme," yelled Spike. "You set yourself up as God to rule over the destinies of a hundred and thirty million people. You are going to bring the horn of plenty, laughter and ease and security. And, damn your soul, you can't even protect the girl you pretend to love."

He drew himself upright by the desk. "You bring a New Era. A New Era of what? Murder, greed, lust. You twist a peaceful nation into one of anarchy, discord and leave it a weak prey to other nations. You're worse than a traitor, you're worse than a dreamer—you're an insane fool!"

It was strange what happened. Hannibal, who had maintained the austere aloof exterior; the man who made his fate and never knew weakness—he, Hannibal, weakened then and tried to excuse himself.

"So many things to do, so little time to do it in," he whispered. "No one man, no fifty supermen could watch over every detail. Power had to be delegated. It was abused and I am to blame. But I can punish."

Spike did not apparently hear. "You murder her brother and now you disfigure her; almost kill her—" Spike's hands rose above his head and he tried to leap the distance to smash the heavy manacles on Hannibal's head. He did not reach his objective and fell headlong to the floor.

Hannibal had not so much as moved; but his blazing eyes had widened and his mouth had dropped ajar.

"Murdered her brother, you say," he repeated. "What do you mean?"

"Norm Carstairs was the Intelligence agent at your meeting in Paris, and you had him murdered by your gangsters."

It was as if much had been made clear to Hannibal. He staggered, braced himself.

"Yes, I did do that," he said. "No wonder she hated me. No wonder she could not understand what I was trying to do. No wonder—"

He broke off and strode across the room. He flung open the door. "Dorsey!" he called.

This time the secretary did not pop out. Instead, George Dorsey, dazzling in his green, silver and gold uniform of a marshal of the Steel Fists, came out of his office and strode toward Hannibal.

"Well?"

Hannibal strode to him. With one motion he jerked the gold epaulettes from Dorsey's shoulders. As the man raised his hands to prevent this, Hannibal struck him in the face.

"You're under arrest, Dorsey, for treason," Hannibal growled, "and the sentence is that you be shot."

27

JOHN HANNIBAL, AMERICAN

DORSEY WHISTLED SHRILLY through his lips. From his office stepped three Steel Fist captains, each carrying an automatic rifle. Hannibal stiffened and turned his blazing eyes on Dorsey. "What does this mean?"

Dorsey's face was peculiarly suffused. His eyes glittered. He snorted through his large nostrils. "I and the others don't like the way things are going," he said thickly. "It's our neck if the thing finally fails, and the way you're running it, it's bound to fail."

"And it will win the way you'll run it?"

"Yes! Your policy is dooming us all to the rope. We can still win—with a firmer hand, a stronger policy, we can quash these sporadic rebellions before they get too important."

"Are you advising me to take a stronger hand?" asked Hannibal, "or are you suggesting that I step aside for someone else—you, for example?"

"I suggest nothing," said Dorsey. "I'm pushing you aside—now."

"You mean," said Hannibal, "that you're going to murder me?"

Dorsey said, "Liquidate you, I believe is the term. And

in such a way that you will be a national hero, assassinated by Brenn and his gang." He laughed mockingly. "And come this day in future years, I'll lay a wreath upon your grave and orate how you saved the country from perdition, started the movement that was the renaissance of the United States."

His control, so far held so carefully, burst at this point.

"And as I speak," he snarled, "I'll be saying to myself, 'I always hated Hannibal. He was the kind of man my kind of man must hate.' You're so damned aloof, so idealistic, so above the cheap sins that you reproach in me. Well, what has it got you?"

"I'm beginning to wonder myself," said Hannibal slowly.

"You're a saint, a martyr," sneered Dorsey. "A martyr who will go to his doom. You had the power and the spiritual strength to move people to follow you. To what end? To a Utopia. Hell! People have been dreaming about Utopia for centuries, written books on it. There is no Utopia."

"No," said Hannibal slowly. His face was pale, and within he felt queer as if his soul were shrinking into a tiny ball. "No, there is no Utopia. Your kind of swine foul it."

As he spoke he was moving slowly backward, always careful to keep Dorsey between him and the three Steel Fists.

Dorsey laughed. "What am I waiting for? Let's get it over, men."

"What about my radio speech?" Hannibal asked. "I'm due on the air in ten minutes."

"That's the point," laughed Dorsey. "I'll make the radio speech. And tell everybody Henderson and Brenn and the rest shot you. That'll put them in the mood for the purge that's needed and the immediate war on Mexico."

He gestured to his men. "Come on."

Hannibal hit Dorsey then, hit him with all his strength so that the mashall staggered back and struck among his men. Before they could recover from this surprise, Hannibal whirled, dashed into the Lincoln room, shut and bolted the door.

He sprang to one side as three shots ripped through the paneling, and half-turned to find furniture to brace against the door and form a barricade. From behind him Spike's voice said, "Okay, Hannibal, it's my turn now. Look around—I wouldn't shoot even you in the back."

HANNIBAL TURNED VERY slowly. Spike was standing, braced against the desk by his thighs. Both his manacled hands were extended and in the right was Hannibal's pistol which he had left on the desk. Spike's face was not smiling; it was grim, and his eyes were thinned as he forced himself to the determination to shoot an unarmed man.

Hannibal faced the gun muzzle coolly. If he was thinking that his temple of dreams lay smashed around him, it did not show on his face. Indeed, he was not thinking of the smashing of his plans; his brain had risen above that.

"Don't shoot, Brenn," he said clearly. "You're playing into their hands if you do."

Spike flung back his head. "You can't talk me out of this, Hannibal. Five hundred men were going to risk their lives tomorrow or the next night to make certain you and Dorsey died. I can't guarantee Dorsey, but I can you."

Hannibal stood quietly. Spike watched him, his finger

tight on the trigger. His face worked with emotion as he tried to nerve himself to shoot.

Finally he said desperately, "Why don't you cry out?"

Hannibal smiled softly. "No, Brenn. I told you not to shoot. You mustn't. Dorsey was going to murder me and blame it on you anyway."

The statement shocked Spike so that he half-lowered the muzzle. From the outside, for the moment, there was no sound.

"What do you mean?"

"Dorsey's made a deal with the Germans and the Italians. He's going to kill me and make himself Seneschal. He's going to blame my murder on you, Henderson, Farnham and the others. Perhaps that will work. If it doesn't, he's got Von Blutcher and Gravi to bring in troops to quell any Steel Fist revolt. And the Germans and Italians, in turn, intend to seize the country, using Dorsey as their figurehead."

Spike knew this was true without stopping even to weigh it. The landing of troops by night, Dorsey's arrest of Kay and keeping it a secret; the shots outside—and last of all, Hannibal's shocked, hopeless face told him it was true. He saw, then, that disaster had come from a most unexpected source.

What use now to cause dissension in the Steel Fist ranks? An army of occupation of nearly a million sealed the doom of American democracy.

As he realized this, his fury against Hannibal mounted to the breaking point. "You caused it all," he growled, "so you can take it the way you're standing."

He had his courage screwed up. His finger pulled the

trigger. But though the gun roared, the bullet did not strike Hannibal. It ploughed into the ceiling. His hands had been knocked up by the slim girl behind him.

Kay said, "Spike, he's right. Killing him does no good. You can't."

Spike went limp from the reaction and half-fell against the desk.

"You shouldn't have done it," he mumbled.

"But she should," Hannibal came across the room but made no attempt to attack Spike. "I was thinking, there, looking into the gun muzzle, that there's one answer. I and I alone can undo what has been done."

"You!" cried Spike. "Haven't you done enough?"

"Listen to him," begged Kay.

THROUGH THE DOOR rattled two shots, which blew off the lock, but did not quite hit the bolt. "Dorsey's coming in," said Hannibal. "You've got to let me do this my own way."

"How?"

"All the German and Italian troops have not landed. He's got, for a time at least, to convince the public that you murdered me. I intend to prove to the public that you didn't, but that Dorsey did."

"Impossible!"

Hannibal strode to the desk where lay the pages of the manuscript he was to read on the air. He ignored the three bullets that thundered through the door. He picked up one telephone and said, "Harry, is everything ready?"

Spike waited in agony; had Dorsey cut the telephone wires? Hannibal read his thought. "Dorsey was going to make this speech. The wires are all right…. All set, Harry? Then put me on the air."

He turned to Kay. His whole demeanor was soft, even his eyes did not blaze any more.

"Bring my son Stephen in, please, Kay," he said. He gestured to the boy's bedroom. To Spike he said, "Guard the door. Shoot any one who tries to come in. Oh, the handcuff keys—here—you can unlock them."

Spike unlocked the handcuffs. Hannibal said queerly, "You once asked me if I loved my country. I told you I did. Tonight—now—I'll prove it."

Spike watched the door. But no more bullets came through at the lock. From out of the night, high in the sky, came the sharp thud of bursting anti-aircraft shells. The dull roar of the fired guns rolled in upon them.

"Hawker and O'Hara!" cried Spike. "They've come. They—"

"Quiet!" cried Hannibal. "I'm on the air."

As he spoke he pressed the button on the microphone that made the connection. Into the room as he did so came Kay leading a yellow-haired boy, sleepily rubbing his eyes and squinting at the light. Hannibal kept his eyes on the boy's face as he began to speak.

"Americans, attention! This is Seneschal Hannibal to speak to you. You have one minute to get the members of your family around the loud speaker, and to tell others that the message you have awaited is coming."

He closed the connection. The *thud-thud-thud* of the AA guns boomed rapidly across the night, and now you could hear the rattle of machine gun fire and the whining moan of high-speed airplane motors. In the room no one spoke for a while.

"They wouldn't have done any good," Hannibal said. "This is the only answer. I had it in mind before you tried to shoot me, Brenn."

He looked at the big radio reporter. "Give me the gun, please. I won't use it on you."

Spike hesitated. Kay said, "Give it to him, Spike. Can't you read in his face that he's playing square?"

Spike surrendered the gun. Little Stephen said, "Daddy, do you wish me to do anything?"

"Just stand there, son," said Hannibal, "where I can see your face."

He pressed the button on the microphone. "Americans all: listen. John Hannibal is giving you his last message." He stiffened at the microphone, ignoring his written manuscript, and with his eyes on the door through which more bullets splintered, began to speak.

28

NIGHTMARE'S END

"I SPEAK," HANNIBAL'S voice was saying, "to those of you
who have stood by while great events have happened and
I address, for the last time, my own splendid Steel Fists
whose record has been marred by the few despicable swine
who betrayed my trust.

"I speak to you as a prisoner. I am a prisoner in the White
House. After I finish this speech—perhaps even before—I
shall be dead. George Dorsey, arch-traitor, has men outside
the room firing through the door at me. Dorsey has sold
out me and the country and you. To become Seneschal, to
wield my power, he has betrayed the nation to the Italians
and Germans who have double-crossed me and you. The
Germans and Italians are sending more troops secretly,
without my knowledge, to conquer America and make of
you their subjects. So I must speak quickly and deliver my
message before Dorsey's bullets silence me forever.

"Now, why, besides desiring my power, did Dorsey sell
us and our New Era movement out to the Italians and the
Germans? I'll tell you. He believes in liquidation—death
for the opponents of the New Era government. He wanted
a purge, a decree that would arrest the ten chief inhabitants
of every village—seventy thousand of them—in America

and unless the Liberators ceased their activities, one out of each ten was to be shot on consecutive days. This was wholesale murder. I would not countenance it. I refused.

"He declares I have withstood bloodshed as much as possible. I have. Many have died, in the home, on the battlefield, but these I was willing to sacrifice for the future good of us all.

"I believed in the New Era government. I believed that democracy was stupid, wasteful, incompetent, and doomed in this changing world. And before the country's resources were wasted, I believed I should step in and take charge. I have done so—and I have failed. I have held my lofty ideals, but those who served me served also their own lustful, greedy, selfish ends and ruined what might have been something splendid.

"If democracy was stupid, futile and incompetent, then my government has been more so, because I also had to trust to human beings and they held not the same dreams that I held, but wanted money and power and revenge.

"So I come to my confession. It was I who conspired to have the Japanese Imperial Crown Prince murdered in Manila waters. The United States had nothing to do with it. It was I who aided and financed the overthrow of Hitler and the assassination of Mussolini. It was I who conspired with the leaders Von Eitel and Della Volpi to make war on this country when we were harassed on the west coast by Japan.

"I did this because—and you must know the truth— the United States was so powerful—and will be again— that no single nation like Japan, or no coalition of nations, Germany, Italy and Japan, could defeat it. If I was to take

command of this government, put in my own New Era
theories, I had to stage an internal revolt which would also
fail unless outside help was had.

"So you see it took my revolt plus the aid of three powerful nations to overthrow this government. In no other way
could it be done and now, warned, it can never happen
again.

"I tell you this and swear by Almighty God that I had
no plan or scheme to reduce this nation to a conquered
province of Germany or Italy. I do not wish it to become so
now. I have made the mistake many dreamers have made;
I have tried to hurry the hand of time, substitute revolution for evolution.

"And rather that you and you and you should become
subjects of a foreign power, I have decided tonight to
appeal to you to stand—not for me—but for President
Henderson, the rightfully elected executive of this nation.
I appeal to the Steel Fists to release the railroads for use
in transporting military supplies and troops. I appeal to
workers in munitions factories not to strike, but to give
everything to force these invaders to leave our shores. I
appeal to the Steel Fists and to New Era executives to turn
back to the rightful authorities the control of the cities and
towns and hamlets of these United States.

"And to the Liberators and my former enemies I appeal
for no retaliation, no revenge. All stand together until
America's shores are rid of those who would hammer the
iron collar of subjection on your throat.

"Democracy may be inefficient; much may be wasted,
much may be stolen, much may be lost in the staggering
cost of maintaining such a government. But at least you

are free men and there is opportunity for all. So I appeal to all to band together and support all those Liberators who have fought for months against my regime.

"I can only say in conclusion that I have loved my country, shed my blood for her. And if I have erred—and I have, criminally—it is because I was blind to the logic of time. That—" Hannibal paused. The door still held but the shouts outside had multiplied.

He looked back at his son who was staring, not understanding the paleness of his father's face.

"Dorsey is entering. I am unarmed. You Americans—fight for the nation! God bless the United States of America!"

JOHN HANNIBAL RAISED the pistol swiftly, yet the motion seemed unhurried. Before the muzzle pointed at his brain, his eyes found the straight figure of his son. Stephen stood near the bedroom door, his expression confused, his eyes imploringly on his father.

With that swift speed with which the brain can work Hannibal saw before him the future of his son. The son of a man who was a traitor, a man to be cursed by history for crimes against the republic. Stephen, he told himself, would be a pariah, a boy to be hounded and persecuted for what his father had done. Stephen would grow up to hear him, John Hannibal, referred to as the most infamous traitor ever spawned.

The boy's life was ruined before it had well begun. He, John Hannibal, owed it to himself, to Bess, to the boy, to take him with him on this unending journey of death.

All this had taken, in John Hannibal's mind but a divided second of time. He half-turned, leveled the gun.

Kay perceived his action, knew what was meant. She flung herself at Stephen, covered his body with her own.

"No, no, you cannot," she cried.

This caused another split-second delay while Dorsey yelled from outside, and Spike leaped forward to wrest the gun from John Hannibal's hand.

John Hannibal knew there was no time for anything else now. There was the microphone; there were fifty million people listening for the thing he had told them would happen.

"You—Kay, take care of Stephen for me," he whispered.

"No, you fool," yelled Spike.

John Hannibal's eyes turned to the boy. And his eyes there, his lips softly smiling, he placed the muzzle of the gun to his temple and pulled the trigger.

The gun's roar was partly muffled by contact with the flesh. Hannibal went back under the impact of the bullet, and whirled and plunged to the floor where the desk hid the horrible sight of his battered skull from the boy on whose face Hannibal's last look had been concentrated. The noise and his father's fall made the boy cry. Kay swept him into her arms.

At this juncture the bolt on the door was shot away. Spike yelled, "Get in the other room with him."

He stooped, grabbed up the gun and faced those at the door. Dorsey yelled, "Brenn killed the Chief, boys, get him."

Spike grinned; and with one movement swept the microphone with a crash to the floor. If that voice went out, then all Hannibal had wanted was achieved. In thrusting the mike away, Spike crouched behind the protection of the desk. He wanted one shot at Dorsey, and for that he would trade all he had.

Whatever else he was, Dorsey was brave. He led the rush into the room. Only he came alone. From the far end of the hallway, a machine gun chattered loudly. Two of the Steel Fists fell screaming. The third flopped and moaned. A rush of booted feet came along the carpet.

All this Spike could see but Dorsey could not. Dorsey had his gun, and he was shouting, "We'll get the kid, too. That'll make it sound worse—killing a kid."

Spike raised up. "You and I all alone, Dorsey," he said. "See how fast you are."

DORSEY WAS FAST but he wasn't fast enough. He fired with a downward snap of his arm and the bullet struck the corner of the desk, ploughed through, tore into Spike's back muscles and on out to plop into the wall. Spike had taken his time, and his shot was good.

As Spike's gun roared Dorsey's chest seemed to deflate. Blood spurted. He pressed his left hand against the splotch and the blood seeped through just the same. He stood for a moment motionless while O'Hara and Hawker, leading the pilots and the regular infantrymen, crowded the doorway, watching, amazed. Then Dorsey went down in segments, first his knees buckled, then his thighs and finally he curled around, lay down and then sprawled out.

He said thickly, "He got me. Can you tie that?"

When Spike moved cautiously toward him a moment or so later, Dorsey was quite dead.

When Spike looked up again he looked into the face of David Farnham. Quite a different Farnham than the quiet man he had known. Farnham's face was powder-marked;

his eyes blazed with excitement, and in his right hand he held an automatic pistol that was still warm.

"I had to come," he said simply. "I heard that Hannibal had captured you both—and I wanted to be in at the end."

"How's things outside?" Spike let his eyes turn to Hannibal's relaxed body.

"We've cleaned up the Steel Fists, but reinforcements are coming—Italians and Germans. We might hold on for a while."

"Then do," said Spike.

He moved his arm and winced at the pain of his wound. "I'll check up on the microphone and the connection. Get on the air and speak in the name of Henderson. Tell them we've killed Dorsey and that we hold the nation until Henderson can arrive."

He turned to the rest. "Fight as long as you can. No matter what happens, we've got to hold on here for five hours."

Back to Farnham again. "Tell Evelyn to steam forced draft. With his sailors, and the railroads opened, we'll move those Germans and Italians out in short order."

The confusion, the panic that had swept the White House staff made Spike's job easier. He had the open connection, and Farnham's speech was broadcast through a quick hook-up to New York. Fighting still went on. But the infantry fire with automatic rifles and the diving planes that used the White House searchlight-lit grounds to find splendid targets, held the Italians and Germans off.

The hours passed when the nation lay in the lap of destiny. But the regulars held on. Toward dawn, by telephone, came a message that Henderson was flying by swiftest bombing plane.

Spike heard it, sitting with Kay and the boy Stephen. He had not realized how keyed up he was until this message arrived. A blackness swept up and over him.

"Dammit," he said huskily, "I think I'm going to faint."

IT WAS FALL again, the crispness of Indian summer when the days are warm but winter comes at night and dawn. Spike Brenn had been up in Connecticut looking at the brilliant colors of the autumn foliage and, incidentally, taking Kay and young Stephen to the Danbury Fair. He was hurrying back now for his 6:45 news broadcast.

All the way back he noticed how the routine of life had resumed just as if no cataclysm had smashed it for a year. Automobiles streamed along the Merritt and Hutchinson River Parkway; and down the Hendrik Hudson into the Elevated Express Highway he saw only happy faces. The repairs to New York needed on account of the bombing raids, had been made; indeed, always in a state of growing, New York was once more tearing down big buildings and erecting bigger ones. Life went on as if there had been no interruption.

At Radio City, when he parked the car, he said to Kay, "Bring Steve and come up and listen. Then we'll plan on a swell dinner."

"Why?" asked Kay. "That is, why tonight as against any other night?"

"Tonight," said Spike, "is the anniversary of the destruction of the *Mutsui;* just a year ago the invasion of America actually began though the troops didn't come until later."

They went up with him, of course, and Spike's secretary

handed him the outline of his broadcast, together with the latest news dispatches for him to comment on.

While he waited, David Farnham came in. A thinner Farnham with suddenly grayed hair and lines around his eyes that would remain there his lifetime.

"I thought we might crack a bottle of wine," he said.

"I thought so, too," nodded Spike. "Wait until I finish this fifteen minutes."

A few minutes later the announcer thrust in his head. "You're on, Spike."

Spike waited until the commercial was finished. Then: "Hello, America, this is Spike Brenn, your roving reporter, giving you the news of the day. And, boy, is it some news! I mean to say yes.

"After a stiff note from Secretary of State Snell, Italy and Germany both agreed to stop their Fascist propaganda in South America and to respect the Monroe Doctrine which has been a part of our policy for nearly a hundred years. The fleet under Admiral Evelyn in the Atlantic probably had something to do with it but, anyway, folks, we have peace and it's likely to endure.

"The Japanese Emperor signed the peace treaty today which officially puts the stamp of approval on the armistice which has lasted since last May. Under the terms, things are at *status quo* except that the United States recognizes Japan as the leading power of the Orient and we have accepted their offer to watch over the Philippines and see to it that Philippine independence is protected.

"They in turn recognize our power in South America and respect the Monroe Doctrine.

"Now, for a look at the home front. Business is booming,

the stock market went up two to five points today and it looks as if that prosperity which has been just around the corner for so long has finally come into sight. What with all the repairs to be made after the destruction of last year's invasion, big industry is reaching a new high in production; Steel reported eighty percent capacity.

"President Henderson has approved the Congressional bill extending amnesty and pardon to all those of the now-destroyed Steel Fists who, on later evidence, have not been found guilty of a crime such as theft or murder.

"On this, the anniversary of the strange sinking of the *Mutsui,* President Henderson dispatched a cable of condolence to the Japanese Emperor.

"The Yankees won again today, folks, extending their American League lead to thirteen games. It looks as if those Tigers have hit a sinking spell, and with old timer Joe DiMaggio in there hitting that apple, I don't see how anybody can stop those Yankees from getting their ninth pennant.

"Oh, yes, you've been reading in Winchell's column about me carrying the torch for Kay Carstairs. Well, so as to let you get the information straight from the feed box, let me say that we're married and tonight leave on our honeymoon for two weeks, and I'll not be broadcasting again until that period is over. So wish me luck, folks, and the same to you. This is Spike Brenn signing off, and I'll be seeing you."

On Fifty-seventh Street Spike led them to a quiet table in the rear of Raoul's a French restaurant that knew how to serve wines. Spike ordered an Amontillado sherry all the way around.

"Even Steve?" Kay inquired. "Now that we've adopted him, we've got to think about him drinking."

"Sherry won't hurt him and, besides, I want him to drink it," said Spike. "A sip, anyway."

The sherry came. Spike lifted his glass toward Dave Farnham. "Peace!" he muttered. "Old Father Divine certainly knew his stuff. It's wonderful. And as far as I'm concerned, we can have a thousand years of it."

Dave Farnham nodded. "The country's been through a terrible ordeal, and has withstood the shocks of it well. Perhaps it was as well for the ordeal to come when it did, because now that we've had a taste of the other, there won't be so much criticism of what we've got. Sobered and shaken, we'll carry on, hanging onto what was handed to us as a precious heritage."

"My daddy used to say things like that," said young Stephen.

They fell silent for a space, looking into his young face.

"Yes," said Spike gently, "I think he did. Your father was a brave man, Steve."

"I think so," said Steve.

Again silence. Kay said finally, "We can drink to his courage, and to the lesson he taught his country."

"Yes," said Farnham. "We can all drink to that."

They raised their glasses.